*She had never
exposed herself
like this before . . .*

By Samantha James

The Seduction of an Unknown Lady
The Secret Passion of Simon Blackwell
A Perfect Hero
A Perfect Groom
A Perfect Bride
The Truest Heart
His Wicked Promise
His Wicked Ways
One Moonlit Night
A Promise Given
Every Wish Fulfilled
Just One Kiss
My Lord Conqueror
Gabriel's Bride

Samantha JAMES

The SEDUCTION Of An UNKNOWN LADY

AVON

An Imprint of HarperCollinsPublishers

This is a work of fiction. Names, characters, places, and incidents are products of the author's imagination or are used fictitiously and are not to be construed as real. Any resemblance to actual events, locales, organizations, or persons, living or dead, is entirely coincidental.

AVON BOOKS
An Imprint of HarperCollins*Publishers*
10 East 53rd Street
New York, New York 10022-5299

First Avon Books paperback printing: April 2008

Avon Trademark Reg. U.S. Pat. Off. and in Other Countries, Marca Registrada, Hecho en U.S.A.
HarperCollins® is a registered trademark of HarperCollins Publishers.

Printed in the U.S.A.

10 9 8 7 6 5 4 3 2 1

To the Rogue Authors—
Victoria Alexander, Susan Andersen, Patti Berg,
Stephanie Laurens, and Linda Needham—
who welcomed me into the fold with open arms . . .
I'd never have been able to finish this book without you.
Hugs and thanks to each and every one of you!

Chapter One

He was back.

I saw him once when I was very young, a creature who was not of this world. Even now I recall the way the hairs on the back of my neck had prickled—as they did even now.

Now, I stood on the balcony outside my room at Raven's Gate and gazed into the light of the moon.

For I could feel it.

I could feel him.

It is not a feeling one soon forgets.

Demon of Dartmoor, F.J. Sparrow

London, January 1852

"Your Grace," intoned Carlton, the impeccably attired white-gloved butler. "Your brother, Lord Aidan."

Aidan McBride strode into his brother's drawing room and without further ado, lowered his long body onto the soft, rich cushions of the armchair that sat before the roaring fire. He leaned forward, rubbing his hands together to warm them.

Ensconced in the adjacent chair, periodical in hand, Alec McBride hiked one dark brow.

"Brandy?" queried Alec without looking up from his reading. "Or whisky?"

Aidan certainly wouldn't refuse either. His brother Alec had a fine selection of both, including an enviable—and extensive—wine cellar. Ah, yes, his brother had both exquisite—and expensive—taste when it came to spirits. And being half-Scots, as a matter of course there was always whisky. Gleneden, in fact, even boasted its own distillery. Alec McBride, Duke of Gleneden, could well afford his pleasures.

"Brandy," said Aidan, "sounds just the thing."

Carlton returned in short order with a generously filled decanter and two finely etched tumblers centered on a gleaming silver tray. The butler poured a perfectly matched measure into each, then retired with a bow. Aidan leaned forward and retrieved the nearest glass. His posture was perfectly erect, courtesy of his rigorous military training and his days as a colonel in the Royal Highland Regiment.

But those days were no more. Now he was once

again a private citizen, on his way to making his own fortune in shipping tobacco and cotton from America, rum from the Caribbean, anywhere west of England. He wouldn't consider the tea trade. God knew he wanted no more to do with India.

His brother's pale blue eyes had finally settled on him. Aidan watched as Alec closed the periodical and laid it on the table—rather reluctantly, Aidan decided. "Well, well," he said lightly, "it appears I've interrupted you at a rather inopportune moment. Would you prefer that I leave?"

"No need. You're already here, aren't you?"

"Well, you appeared quite engrossed in your reading material—what is it? Ah, *THE MONTHLY CHRONICLE* . But what article were you reading that holds you in such fascination?" Curious, Aidan picked up the periodical his brother had laid on the table but failed to close, as if to mark his place—as if loath to forget it.

His brows shot high. "What the devil! *Demon of Dartmoor*," he quoted. He couldn't withhold a laugh. "Who has taken the place of my brother? Perhaps the devil himself! Or—dare I say it?—a demon? I confess, Alec, you astound me. I rather thought you should be reading the classics."

"The devil indeed. Or just as you say, perchance a demon. And it's not an article, Aidan, but a novel. Rather, a serialization of a novel."

Aidan glanced at it once more. "F.J. Sparrow? I've never heard of him."

"Yes, well, is it any wonder?" Alec asked dryly. "You were in the Punjab so long it's a miracle any of us recognized you."

The Punjab.

Touched by echoes from the past, Aidan managed to maintain his smile. He held himself very still. He didn't try to stop the painful tightening of his gut. He'd long since discovered that to try merely made it worse.

No, there was no turning back the past. No escaping it.

Lord knew he'd already tried.

He also knew that Alec meant no harm by the offhand comment.

Like Alec, his complexion was almost swarthy. But the Indian sun had darkened Aidan's still more, so that his skin was a dark, burnished hue that made him appear almost a foreigner—particularly when combined with the beard he'd grown, the patch he'd still worn over one eye upon his return home. Aidan recalled with a faint amusement how their poor mother had appeared severely distressed at the notion that perhaps her second son had not returned on this particular ship after all. She'd passed by him on the dock fully half a dozen times over, fretting aloud, before Aidan finally took pity on her, picking up her dainty form and whirling her around. He knew, from the hint of mirth that tugged at Alec's mouth, that Alec was thinking of that moment, too. And of course Mama had also been delighted when he shaved his beard off the following day.

It was Alec who'd told him how disappointed she had been when she'd learned of Aidan's decision not to return home immediately upon resigning his commission. In fact, nearly a year had passed before he'd come home.

It wasn't, as he'd cited to his mother in his letter not long after he'd resigned his commission, a continuing need for wanderlust that delayed his reunion with his family.

It was shame. Shame and guilt and—

Unfinished business.

And once that was done, well . . . he still hadn't been able to return.

He couldn't. Precisely why, he couldn't say. Perhaps he'd been running. Hiding. Trying to heal.

It took a moment before he realized Alec was still talking about that damned author. What was his name? Wren?

"At any rate," Alec continued, "since the publication of *Satan's Path*, F.J. Sparrow has enjoyed enormous success."

F.J. Sparrow. That was it.

"*Spectres of the Dark* followed, I believe, then *The Devil's Way. Howls at Midnight* was the last." Alec pointed to a cabinet in the corner. "Alas, I've the entire collection thus far except *The Devil's*

Way. I read it, then lent it to someone and it was never returned. And now it's almost impossible to come by."

He sounded most indignant. "Let me guess," Aidan drawled. "His characters battle almost unspeakable evil."

"But of course."

Aidan silently contemplated. *Satan's Path. Spectres of the Dark. The Devil's Way* and *Demon of Dartmoor.* F.J. Sparrow must surely be a queer, twisted fellow, to pen such grisly-sounding tales. But he kept his opinion to himself.

His eyes, thick-lashed as were all the McBrides', blue like all of the McBrides'—though all of them hued in various shades from palest blue to deepest sapphire—began to sparkle.

He tapped a finger atop *Demon of Dartmoor.* "Tell me," he invited, "what entrances you so."

"It's not just me, it's the whole of England, man. F.J. Sparrow is all the rage. Walk into any club, and you'll no doubt find a dozen copies of the latest *CHRONICLE* with the latest chapter of *Demon of Dartmoor.* Attend any party, any gala affair, and his name will surely crop up, for again, I say, he's captivated the whole of the British Isles. The master of murder and monsters and mayhem he's called."

"And no doubt his novels are full of phantoms and apparitions, creatures of doom, creatures of gloom, secret passageways, trapdoors, and the like. And in secluded, ruined castles. My God, you're reading Gothic horror novels—my brother, the duke of Gleneden!"

"Well, would you expect anything else from such a novel?" A faint smile curled Alec's lips. "The thing is, no one really knows who F.J. Sparrow *is.* His identity. And that but fuels the mystery even more—and his sales, no doubt."

Aidan fought the urge to erupt into laughter. It must have shown, for Alec cast him a look that clearly proclaimed his recalcitrance.

Aidan schooled his features. "Since this is clearly a passion of yours, tell me more."

Alec took a sip of brandy. "Well, our intrepid heroine is a young, virtuous woman in incessant danger."

"I find the idea of young, virtuous, innocent ladies immensely . . . appealing." Aidan arched a well-shaped brow. "But I'm surprised that *you* of all people should take to reading such drivel."

Again that withering look. "One should never criticize what one has not read," Aidan was haughtily informed. "Besides, they are not drivel. They're surprisingly well written, Aidan. I think of them as novels of hair-raising adventure— they're most certainly not for the faint of heart. Indeed, while some of his monsters are deviants whose deeds are of horrendous proportion, one of his previous works featured a villain who had been shut up beneath the house he'd been born in for ten years. When he was a child, his father cut off his fingers one by one for daring to snatch a biscuit—and then his tongue as well, so the child could not protest when his father shut him away in a closet so tiny he could not stand upright. He was an outcast from society. An outcast of his family. When his father died, and he managed to escape, it wasn't just his outward body that was crippled. It was as if his heart was crippled as well—a crippled soul, if you will. Vile as he'd grown to be, it was really rather sad that he was such a tragic figure of a man."

A crippled soul. Well, he thought, *that was something he understood.*

He lowered his glass to the table. "I confess, I am all agog."

Alec pretended to frown severely. "Do you mock me?"

Aidan's smile was purely devilish. "Only when I am able."

"Well," Alec said wryly, "I doubt you'll find anything in England so exciting as defending the masses in India, but Raven and Rowan certainly have—in the moors of jolly old England."

"Raven and Rowan?" Aidan queried.

"The characters in *Demon of Dartmoor.* Amateur sleuths."

"Ah, those who do battle against the creatures of infamy."

"Yes. They worked together in *The Devil's Way,* you see, quite closely. Rowan owns the estate next to Raven's. When she came into her inheritance after her father's death, she bought a country manor. Raven's Gate, she decided to call it. But Raven's Gate was haunted, you see. Together, Raven and Rowan hunted down the villainess—the housekeeper, can you imagine?— a reincarnation of some spawn, a creature of sadistic madness. I confess, for a day or so, I was given to regard Carlton's behavior quite closely. And then Raven and Rowan appeared together again in *Howls at Midnight*. I daresay their escapades are awaited most eagerly by nearly everyone in the kingdom."

Aidan smothered a smile. He tipped his head to the side. "Raven," he repeated. "A woman?"

"Why, however did you know?" Alec feigned shock. "Despite the name, Raven is a flame-haired beauty."

"But of course." It was Aidan's turn to echo his brother's earlier statement. He wasn't quite sure he would ever grasp his brother's passion, but he would humor him. "So. We have a flame-haired beauty," he mused. "Petite and delicate?"

"Mmmm."

"And her cohort? Rowan, you say?"

"Indeed."

"A splendid-looking fellow," Aidan mused, "no doubt a well-skilled pugilist and more than able to protect the lovely lady Raven."

"Indeed, but there's the thing. The lovely Raven usually does not *want* Rowan's protection.

She's quite able to take care of herself, thank you very much. And *that*, dear brother, is an exact quote from our beauteous heroine."

"So no one knows the identity of the mysterious F.J. Sparrow. Could it be that *you* are the author?"

Alec rolled his eyes. "You were gone too long, my dear brother. I do believe the heat has damaged your faculties." Alec tapped a lean finger against the center of his lower lip. Now it was he who smothered a laugh. "Although I do remember calling you dim-witted a time or two when we were children."

"Not," Aidan countered with nary a blink, "when I had you pinned to the ground. Much to dear Mama's distress. And Annie's delight."

"Yes, Annie did seem to delight when either of us were in a pickle."

"Or especially *both* of us."

"At any rate, regardless of your opinion of my reading tastes, the fact that these two are at odds is part of the readers' attraction to Raven and Rowan. Or perhaps more aptly, the attraction the two of them share—though each pretends otherwise, of course. It was evident at their very first meeting in *The Devil's Way*, and with each successive novel, it's become ever more pronounced, this new element between them. It's not just the hair-prickling adventure. It's the relationship between the two of them. All await their newest adventure—and the next installment of *Demon of Dartmoor*. I predict Raven and Rowan shall

. . . well, we shall see. It's not only their extraordinary encounters with all manner of unearthly creatures that hold everyone enthralled, but the pull between them. All I can say is that when the two are together—the combination of peril and passion—well, one can fairly feel the way they *sizzle*—and so does my flesh!"

"My God, you make it sound as if they're real people!"

"An acknowledgment to the author's talent to think of them so, don't you think?"

"Perhaps, but it sounds like an erotic novel, not a horror novel, or even a Gothic novel." Aidan tipped his head to the side. "Knowing you, Alec, now I begin to see why *you* are so entranced."

Alec laughed. "Well, perhaps it's a bit of all three!" He paused. "But enough of Raven and Rowan," Alec said after a moment. He studied Aidan. "How is the eye?"

Aidan braced himself. Alec referred to the vision in Aidan's left eye. It had happened that horrible night . . . his rifle backfired, leaving behind burns that would never heal. Though no outward sign of the impairment was evident, things were still fuzzy on the left, and his peripheral vision had been affected. Upon his mother's insistence, he'd seen a surgeon after he'd returned to England. The man merely told him what Aidan already knew, that there would likely never be any improvement in his vision.

Aidan shrugged. "The same." The physician in

London advised against the patch. He said it but weakened the eye even more.

There was a long, drawn-out silence. Aidan sipped his brandy, aware of his brother's regard. "You've changed," Alec said finally. "You're—" Alec seemed to hesitate.

Aidan had no such qualms. One corner of his mouth turned up in what could hardly be called a smile. "Harder?"

Alec neither agreed nor disagreed.

As a lad, Aidan never had any doubts about his abilities to do whatever he set his mind to. Yes, Aidan reflected rather cynically, after so many years away from his homeland, he supposed it was true. He *was* harder than when he'd left. Tougher. God knew he felt infinitely older than his thirty-one years. Why, it seemed a lifetime had passed since he'd joined the Regiment as a green youth of twenty.

Ah, yes, he'd returned a changed man.

A guilty man.

Once again he was aware of Alec's scrutiny. Aidan drank deeply, once, and then again.

"You abandoned a brilliant career," came Alec's inevitable observation. "Still no regrets?"

"Regrets?" Aidan gave a brittle laugh. "What, man, are you mad? Besides, if you'll recall, I'd been considering leaving the Regiment for a number of years already—shortly after Annie married Simon."

"We both know why you left, Aidan."

There was no accusation in Alec's tone, no judgment. Nonetheless, Aidan didn't appreciate the comment, and it showed in the fulminating glance he cast toward Alec.

Alec ignored it. Instead, he leaned back. "Which brings to mind the question . . . How are you, Aidan? How are you really?"

"I'd be perfectly fine if you'd cease your talk of India and the Punjab!"

Alec merely looked at him. Aidan released a puff of air. "Sorry," he said gruffly. "I didn't mean to bite."

"No need to apologize. Point taken," Alec said lightly. "I have just one thing to say, however."

Once again, Aidan steeled himself. Damn! Why couldn't Alec leave well enough alone? Oh, he knew it was concern that motivated him, but still . . .

"It wasn't your fault those men died, Aidan."

There. He'd known what Alec was going to say. It didn't, however, make it any easier. The pain that sliced through Aidan's chest was as sharp as ever.

"I beg to differ, Alec." His lips barely moved. His tone was no less than terse. "It *was* my fault. I was their commander. I was careless. I was greedy, and I led them into a goddamned massacre. I will always—*always*—have their blood on my hands. And those men numbered forty-seven, Alec. Forty-seven souls who died needlessly. Because of me. So yes, it *was* my fault."

The silence ticked out. Alec held his gaze steadily.

"You're still beating yourself into the ground, I see," Alec said softly. "Someday, Aidan, I hope you'll forgive yourself. I can see it won't be today, however. Therefore, I salute your past adventures"—Alec smiled and raised his glass—"and wish you luck in your new endeavors."

Aidan felt the tightness in his throat ease. "To new endeavors then." The two brothers clinked glasses.

Their conversation turned to other things. Aidan's first successful quarter at his new business, his newly completed purchase of a home. Their sister Anne, her husband Simon, and their children.

"That's the answer to what ails you, man," Alec said suddenly. "A woman for the night."

Aidan blinked. "A woman?"

"Exactly! I think what you need, dear brother, is the gentle touch of a woman to soften those hardened edges of yours. Lose yourself in her eyes. Lose yourself in her arms."

Aidan couldn't help but laugh. They fell back into their usual banter. "The touch of a woman cures all, eh?"

"That's been my experience," Alec stated suavely. "I do believe I've heard you haven't lost your touch. I recall hearing rumors several years ago that you'd taken a fancy to the daughter of the Governor-General. So much so that I thought perhaps marriage was in the wings."

Aidan snorted. "Marriage? You're the Duke of Gleneden, brother, and you've yet to find your duchess."

"All in good time," Alec retorted glibly. "Now tell me of this woman."

"Well, she was most definitely not the daughter of the Governor-General," Aidan informed Alec smoothly.

Alec wasn't to be dissuaded. "Who then?"

"I rather suspect you refer to a relative of a member of the diplomatic corps. A widow, in fact. The lady pursued me, and that is all you need know, dear brother."

In truth, Englishwomen were relatively rare in India, a beautiful one still more rare. Aidan might have eyed the daughters and wives of high-ranking officials, but he wouldn't allow desire to hold sway over him. He had too much discipline for that. But while he still possessed the same physical urges of a man for a woman, he was discerning enough to spend his needs with one who didn't smell of musk and grime and dust.

Alec appeared to take great delight in the admission. "You were always the ladies' man when you were young, Aidan."

"Only because I observed my brother. And from the talk I hear, it's still true. I was at a dinner party the other night with an old friend, and I overheard a woman talking most avidly about a man called the Black Scotsman. She'd had one glass of champagne too many, I suspect, but I listened most keenly when she mentioned the Black Scotsman. Isn't that what the lovelies used to call you when you were young?"

Alec gave a burst of laughter. "Good heavens! Don't tell me that particular moniker has resurfaced?"

"It would seem so."

"Why, I haven't heard it in years!" Alec hiked a black brow, a half smile on his lips. "Dare I inquire what else this lady ventured?"

"I believe something about the Black Scotsman's charm being exceeded only by his . . . how shall I say this?" Aidan feigned a great pondering. "Now I recall! His charm was exceeded only by his masterly achievements in the boudoir."

"Masterly, eh?" Alec laughed with gusto. "And you divined they referred to me? Well, then, I thank you for the compliment. Though I do hope *you* didn't learn how to become a ladies' man by—oh, how shall *I* say this?—er . . . by direct observation when you were a boy trailing in my footsteps."

It was Aidan's turn to arch a heavy brow. "Set your mind at ease," he said bluntly. "I should like to think I've acquired my own brand of technique rather than imitate my brother's."

"Then use it, man! I'm in no position to judge,

but I should imagine the right woman would go a long way toward what ails you. Aye, perhaps a strong, healthy dose of lust is all you need, Aidan. And not just for tonight."

"An affair?"

"All the better." Alec slanted him a rather wicked grin.

"Ah. Sage words of advice from the legendary Black Scotsman, then?"

"Aye," Alec declared. "But remember, discretion is everything."

Aidan chuckled. A few moments later, he glanced at the clock on the marble mantel. "Gads, look at the time! I'd best be off if I'm to find a woman for the night."

Alec laughed and clapped a hand on Aidan's shoulder.

In the grand entrance hall, Carlton appeared with Aidan's greatcoat. The butler frowned. "It's quite dreadfully cold, Lord Aidan. Shall I summon the master's carriage?"

Aidan shook his head. "No need, Carlton."

"A hack then," Alec started to say.

Aidan dismissed them both with a hand. "Thank you, no. I shall return home the same way I came."

"What! You walked?" Alec shot him a look that proclaimed he was surely convinced Aidan had gone daft. "Mother commented today she wouldn't be surprised if the Thames froze over, the way it did the year she and Father married."

Carlton assisted Aidan into his greatcoat. He was still frowning severely as he took up a post near the front door.

"You're welcome to stay the night," Alec told him.

"No, I shall let you return to your tales of demons and darkness by the famed—"

He stopped short and glanced at Alec inquiringly. "F.J. Sparrow," Alec supplied.

Aidan feigned a shudder of fear. "There, you see? I vow, with your talk of devils and demons—why, the very name F.J. Sparrow—you've frightened me half to death. I dare not stay the night. I'd neither close my eyes nor sleep a wink, for fear of some vile creature walking straight from the pages of your cursed novels!"

Alec merely hiked a black brow.

"Besides, what if *you* should find a female companion for the night?" Aidan added. "We'd have to share her."

"We've shared many things, brother, but never a woman. And I daresay, we shall not. Now, let Carlton have the carriage brought around."

"Nay, my lord duke. I fancy a brisk walk instead."

"Mad, man, that's what you are," came Alec's muttered observation.

The memory came unbidden . . . All at once Aidan recalled the intense heat shimmering over the deserts in India, the gritty sand finding its way into his mouth and flesh, stinging his skin and burrowing into his pores even beneath his uniform.

"Strange as it may sound to you," he said with a faint smile, "during all those years in India, the one thing I longed for most of all was the chill of a British winter. Mist, frost, snow, I'd have welcomed any and all."

And with that, Aidan ventured outside . . . and into the blackest depths of the night.

Chapter Two

Word spread quickly, as I knew it would. That somehow he has escaped that place where no one said he could escape. No matter that it was an accident. That it was never meant to be.

In walked a man.

And out slipped a demon.

I will need help with a creature as vile as this.

A message, I thought. I must dispatch a message to Rowan. And quickly.

Demon of Dartmoor, F.J. Sparrow

Someone is watching me, Fionna thought, trying desperately to determine if she was right.

She was. She felt it in every fiber of her being, every pore of her soul.

She was being followed.

Something was afoot. Some*one* was afoot, for

she knew she was not alone. And this had nothing to do with the fearful creatures created by Miss Fionna Josephine Hawkes.

Ah, yes, Fionna was a teller of tales, tales of the dark side of the soul, of supernatural beings that transcended belief. Without question, she possessed an imagination most vivid. Yet every sense inside screamed a warning. And Fionna had the terrifying sensation that someone lurked near.

Following with stealthy step. Moving when she did. *Stopping* at almost the precise instant that she did.

This was not within the pages of a novel. This was here.

This was real.

This was now.

Thoroughly unsettled, Fionna whirled, ready to confront whoever it was.

There was about the night a sense of eerie stillness. Even now, the darkness seemed to creep in, closing all around her. Indeed, as she had oft written, the depths of the night could be terrifying—though Fionna did not find it so. What she did find terrifying—no, disturbing, for "terrifying" was far too strong a word—was that absolute stillness. That sense of waiting—for something to happen, knowing not *what* would happen . . .

The world seemed to have stopped in time, like a heart that had ceased to beat. There was nothing, no breeze to stir the air, ruffle the treetops, for the limbs were barren of life and would remain so until spring. There was no moon to cast out even the most feeble slice of iridescence. What light there was came from a trace of snowfall that had fallen earlier; it was as if all the earth were laden with silvery crystals, frozen in time. Beautiful, almost unearthly so. Yet cold—so very, very cold . . .

She shivered, yet this was a shiver that came from the innermost depths of her being—and had not a whit to do with the bone-chilling temperature. She even thought the stark, withering limbs of the trees seemed to stretch out toward her, seeking to close around her, to squeeze the life and breath from her—though she well knew that was given to sheer imagination.

Yet all the while her eyes strained, as if to see through every tree, through the heavy darkness, around every corner.

All that she heard was that chilling, absolute silence.

Then, the hollow chimes of a clock tolled through the night . . . the very stroke of midnight. So unexpected was the sound that Fionna actually started.

Turning on her heel, she began to walk once more.

It came again, the sound of footsteps, almost attuned with hers—no, it was more of an echo. As if when *she* stopped, *he* stopped.

Had she been running, she'd have felt . . . pursued. As it was, she felt . . . violated.

And furious. Yes, most of all, she was furious.

For Fionna relished the night, cherished its solitude. When darkness veiled the world, she felt . . . free. Oh, but there was no other way to describe it! As if the dark let free her imagination.

Yet she was certain she heard footsteps for—oh, perhaps at least three times. Sensed a presence that made her skin prickle—and that not an easy task, to be sure, given her occupation.

It had crossed her mind to speak to a constable. But she hadn't actually *seen* anyone, so how silly would that sound? No doubt he would merely gaze at her as if she were an hysterical female. Besides, if she contacted the police, she could not—*would* not—convey her alternate identity. Oh, but someone would have a rousing good chuckle with his comrades. He'd surely have laughed in her face. For all that Fionna was firmly grounded in reality, they might consider her . . . *mad*. No doubt a constable would boorishly advise that she remain indoors, which would only make her fume.

No, Fionna Josephine Hawkes wouldn't hide behind closed doors. She wouldn't cower.

She had a living to make. Her nightly jaunts allowed her to think, to shuffle and ponder and plot.

Steeling herself, she stopped again. Her gaze swiveled in all directions. She held her breath, not even daring to exhale. All she could hear was the drumming of her own heart pounding hard in her ears.

Chiding herself for her folly, she gathered herself in hand, turned, and resumed her journey toward home.

But she couldn't lie to herself. She was nervous. Skittish. Was it folly after all? Was it nonsense?

Rubbish! she chided herself. *What would Raven do if she were being followed?* she asked herself. What *would* Raven do? *Raven,* she reminded herself, *was unafraid of anything, adventurous to the point of being reckless . . .*

And Rowan would have been directly behind her, ready to step in should she need him.

There! She heard them again, firm, rhythmic footballs, quickening now with their approach.

Rounding the corner, Fionna ducked behind the next doorway—it shielded her from view. She lived in one of the very best neighborhoods of London. There was little crime, either day or night. She was still frightened, but suddenly angry as well.

The footsteps halted. The intruder was close. She could just make out the outline of his form—shoulders wide and brawny beneath the layers of his greatcoat. Between his top hat and the shadows, she could detect virtually nothing of his features, his age, or naught else. Only that his face was a mass of shadows and his form a powerful one.

She braced herself, both inwardly and outwardly. *Drat!* He was almost upon her now.

She gripped her parasol hard, with both hands, bringing it up to rest near her shoulder. It had been snowing lightly when she'd left home. Thank heaven she'd brought it! Her heart was beating like a fury. By heaven, if necessary, she would use this as a weapon. She would—

"Hello?" came the sound of a man's low baritone. "Madam, are you—"

Fionna didn't wait to hear any more. Here was her tormentor, in the flesh. Gritting her teeth, she sighted his midsection . . .

And swung her parasol with all her might.

Aidan's conversation with Alec was still fresh in his thoughts when he departed Alec's town house that night.

No matter how he tried, the memory of that night in the Punjab never quite left him. Neither his mind . . .

Or his heart.

Bitterly he wondered if it ever would.

Rajul.

Even dead, the man had the power to fire the blood in his veins to boiling. The rebel leader's image filled his brain—the arrogant tilt of his turbaned head, that ever-taunting gleam in coal black eyes.

He'd wanted Rajul too badly. Glory or gain had nothing to do with it. When word came that Rajul was near, he'd reacted too rashly. *Unthinkingly.* He should have waited for the troops he knew were less than half a day's ride away.

His steps continued, echoing through the frigid London air.

Turmoil raged in Aidan's breast. Self-loathing poured through him, boiling through his veins. He'd never had any shortcomings when it came to his abilities. After all, he was Colonel Aidan McBride, the pride of the British Empire. The man whose military career had been built by the fact that every decision he made was thorough and calculated and deliberate, the fact that he anticipated with an almost uncanny perception the actions and reactions of the enemy.

But not that night. *Not then.*

Rajul had escaped.

His mouth twisted. God, how he'd fooled them all. His men. His superiors. Even himself.

And to think he'd been offered a medal. Offered a promotion, for the Command considered the toll on the rebel forces a major blow.

To Aidan, it was a travesty. A joke.

It changed nothing. It didn't erase the deaths of forty-seven men whose blood had been spilled needlessly. Whose blood would forever stain his hands.

And that was why he'd forsaken his so-called brilliant career.

Deliberately he forced the tension from his jaw. Alec was right. He needed to forget. This was London, and by God, that part of his life was no more.

The merest trace of a smile broke the taut line of his lips. A strong healthy dose of lust had been Alec's precise words. Well, perhaps he was right. Perhaps he needed a woman whose skilled lips and warm hands would shatter the past. Purge the ache inside and replace it with another, one that might be filled, at least for a while.

Rounding the corner, a muffled sound brought his head up sharply. He spied a lone figure gliding along the walkway before him. Almost in spite of himself, he couldn't help but be reminded of Alec's admiration of F.J. Sparrow's ghoulish tales.

Bedamned! he thought. He squinted a little. Granted, his distance vision wasn't what it used to be, but . . . speak of the devil . . . By heaven, it was a woman!

But this wasn't a neighborhood that was frequented by ladies of the evening, selling their bodies. And if he weren't mistaken, *this* woman appeared to be respectably dressed. He was suddenly impatient, almost angry. So why the devil was she out walking alone, with no escort . . . at the hour of midnight?

He began to walk faster. Then she disappeared from view around the corner.

Aidan hastened his pace.

"Hello? Madam, are you—"

Aidan had one single view of her clutching her parasol—as if it were a cricket bat.

That was his last thought before he heard a *whoosh* of air.

He sensed it, more than he saw it. His hand shot out, propelled by sheer instinct, at precisely the right instant. He caught the parasol squarely in the middle, holding it away from his body— squarely between them. His attacker gave a little scream of frustration at being thwarted and sought to yank it from his grasp.

Had his reflexes not been so quick, he realized, he might have suffered a good wallop in the belly. The woman twisted the parasol fiercely. Aidan refused to release it.

"My good woman, it'll take more than a parasol to bring me down." Aidan hadn't yet decided if he was more amused or angry.

It was as if they had faced off against each other in order to do battle. Indeed, she appeared ready to do exactly that. Her expression was fierce, her determination evident as he caught a glimpse of her face beneath the wide brim of her bonnet. She was still grappling with him, trying with all her might to wrest the parasol free. "Let go!" she cried.

"Not until I'm assured you won't try to use it against me again," he stated grimly. "For all I know, you've a pistol in your reticule."

"I'm not carrying a reticule! And you were following me!" she accused. "Why?"

"I wasn't following you. I was merely on my way home when I saw you. I thought to lend assistance if you were in need of it."

Something flashed in her eyes. She made a small, choked sound—a sob? Was she trembling? He couldn't quite tell, but he suspected she was on the verge of it.

Something within him softened. "I was concerned," he said again. "I thought perhaps you were hurt." He paused, then added quietly, "I didn't mean to frighten you."

"I wasn't frightened!" she denied, yet with such vehemence that he knew very well she was.

He released his grip from the parasol. She immediately snatched it back.

Aidan indicated the parasol with a swirl of a gloved fingertip. "May I suggest the very tip might be quite useful as a weapon if need be." He lifted two fingers upward. "Lunge at the face. The eyes, if you are able. The chest or belly or . . . parts thereunder." Another swirl below his waist.

He ignored her gasp of shock.

"A knee there is particularly effective if you are not carrying your parasol. It will bring a man down to his knees in a heartbeat, if not to the ground itself. And if you are carrying it and if you were behind your assailant, then swing as you did. At the back. The head. Or squarely behind the knees. Vulnerable areas, all of them. And if you are in front, then swing as you did with me. At the belly, hard as you can. It likely won't bend a man completely double, but it just might give you the chance to bring your knee up and into his face. Hopefully that, at least, will give you the chance to run and scream your bloody head off."

"Really. And what if I'd intended to do all of those things?"

What a defiant little creature she was! "Then I should call you a resourceful woman—a woman well prepared indeed."

His observation seemed to reassure her. But she was still a trifle frightened, though he sensed she was doing her best not to show it.

His eyes flicked over her. "Do you have any idea of the hour?"

She blinked. "What?"

"A woman like you should not be strolling alone at this time of night." His tone was sharp. He didn't care.

Her eyes lit like sparks again. He couldn't quite make out their color—and suddenly wished that he could.

Aidan arched a brow and continued, "My dear lady, when a woman is alone at night, wandering the streets . . ." He paused, that she might take his meaning.

He recognized the very instant she did. "I am not wandering," he was haughtily informed. "I know precisely where I am going. Nor, sir, am I a light skirt. So if you're in an amorous mood—"

"I am not," he interrupted coolly. "And I was not implying that you are. Were that the case, I imagine you would be trying your best to lure me close—not bring me down instead."

She said nothing, merely matched his stare with a boldness that bordered on fury.

"As for you, young woman, it's after midnight."

Her chin came up. "I'm well aware of the time. Not that it's any of your affair, but I . . . had a late engagement."

Aidan assessed her with an unflinching regard, taking in the way her eyes flitted away. He studied the slim line of her jaw, slightly square—and also noted the way she fiddled nervously with her parasol.

She was lying. Furthermore, she wasn't accustomed to lying.

"Then you should have hired a hack," he said bluntly. "At the very least, your gentleman friend should have sent you home in his coach."

His censure was sharper than he intended. She didn't like it—not one bit, he saw. Not that it appeared there was anything she liked about him . . .

"Well, *sir*," she stressed, "not that it's any of your affair, but I wasn't with a gentleman. Nor do I take kindly to strangers—or anyone else—telling me what I should and should not do. I'm quite able to take care of myself, thank you very much."

I'm quite able to take care of myself, thank you very much. Aidan discovered himself unexpectedly amused. Wasn't that what Alec had said the lovely Raven told her counterpart Rowan?

He conceded that women were changing. They were more independent than when he'd left for India, capable of seeing to themselves and their needs.

"So I see. As for who I am, my name is Aidan. Aidan McBride." He bowed low. "And now I am no longer a stranger."

Judging by her silence and the set of her jaw, she didn't agree.

Aidan gestured over his shoulder, and went on pleasantly. "A pity we must make introductions at this time of night. I've just moved into the town house down the street, you see."

"Excellent." She spoke through her teeth. "Then it won't take long for you to get home."

"And I won't be returning home until I escort *you* home." He held up a hand. "I see you are tempted to argue. However, I insist."

Her back was ramrod-straight. "Sir, as you must surely be aware, this is a highly respectable neighborhood. Therefore, you may leave."

Drat, but the woman was stubborn! "I couldn't call myself a gentleman if I left a woman alone on the streets at this hour of the night, no matter how respectable the neighborhood. I should imagine my mother would be quite disappointed were I to do so." He didn't bother disguising the steel beneath his polite statement.

He knew that *she* knew it too. "While I should hate for your mother to be disappointed in you, I say again, sir, you may leave."

They continued to lock horns.

"Nonetheless, I am compelled to escort you to your home," he said quietly. "I warn you, it will do no good to argue."

She wanted to—oh, how she wanted to. Aidan saw it in the way she tightly compressed her lips. Yet the strangest thing happened—something flitted over her face. He had the oddest feeling that she was warring within herself.

"There is no need to escort me further. You see, I . . . *am* home."

It was a grudging admission.

Aidan glanced up at the sign dangling above. "Every Book and Cranny," he read aloud. He squinted, then looked down at her. "But—this is a bookshop."

"So it is," she returned pleasantly.

His gaze narrowed. "You live here?"

"I do."

"Abovestairs?"

"I don't believe that is any of your business, sir."

"Well—" Aidan was at a rare loss for words. "Then at least allow me to know that you are safely inside, Miss . . . " He paused expectantly.

"Hawkes," she said finally. "Fionna Hawkes."

Yet another grudging admission. Lord, but it seemed the chit guarded herself closely!

"The pleasure is all mine, Miss Hawkes."

Somehow he didn't expect her to return the courtesy.

And she did not. She merely regarded him with that same wariness that marked the whole of their encounter.

"What makes you so sure it is 'Miss'?"

"You denied having a gentleman friend. I believe if you had a husband, you'd have very promptly pointed it out to me. And," he said smoothly, "you are not wearing a ring."

"I am wearing gloves! You couldn't possibly see whether or not I wear a ring!"

"A vehement denial," he said softly. "And you've just now given me good reason to believe I am right."

Her entire body stiffened. "You presume too much, Mr. McBride."

Her lips barely moved. She had fire, Aidan decided. She had spunk.

And Aidan liked that. The admission startled him a little. Moreover, the woman piqued his interest more with every word.

"Perhaps," he said with a shrug. "But you've taken a dislike to me, I see."

He was surprised when her gaze skittered away. He heard the ragged breath she drew. "It is not dislike, sir," she said. "I . . . We do not know each other. I am, by nature, protective of my private life."

Aidan was silent for a moment. He could respect that, he found himself admitting. God knew, he'd grown protective of his own. "Well, then"—he gave a slight bow—"I shall bid you good night."

The words declared an end to their encounter. He executed a slight bow.

The chit said no more. His hands behind his back, Aidan remained where he was, watching as she retreated a few steps, then extracted a key from the inside of her cloak.

He noticed the way she glanced over her shoulder several times as she fumbled a little with the key before the lock finally turned and she opened the door. He also noted the way she did not turn her back on him fully, as though to make certain he made no sudden move to follow as she slipped inside.

The click of the lock seemed unusually loud.

Only when he saw the glow of a lamp inside the shop did he turn and amble toward his town house, his mind on the woman he'd just met.

Fionna Hawkes was a most untrusting woman. A most cautious woman. All in all, a most curious one, to be sure.

And, he realized with a vehemence that was almost startling, quite the most fetching one he'd seen in a long, long time.

Of that, he was most certain of all.

* * *

Fionna loved the dark, for it lit her mind, her muse; it was truly her inspiration. It fired her imagination as nothing else could. She had never feared the depths of night, not even as a child. She reveled in it, particularly on those moonless nights when all the world lay closed and sleeping, while *she* lay awake and dreaming—of legends and myths, and stories yet to be told. That was when her mind came alive, when *she* came alive.

Climbing the stairs to her apartments above the bookshop, she couldn't forget the incident. Had she acted like a fool? No, she decided, it was better to be prepared. And she would not remain closeted behind closed doors, cowering like a frightened little mouse. She'd never been the sort to frighten easily, else she could never write the stories she did.

No, she was not easily frightened, which made her wonder if she had been followed last week.

There was no logic to it, unfortunately. She had sensed a presence, with all that she possessed. She'd known, even before she whirled to confront whoever it was that followed, that she would see nothing. Yet that very same sense warned that something—some*one*—was near. Following. *Watching*.

It was quite unnerving.

Distinctly unsettling.

Too much like *Demon of Dartmoor* for her peace of mind.

And Aidan McBride . . . he was nearly as unsettling as well, though in a far different way. She pictured him again. His manner grated somewhat. So confident, so sure of himself, so determined to play the gentleman/protector. She'd caught a glimpse of his profile, arresting and handsome, from what she could see of him. Somehow she sensed that had they met in the light of day, she would have found him a most striking man. His image swirled anew in her mind.

In irritation, she wrenched thoughts of him far away, relegating him to the distant corner of her mind. Mr. Aidan McBride was gone. And she vowed to give him no further thought.

Her dander rose as she recalled his insistence that he escort her home. His manner conveyed displeasure at her refusal—that she was out at midnight. She would certainly not entertain the notion that she cease her nightly walks. She'd been doing it for several years now, even before she'd moved to London. She never ventured far from home. By heaven, she would not be confined! She couldn't. She wrote of all that lay secluded in the night, of all that lay hidden in the darkness of the soul, and . . . well, it put her into the proper frame of mind. It helped to set her thoughts to rights, for she was at her most creative at night.

Even when she was very young, Fionna had always been given to dreaming; an only child, she and her parents lived in a village just south of Lon-

don. Once in church she'd sat through the service
and hadn't even noticed when at last the church
had emptied, or even the sound of Vicar Tomlinson's voice until he shook her shoulder, startling her. In school, she'd been scolded soundly
for her lack of attention. But oh, how she loved
the hours between sunset and sunrise! How she
loved the night! And from the depths of the dark,
her dreams of becoming something more than
she had ever aspired to had been achieved.

The neighbors in the village would have been
shocked to discover that Fionna Josephine Hawkes
was the authoress of tales dark and twisted and
tormented—of the fiends and monsters and demons conjured up. So would her neighbors in
London, she suspected. No doubt at all, everyone
considered her quite bizarre, for Fionna had little
interest in finding a husband, either then or now.
At six-and-twenty, she supposed she was now
consigned to the role of spinster—not that she
cared a whit.

Snug at home in familiar, comfortable sur-
roundings, her earlier anxiety seemed rather silly
now. Sternly she reminded herself that she'd
never actually *seen* anything, nor had she been
approached by anyone threatening—except for
Aidan McBride. True, she'd been frightened, and
yes, he'd nearly scared the very wits out of her.
But *he* had not been frightening.

Annoyed with herself for thinking about him
again, she headed to the kitchen. She boiled a

kettle of water, brewed a pot of tea, and walked to her desk. In her hand was a dainty, flowered teacup that was part of her mother's china set.

No, Fionna thought. She would not be cowed. She was a woman of routine, of regularity. She was, she admitted, a very private woman. A young girl, Glynis, came several days a week to do the occasional chore and see that her gowns were kept clean and pressed. Fionna preferred to do her own tidying up. So she cooked for herself and cleaned for herself, though her monetary situation was hardly such that she must watch her pocketbook. Indeed, quite the opposite at present.

Perhaps, she decided, she was even wrong about being followed.

For there was a need for Fionna Hawkes to guard herself closely. To preserve her privacy in the same way she safeguarded her identity. To protect her secret to the utmost.

A tiny little smile curved her lips. It had long been a dream of hers to explore the world to her heart's content. The pyramids in Egypt. To turn her ear to the chattering singsong of Chinese and wander amidst the markets as she wished, fingering lavish, delicate silks. Perhaps even to experience the wildness of an African safari—or see the majestic rise of the towering peaks in the American West.

But not now. Not just yet. For this was a dream that would simply have to wait . . .

Her mother must come first.

For now, she reminded herself, she must be content. She had a responsibility to her mother. When she'd brought Mama to London, they'd had to sell the house and lands. They had lived in comfort but not in luxury, for Papa had been but a modest landowner—and, as she discovered upon his death, he'd been a most lenient squire, dismissing many a debt from his tenants. But now that she was well established in her chosen vocation, her work had proved to have its rewards. She was well paid. She lived in ample comfort. And so did her mother.

That was the most important thing of all.

Slowly she lowered the teacup. An empty ache spread in Fionna's breast. Her throat caught. Her mother . . . ah, but it hurt so to think of her! And her father . . . He had been her staunchest champion.

Rising, she went to the bookshelf next to her desk and pulled out a copy of *Satan's Path*. How proud he'd been when she'd torn open the wrappings around that very novel. That moment was etched in her mind forever. Papa had been beaming, so very, very proud! And she had been so happy, happier than she'd ever been in her life.

She had always been a rather solitary person. Her father had always understood her best, and Fionna missed him dreadfully! Never had she dreamed—never in the world—that she would be quite so alone, the way she was now.

For her mother . . . oh, Mama was still in this

world . . . and yet she was not. A twinge of bitter-sweet pain closed around her chest. Her mother had always possessed a certain fragility about her. But when Fionna's father, tall and stalwart and hardly ill a day in his life, had suddenly died in his sleep one night, no one expected it. No one.

It was then that Mama took to her bed for days, refusing to leave it, refusing to acknowledge that he was gone. Her father's death had dealt a blow from which her mother never recovered, Fionna realized.

Rising, she raised a hand and moved aside the lovely lace curtains to stare into the frigid night.

No, she thought achingly, *Mama never got better. Not really.* And when Fionna thought about her mother's . . . illness, for she could not bear to think of it—to *call* it otherwise—her throat clogged tight with emotion.

It had been serendipity, she supposed, when the offer to serialize *Demon of Dartmoor* had come through. By then Fionna had authored four novels, but this offer surpassed all others by far. She could hardly refuse—for several reasons.

She had already sought help for her mother from the best physician in London, Dr. Colson. Cases such as her mother's were his particular specialty. When he had suggested he could care for her better in his facility in London, Fionna had balked. Yet in time she had yielded, for her mother's condition continued to worsen. Fionna knew then that it must be done. And if her mother must be moved to London, then she would move as well, for it was imperative that she remain close to her mother. That Mama not feel as if she'd been deserted.

Fionna shuddered. That would surely have sent Mama over the edge.

It was also then she came up with the idea of opening Every Book and Cranny. Her position as bookshop owner afforded her the opportunity to maintain her anonymity as F.J. Sparrow, to continue the ruse even with her publisher—she "acted" as go-between, both with delivery of her manuscripts and payment.

Keeping her mother in the very best institution—faith, but she refused to call it an asylum for she loathed that word!—was expensive. But this opportunity, coupled with the moderate proceeds from the sale of the house—assured that she could keep her mother in comfort for some time to come.

Until the time when Mama was well once more, she told herself firmly.

Gathering her manuscript in hand, Fionna tapped the sheets on the desk top and gathered her thoughts as well. It was taking a little longer than usual to settle in tonight after her walk, for she was still a trifle nervous. Her gaze was drawn to the window—her glance through the frosted pane lingered.

Yet tonight had been different. Tonight had

stepped forth a man named Aidan McBride. And it certainly didn't appear as if *he* had been trying to hide either his identity or his presence. Fionna fancied herself a fair judge of character and details—it helped immeasurably in her work.

Aidan McBride's image danced before her eyes—her vivid recall was most irritating. His mouth was set in a stern line, yet there was something about his manner that warned he could be quite the rogue if he wanted.

And if ever there was a bold, aggressive man who was sure of himself and all within his world, it was Aidan McBride.

Damn the man anyway! Why did he persist in cropping up?

Squaring her shoulders, Fionna drew up her chair a bit closer to her desk, then picked up her quill. There was, after all, she reminded herself pointedly, the need for gainful employment. She twirled the quill between her fingertips, her eyes narrowed in thought.

An instant later, the tip of the quill dipped into the pot. She began to write:

I knew, of course, that Rowan . . .

Chapter Three

It is difficult to put the image of that poor wretched soul from my mind. I trembled when I saw him.

Both of us knew, Rowan and I, that this was a place of death, a place of chilling silence.

A place of evil.

Alas, it is true, I fear. A demon has been set free.

He has claimed his first victim.

Demon of Dartmoor, F.J. Sparrow

The tinkling little bell at Every Book and Cranny gave a cheery little sound as the door opened and closed. A floorboard creaked beneath Aidan's weight as he stepped inside and glanced around curiously. The shop was long and narrow, with floor-to-ceiling shelves that formed the perimeter of the room on all sides. Another three paralleled the length of the building, with several aisles in between.

Aidan began to leisurely browse the shelves, for neither the proprietor nor any clerk had yet to appear.

From the rear of the building, he heard brisk footsteps. A figure emerged from the back room, briskly dusting off her hands.

"Hello!" came a cheery greeting. "Feel free to have a look, and should you need—"

The lady regarded him with narrowed eyes. "You're back!" Her tone was no longer so cheery. Indeed, she looked—and sounded—damned displeased.

Aidan was down on his haunches. He held up a novel. "What!" he said lightly. "Did you think I'd come to see you?"

In all honesty, Fionna *had* thought he'd come to see her. Her lips tightened. How silly, she decided, chiding herself for her foolishness. Why ever should she think he'd come to see *her*?

She didn't dare back down at his bold, unrelenting regard—for oh, there was no question, he *was* bold and quite the man of self-assurance. Despite the fact that he remained where he was on his haunches, despite his tone—despite her position above him, there was no question that here was a man who might easily have put many *another* man to quivering in his boots with only a word or a look.

His hair was cropped so that a dark lock fell over his forehead. His brows were just as dark and one remained quirked high. Fionna ran her tongue over her lips. She felt the fool, surely looked the fool. But by God, she would not *be* a fool.

Had *she* been any less assured, that air of authority that surrounded him might have set her aback. She could well imagine some silly young maid fanning herself feverishly—at either his approval, or his *dis*approval.

He rose to his feet; his height was staggering. Fionna sucked in a breath. She wasn't quite so confident as she appeared. He seemed even taller than he had last night when he wore his top hat, now tucked under an arm. Perhaps her own short stature made him seem so. And she was surely losing her mind, for in all honesty, the man was quite splendid-looking—though in a rugged sort of way, not a *perfect* sort of way. Her breath was lost as she took in the width of his shoulders; they seemed to fill the entire gap between the shelves. Every part of him, every inch of him was so blatantly masculine it nearly set *her* heart to fluttering.

His face was deeply tanned, leaving her a trifle puzzled given that it was the middle of winter. His eyes were several shades deeper than turquoise, like blue ink, set off even further by the bronzed hue of his skin.

It wasn't just his features either. He wore no

greatcoat but a warm navy wool frock coat and shiny black boots. His posture was every inch as straight as she recalled. Of course she'd heard the phrase—*he cut a fine figure of a man.* But for the first time Fionna was truly aware of its meaning—why one would use it and precisely when one would use it—and it was all she could do not to stare.

In shock. In . . . oh, but she was surely losing her wits! . . . in admiration.

"Perhaps I can help you. Is there a book in particular that you're looking for? An author, perhaps?" It wasn't like her to babble, and she prayed she wasn't.

A slight pause. "Frank . . . Crow? Wren? No, that's not right either." Another pause. "F.J. something or other, I believe." He shook his head. "Damn, I can't remember."

But Aidan hadn't come to buy a damned novel by the man, or anyone else, for that matter. He'd come to see *her.* Fionna Hawkes. In the flesh again. In the light. Without the bundling of cumbersome winter clothing.

He thought of Alec's advice last night—that he find a woman. *Lose yourself in her eyes. Lose yourself in her arms.* He found himself unwittingly amused. Somehow he didn't think Miss Fionna Hawkes was quite what Alec had in mind.

But Aidan liked what he saw, heaven above, he did. She wasn't a silly debutante out to snare a husband—she was too old for that. Not that she was *old*. He guessed her age to be—oh, some-where in her midtwenties, perhaps.

He also liked the fact that she possessed no vanity about her appearance—there was too much that gave it away. Her eyes were a shade between amber and brown. Her face was scrubbed clean, void of any of the creams that some women favored to add color to their lips and cheeks. She had made no effort to hide the smattering of freckles on her nose, as some women were wont to do. He felt something inside him tighten. Oh, but she was a beauty, a sweet, natural beauty—not perfection. And it was that very unadorned quality that made her more beautiful still.

Little tendrils of hair, the color of chestnuts turning in the sunlight, trailed from her nape and her temples. And there, in front of her ears. It was as if she'd wound her hair in a loose topknot and hadn't given it another thought. He wondered if she was the absentminded sort.

"Do you know the author I mean?"

"Possibly," she said slowly.

He snapped his fingers. "Wait! The author's name is some species of bird . . . Sparrow! That's it, F.J. Sparrow! Have you any of his works? I understand he's quite the storyteller."

Oh, now what was she to say to *that*? Fionna resisted the urge to laugh.

It was her father who had encouraged her to write whatever she wished. Oh, how they had laughed, that no one else knew that *she* was F.J. Sparrow. Considering the dark nature of her work, she didn't want the villagers all agog, so she'd chosen a pen name, knowing people would assume the writer was male.

Success followed, and who could argue with success?

"Are you acquainted with his works?"

"Intimately," she said rather demurely. "Is there any title in particular you're after?"

His brow furrowed in consternation. "I fear I cannot remember," he muttered. "*Spectres in the Night? Satan's Tale?*"

Fionna smothered a laugh. She wasn't sure if he meant *Satan's Tale* or *Satan's Tail*.

"Well," she said lightly, "there is a novel called *Satan's Path*."

He was still in the throes of concentration, rubbing his chin now. Suddenly he snapped his fingers. "No, that's not it. Wait . . . There's more. Now I recall. The novel he wrote . . . There's a woman named Raven, a man named Reginald."

Fionna nearly clamped a hand over her mouth to hold back her mirth. It was amusing; no, more than amusing. Of course there were occasions when it was irritating, but how very like a man—and the rest of Britain—to assume that the author was a man. As if women had no minds or imagination and were unable to think of anything but household affairs and children. But mostly it was just absurdly amusing to keep such a secret, with no one but Mama the wiser.

If Mama even remembered.

She willed away the bitter pain that crept around her heart.

It was all she could do to get out, "I believe you mean Raven and Rowan. And there are several novels by F.J. Sparrow that feature the pair. *The Devil's Way* was the first. Unfortunately, it's become rather difficult to come by."

"Damn. That's the very one my brother Alec covets."

Fionna thought of the ten copies she had in her apartments upstairs. She was loath to part with them, not until there were more copies available.

Fionna hesitated. "I've heard rumors," she allowed slowly, "that it may be reprinted."

"Soon?"

"Well, of course there's no way I can be certain. But I've heard rumors."

"Excellent. Perhaps then you'll be able to conjure one up for both of us."

Conjure up? She could conjure up ghouls and monsters, phantoms and wraiths. Fionna found herself possessed of the strangest urge to giggle. Giggle? *Her?* Oh, heaven help her, it was so unlike herself that she gave in and smiled.

He ran a finger along the line of her jaw. "Are you familiar with *The Giaour* by Lord Byron?"

She nodded, rather stunned by his bold, unexpected touch.

> *"'But first, on earth as vampire sent,*
> *Thy corse shall from its tomb be rent:*
> *Then ghastly haunt thy native place,*
> *And suck the blood of all thy race;'"*

Fionna blinked, still pondering the reason for his quote, the mention of Byron's poem.

The corners of his mouth turned up ever so slightly. "Well, my lady of midnight, I am pleased to see you smile, for I'd begun to fear last night that perhaps I'd encountered a vampire."

As if he feared anything!

Fionna led the way to a special display near the back counter; her privilege as the author, she had decided. "Perhaps if you're not familiar with F.J. Sparrow's work, you'd like to begin with his first, *Satan's Path*. Or the second novel featuring Raven and Rowan, *Howls at Midnight*."

"I shall take one of each," he declared.

Plucking a copy of each off the shelf, she handed them to him.

"Will you let me know if and when *The Devil's Way* becomes available?"

"Certainly. You may stop in anytime."

"I look forward to it. A pity, though, that the first edition is not available. As I mentioned, my brother is quite the devoted admirer of F.J. Sparrow. I vow, surely his most dedicated fan, if you could listen to his praises."

Fionna hesitated. "I can make no promises that it will be printed again. But I am acquainted with another bookseller, who knows another, and there is a chance—the very, very slightest chance, mind you—that I might be able to locate one before that."

"Wonderful!" He went on rather thoughtfully, "Alec tells me this fellow F.J. Sparrow is quite mysterious. Indeed, I believe he said that no one really knows who he is."

"Yes, I've heard that as well." They were getting into dangerous territory here, Fionna decided.

It appeared Aidan wasn't yet ready to leave the subject behind. "I vow Alec would be over the moon to have a signed copy. My brother-in-law Simon is a collector of rare volumes, and I fear he's turned Alec into yet another." He shrugged. "I daresay, in my mind, F.J. Sparrow is quite the freakish fellow, given the subject matter of the novels he writes."

Fionna very nearly snatched back the copies of *Satan's Path* and *Howls at Midnight* he held at his side.

Her smile had frozen. Freakish? *Freakish?* A tad eccentric, she might have called herself. But what the blazes would he know about it? she nearly snapped. "Perhaps F.J. Sparrow merely values he—" Ye gads, she caught herself just in time! She'd almost said *her*. Oh, but she must watch herself with him. Many a customer had come into Every Book and Cranny seeking F.J. Sparrow's novels. But this man rattled her to the bone.

Striving for the decorum that had so eluded her an instant earlier, she tried again. "Perhaps," she finished icily, "he values his privacy."

"So it would appear."

Those deep blue eyes flickered keenly over her—drat, a little too keenly for Fionna's peace of mind.

"*Miss* Hawkes. We settled that last night, I believe?"

Oh, the rogue! He didn't ask, he stated, which set her to sizzling again. "It is." *Bedamned*, she thought. She'd let him wrest her name from her last night. If she wasn't careful, the next thing she knew, he'd be standing in her parlor! And why the blazes hadn't she allowed him to believe she was wed!

"And yours, sir?" Her tone was decidedly tart. "I fear I've forgotten it." She hadn't, of course.

"Then I'm happy to oblige once more." He swept her a bow. "Aidan McBride."

Aidan McBride. It had seemed almost familiar last night, only she hadn't been able to place it . . . but now, all at once she did. By the time he'd straightened to his full, impressive height, Fionna was never quite certain how she stopped her jaw from dropping in either amazement or horror.

Aidan McBride. Why hadn't she realized it last night? He'd said he'd just recently moved here. He was *Lord* Aidan McBride. Mrs. Chalmers, directly across the street, had been going on and on all week about the gentleman who had just moved into the town house next to her.

And of course, Mrs. Chalmers eagerly informed everyone she encountered that her new neighbor, Lord Aidan McBride, had recently returned from India. And most importantly—that he was brother to a Scottish duke—the duke of Gleneden.

"Ah, yes. You are the talk of all the neighbors, Lord Aidan—"

"Please," he interrupted. "It's Aidan. Just Aidan. The formality is not necessary. After all, we've been in each other's company in the dark before."

Fionna gasped.

"Miss Hawkes, you surprise me. I didn't think you were a woman easily shocked."

The merest light flared in his eyes. Fionna's narrowed. "I think you meant to shock me."

One corner of his mouth turned up. "I do believe I did."

For a fraction of an instant, his gaze met hers with that boldness she found so disconcerting. Then, to her further shock, his eyes trickled down her features, settling on her mouth. Something sparked in those incredible blue eyes, vanishing by the time she recognized it. Yet that very spark of something set her further on guard . . . and further on edge.

Fionna wet her lips. If he could be bold, then so could she. Her chin tipped. "I should like to know what you're thinking, my lord."

His smile was slow-growing. "I'm not so sure you would, Miss Hawkes."

"I believe I know my own mind." Fionna was adamant.

"Very well then. I was thinking that I am a most fortunate man."

"Why?" she asked bluntly.

Again that slow smile—a breathtaking one, she acknowledged. All at once she felt oddly short of breath. And there it was again, that smolder of something in his eyes. And now it was evident in the glint of his smile, too.

"Perhaps fortunate is not the best way to describe it." He pretended to ponder. "No, that is not it at all. Indeed, I must say, I relish my luck."

"Your luck, my lord? And why is that?"

"It's quite simple, really. I relish my luck . . . in that I have found you before my brother."

Fionna's cheeks heated. Oh, heavens, the man was outrageous! He was an accomplished flirt—but surely he wasn't flirting with her. No one flirted with Fionna Hawkes.

"And another thing, Miss Hawkes." He traced a fingertip around the shape of her mouth, sending her heart into such a hammering rhythm that she could barely breathe.

She could not have moved if the earth had tumbled away beneath both of them.

"I am immensely delighted," he murmured, "to discover that you are most definitely *not* a vampire."

No, she was not. Still, Fionna didn't know whether to laugh or cry. Ah, she thought, if he only knew . . .

It was a dark red brick building toward which Fionna directed her steps the next afternoon. It sat at the end of the street, surrounded by lawn covered with a blanket of white; it had snowed last night. Sunny and bright, a stream of sunlight seemed to cast glitter through the air. Fionna found herself praying as she approached. In the summer, she'd been told, there was a lovely, secluded garden where the patients could walk. Indeed, the façade was beautiful and so stately that one would never have guessed what it was—or who lived there. Dr. Colson called it a private hospital, catering to exclusive patients. As she climbed the wide stone steps to an ornately carved door, a bitter thought took hold. It was not at all grim from the outside. Indeed, it was a rather stately-looking building.

But the inside . . . She shuddered. It wasn't like Bedlam perhaps. Not that she'd ever seen Bedlam, nor would she. Or more aptly, she would see that her mother never would.

Raising a hand, she took hold of the brass knocker and rapped firmly three times.

The door was opened by a matronly-looking woman named Eunice.

"Good evening, Miss Hawkes," the woman said cheerily. "Come to see your mum?"

Fionna nodded.

"I believe she's in her room, miss."

Fionna walked down an adjacent hallway. There was a common room, filled with several other patients. One man sat alone in a chair, jabbering nonsense. Another knocked his head repeatedly against the pristine white trim surrounding the window, while a nurse sought to pry him away.

Fionna longed to clap her hands over her ears and squeeze her eyes shut. She hurried forward, rapping lightly on the door before entering.

Her mother sat in the middle of a small, cushioned sofa. There was a wide, comfortable bed on the far wall, a teakwood table before the sofa. Dr. Colson did not spare comforts for his patients.

"Hello, Mama." Fionna summoned a bright smile.

Her mother stared at her for a moment. She searched Fionna's features, her expression one of confused consternation. Fionna's heart sank. Some days were better than others; of late they had not been good.

"Fionna?"

The sofa was situated before the window. As she approached, Fionna noticed a cool draft emanating from the glass. She would have to speak to the staff and see that the sofa was moved— perhaps to the far corner.

There was a warm shawl on the rocking chair opposite the bed. Fionna retrieved it and wrapped it about her mother's shoulders, knotting it firmly at her breast.

"Mama," she said gently. "You must remember to wear your shawl and a warm gown. It's rather drafty here by the window."

"Drafty? But it's summer, Fionna."

"No, Mama." Fionna pointed at the window. "It's winter. January, in fact. Remember the embroidery I bought as your Christmas gift? See the snow? Lovely, isn't it?"

"January? I thought it was June." Her mother suddenly seemed crestfallen. "I forget things, Fionna. Why do I forget? This morning I could not find my slippers. You know, those lovely yellow kid slippers you bought me last week."

It hadn't been last week; it had been at least three years.

And the slippers on her feet were black.

Her mother's face suddenly brightened. "I had a visitor yesterday, dear."

"Did you, Mama? How lovely! Who was it?"

"It was Vicar Tomlinson. He chided me for not coming to church, Fionna. For failing to sing in the choir. But I am too tired."

Vicar Tomlinson from the village. Highly unlikely, Fionna decided.

Fionna regarded her mother with a mix of tears and endless regret.

Her mother had always been of a frail constitution. Painfully she recalled those days after her father had died, when Mama's frailness extended to the mind. She fell into a debilitating bleakness that could not be breached. She had to be coaxed to eat and to dress. She took pleasure in nothing. Previously, the highlight of her week had always been church on Sunday, when she sang in the choir—she loved singing above all else. Her mind wandered—and *she* wandered, once in the middle of the night. Kindly old Vicar Tomlinson brought her back after finding her in the church.

For a time after her father's death, the other villagers would come to call, or send baskets of food. But Mama said little. She sat in her chair, rocking . . . rocking.

And as Mama retreated further and further into herself, eventually the neighbors stopped visiting. They stopped asking after Mama's health. Once she heard a woman whispering as she coaxed Mama out for a brief walk near their house. The woman had called her "touched in the head." Fionna was furious. Finally, their only caller was the vicar. Only Vicar Tomlinson treated Mama with kindness.

Fionna had been at her wit's end. Her mother's prolonged state baffled the local physician, a simple, country doctor.

Dr. Colson's institution was Fionna's last hope.

Vicar Tomlinson had corresponded with her several times since the move to London, inquiring as to her mother's condition. But somehow she doubted the vicar had come to see her.

For Mama's periods of lucidity were growing fewer and fewer.

Fionna laid her hand atop her mother's fingers. "Perhaps you would not be so tired if you would eat more, Mama." Fionna knew from the nurse that her mother's appetite was almost nonexistent. She barely ate enough to subsist.

"I will, dearest. But your father did not come to tea today." Thin fingers plucked the folds of her gown. "Nor did he come yesterday or the day before. I shall have to have a word with him. My William . . . well, he makes me so angry sometimes."

Despair descended, thick and unrelenting. Fionna spoke with painful truth. "He is gone, Mama. Do you not remember the day we buried him in the churchyard?"

"No!" Her mother's outburst startled her. "You must tell him, Fionna. Tell him that I am angry at his disregard! I will not stand for it, do you hear? Tell him that when you see him!"

Her mother leaped to her feet and paced, calling her dear, departed husband disparaging names. It wasn't like her mother—it was as if she *wasn't* her mother. It was clear she was growing increasingly agitated. Fionna sought to soothe her, to urge her to sit once more.

Someone must have heard her. Very soon the door opened. A nurse hastened into the room, a small glass in hand. "Mrs. Hawkes? It is time for your daily tonic. Drink it, dearie. You will feel better soon. There you go, just like that." The nurse managed to calm her. She helped Mama into the chair in the corner.

After the nurse was gone, Fionna waited a few minutes, but she could coax no further speech from her mother. She gazed outside the window, ignoring her. Or perhaps she didn't even realize Fionna was there. It was so much like before, Fionna could have screamed. At last, she rose, kissing her mother good-bye.

Mama never even noticed.

Dr. Colson was just coming down the hall.

A gentleman in his forties, his eyes were nearly black, cleanly intelligent. His nose was prominent, his lips a bit thin but tipped up in a faint smile, as they usually were, as if he were disposed to put on a cheery front for his patients. His manner toward her had always been that of the utmost politeness, and to her mother, that of the utmost patience.

Perhaps that was what led her to trust him in the first place.

"Miss Hawkes. How good of you to come see your mother."

Fionna visited without fail, Tuesday and Thursday afternoons and Sunday mornings.

"It is not a good day for her," Fionna admitted.

The doctor shook his head. He must have seen her despair. "Do not lose hope. I've seen cases that took many, many months before improvement was evident."

Fionna wanted to cry out with pain.

"She is so thin. It's almost as if she is wasting away."

"Yes," he said thoughtfully. "Her appetite has not been particularly stout of late."

"The last few weeks, she speaks incessantly of my father. As if she still cannot comprehend that he is dead."

"In her mind, he is still very much alive. The mind refuses to accept what it does not want." He paused, then repeated. "Do not give up, Miss Hawkes. It is far too soon for that. It may take time, but I truly believe she can be cured." They talked for several more minutes before Fionna left and started for home.

But inside her heart was breaking apart.

For she could not hide the dread that had taken root inside her. In her heart of hearts, she was desperately afraid her worst fears were coming true.

That Mama would never get better. *Ever.*

Chapter Four

Is it any wonder that the people of Dartmoor
fear for their lives? No one is immune. No one
is safe.

God knew there was room enough for evil to
roam free.

For the demon to roam free.

Demon of Dartmoor, F.J. Sparrow

The next few days dragged endlessly.

Fionna was not usually given to moodiness, but
worry about her mother was never far from the
back of her mind. Adding to her strain was the fact
that Raven and Rowan were not behaving. They
were squabbling ceaselessly, when they should
have been hunting down their quarry. Usually
the words flowed fast and furious at night, and

she would look over what she'd written the next day, making changes as needed.

Shortly after opening the shop one morning, she sat at her desk in the back room. If anyone entered, the bell gave enough notice that she could be up and on her feet.

But it wasn't only worry about her mother that disrupted her concentration. It was *him*. Aidan McBride. It was silly, for they'd only met twice. When he appeared at the shop the day after they'd met, he'd told her right out that he hadn't come to see *her*. Yet somehow she'd convinced herself it wasn't true. But really it was probably just as he'd said—he'd come to buy—marvel of marvels—a book.

Yet Fionna continued to think of him at the oddest moments, in particular when she was writing about Rowan, she kept picturing *him*.

Aidan McBride.

It was disconcerting to the point of distraction. Distracting to the point of frustration. Furthermore, every time the shop bell rang, her pulse leaped. Did she fear it would be him . . . or did she *want* it to be him?

She stared down at her manuscript. Drivel. All of it. She would have to write the entire scene over.

Just then the shop bell tinkled. Fionna found she was relieved for the interruption.

Sweet heaven, it was him. *Aidan McBride.*

"Hello," he greeted with a faint smile that set her heart bounding. He was even more devilishly striking than she remembered. He removed his top hat and tucked it beneath his arm.

She inclined her head in return. "Good day. Is there something I can help you with, my lord?"

A brow cocked high. "I thought we'd resolved that," he stated smoothly.

"What is that?"

"The subject of my name. I should prefer it if you call me Aidan."

Fionna said nothing. She repeated, "Is there something in particular you're looking for?"

"I think I'd just like to browse for now."

"Certainly."

Fionna took her place behind the counter, pretending to rearrange the books there.

It wasn't more than five minutes later that he presented himself there again, a glint in his eyes. Fionna eyed him warily.

"Miss Hawkes, I fear I cannot find the book I'm looking for."

"What is it? Do you know the author?"

"I do. His name is Vatsyayana."

Oh, but he was horrible. Hateful! It was Fionna's dearest wish to slap him, but he was too far away.

And if he thought to rattle her, he was sorely mistaken. "Ah, yes, I know his work."

His smile widened slowly, an unmistakable

gleam in his eyes. For an instant he looked almost boyish. Under other circumstances, it might have been utterly engaging. As it was, it just infuriated her more.

"But I must inquire . . . you didn't find F.J. Sparrow to your liking?"

"It wasn't that. I simply found I wasn't in the mood for ghouls and monsters."

"And I am not in the mood for *you*, sir. Since it's *Kama Sutra* you're after, I suggest you find the nearest brothel. You may well find it there. Now please remove yourself from my establishment." She started to stalk around the counter, intending to wrench open the door and push him out if need be.

"My, my, you'll be going to the poorhouse if you keep turning away all the customers."

"And that would be my affair, wouldn't it? Not yours, *Lord Aidan*. You are the most intolerable man I have ever met, and I hope I shall never meet another like you. Furthermore, if you ever come into my shop again, I shall call the constable." This time she did march to the door and drag it open.

To her shock, he reached out and closed the door firmly with the heel of his hand.

Fionna whirled—only to stop short when she found herself confronting a broad, wool-covered chest.

He gave a slight bow. "My apologies, Miss

Hawkes. I stand duly chastened . . . and duly charmed."

She looked him up and down. "Charmed, is it?" she snapped. "Well, sir, I am not charmed. And I am certainly not impressed with your impertinence. Furthermore, I advise that if you wish to charm a lady, you might employ a drastic change in tactics."

"I do believe you are right, Miss Hawkes." The gleam faded from his eyes. "It was in poor taste, and I truly apologize. The truth is, I spent the span of eleven years in India, most of them in the Punjab, where ladies such as you are in short supply."

If it hadn't been *un*ladylike, Fionna would have snorted.

"I suppose," he went on, "in all honesty, it was an attempt to gain your attention. I believe you were ignoring me."

"Ignoring you? I was merely letting you do as you stated you wished to—browse freely."

"I should like to make it up to you," he said quite seriously.

"Impossible," she stated coolly. Fionna tried to step past him, but he'd angled his body slightly so that it was . . . well, impossible.

Little did she realize what Aidan was thinking. What the *hell* was he doing here again? He was impressed by her speech, her diction. He was also impressed by his reaction to her. He'd returned to see if it was the same, if he was as drawn to her as he had been the other times he'd seen her.

By God, he was.

If anything, he found himself more taken with her than ever. In all honesty, he didn't know *when* he'd been so damned attracted to a woman.

It was ridiculous because he couldn't even see her figure. She was covered by one of those damnable Paisley shawls. Aidan's estimation was that she could have surely wrapped the wretched garment about her body at least four times. He leashed the very impatient urge that clamored inside him. He'd like very much to unwrap that unwieldy, shapeless shawl to see if he was right—that beneath all the silly, ruffled petticoats and starch that defined women's fashion these days was a woman who was far from shapeless. A slim, lithe woman with softly rounded breasts and warm, silken limbs.

For the love of God, he didn't quite understand his fascination with her. For all that the companionship of a woman was enjoyable, he wasn't sure he wanted or needed the complications of a woman in his life right now.

As for the lady, she was hardly an exquisite beauty. Hers was of a sedate quality, though it appeared the woman herself was not! Her hair was pinned up primly, her gown buttoned up clear to her chin.

It made her no less desirable.

If anything, it only made her *more* so.

"Let me pass," she said sharply.

Aidan moved to accommodate her request. Once she'd resumed her station behind the counter, she tipped her head back and stared him straight in the eye.

"Must I remind you I asked you to leave?"

Aidan arched a brow before turning and curling his fingers around the doorknob.

Behind him he heard her voice, rather shrill this time. "I meant what I said, sir. You are hereafter banished from the premises!"

Hereafter banished? He nearly threw back his head and erupted into laughter. Such melodrama! Why, the chit should have been on the stage instead of owning a bookshop! Aidan donned his hat and sauntered through the door.

"Good day, Miss Hawkes."

His tone was mild. The emotions running through him were not.

She enticed him. She intrigued him. By heaven, she entranced him.

A woman, he thought again. Aidan hadn't been convinced, yet maybe Alec was right. Perhaps a woman was just what he needed.

But he rather suspected this prickly chit wasn't what either of them had in mind. No, he strongly suspected Miss Fionna Hawkes was not the kind of woman with whom one had a hot, torrid affair.

Yet there was no denying the desire that scalded his veins like fire.

He wanted her, the lovely Miss Fionna Hawkes.

Around him. Beneath him. Atop him . . . he didn't care how.

And that certainty shocked him, as much as he was sure it would shock the fetchingly lovely Miss Hawkes.

Inside the shop, Fionna's thoughts were not quite the same. She stared daggers into the straight lines of his back as he strode boldly down the street, still seething. And to think when he'd first walked in, she had entertained the notion of giving him a signed copy of *The Devil's Way* for his brother!

She'd obviously made a grave misjudgment about his character. No matter that he was part of a well-respected family—not just a well-respected family, but the aristocracy!—he was the worst kind of rogue. Which was probably why he'd spent so many years in India—in the Punjab, no less. No doubt his family had sent him away in exile!

And now her morning was ruined. But she'd learned her lesson. Never again would she allow thoughts of this ever-so-handsome wretch to enter her mind.

I stand enthralled.

From behind the shelter of a tree, he lifted his head ever so slightly, peering at her from beneath the brim of his hat.

It was as if he'd known her forever. She belonged to him. He saw the way she paused, as if she sensed his nearness, as if she knew he was nearby . . . watching.

It was amusing, this game he played, and he knew that once they were together, she would find it just as amusing.

He'd known they belonged to each other, for . . . oh, ages now.

He thought of her mother. Quite delusional, the poor thing—he'd seen other such creatures before, before he came to his present position. But there was the occasional period of complete sanity.

And he knew that Fionna hoped to someday have her back.

She wouldn't, of course. Her mother . . . well, she had gone too far into the most distant realms of the mind to ever return.

But Fionna was, as much as he, a creature of the dark. A creature of the night.

Sometimes he walked with her, her silent companion. Sometimes he just watched, unmoving.

For they were meant for each other. To be together. Forever.

For always.

With that, he rose and slipped into the shadows as silently as he had come.

Fionna tucked up her hood and buried her chin in the warm depths of her fur-trimmed mantle, pulling the velvet-lined interior tighter around her body.

It was horridly, wretchedly cold, so cold she fancied she could almost see her breath freeze as she expelled a rounded puff of air. She wished she'd stayed indoors tonight, where the fire burned warm and cozy . . . but Raven and Rowan had finally settled in over the last few days, and she was quite happy with the way *Demon of Dartmoor* was coming along. She needed one of her nightly walks to inspire her creativity.

And then, all at once . . . she felt it. A shiver touched the base of her spine, a chill that had nothing to do with the frozen air ran up her back until it prickled the very hairs on the back of her neck.

She paused, every sense screaming, then glanced quickly around, executing a full circle that she might see in all directions.

There was nothing. Nothing but the endless blur of the night, the eerily patterned glow of the gaslights behind ice-encrusted panes. Across the street, naked, gnarled branches twined in a mating that was almost macabre.

Good heavens, what was she thinking? It was like something out of one of her books. She was being utterly ridiculous.

Nonetheless, Fionna quickened her pace. But only to warm herself, she told herself stoutly. She rounded the corner. Four more houses and she would be home.

But then there was a crunch of snow. She spun around. And then she saw it . . . a shadow trespassed on the frozen walkway. In her mind it was black as the devil's soul . . . Her stomach churned. She hated the way she suddenly felt . . . as if the night was no longer her own . . . and she was angry, bloody angry.

And terrified as well.

"Come out, you wretched dog," she cried. "Show yourself."

A form stepped from the shadows just as she whirled. A man, she realized. Big. Dark-skinned . . .

Fionna screamed.

Hands clamped down over her shoulders. To her they were like iron manacles.

She twisted madly, but she couldn't escape.

"Fionna! Fionna, stop! It's only me—Aidan. For pity's sake, stop before you wake the entire city."

Aidan. *Aidan.* "It's you, isn't it?" A cry. A gasp. An accusation. "You followed me before. You came to the shop. You follow me now! Why? *Why?*"

"I did not follow you, Fionna! I was just returning from my brother's. I usually walk from there. Then I saw you—again."

Oh! How dare he accuse *her*?

"So you followed me out of concern? I don't believe you!"

His town house was directly to the right. Taking her arm, he guided her up the stairs. A sleepy butler opened the door. Aidan dismissed him with a nod.

In the drawing room, he guided her to a settee angled before the fire. "Sit," he ordered.

Golden eyes sparked like fire. The air of command he possessed grated.

"You were a military man, weren't you?" she demanded.

"Whether I was or wasn't has nothing to do with . . ." He suddenly caught her meaning.

"Please," he said grittily, "please sit."

He lit several lamps, then stirred the fire with a poker. The fire blazed anew, orange tinged with blue. When he turned back, his expression was still stony.

Fionna sat on the edge of the settee, her features schooled into an expression of decided defiance as she peeled off her gloves.

"You are the damnedest woman I know!" he growled. "And I believe you owe me an explanation."

"I owe you nothing, my lord."

He made a sound of extreme exasperation. "Why are you so frightened?"

"I'm not frightened. I'm angry!"

"Because you thought I was following you?"

"You admit it then!"

"I admit nothing of the sort. I've given you my explanation. I have yet to receive yours, Fionna. Why were you out again at such an hour? Why were you out *alone*?"

"It may have escaped your notice, but I live alone."

"Pray do not patronize me, Fionna. Something frightened you, Fionna."

"Yes. *You* did."

"I'm not talking about just tonight," he said grimly. "The other night as well. Why, you're still shaking."

"I'm shaking because it's wretchedly cold out there!"

At the sideboard, Aidan studied her from the corner of his eye. Once again, she proved herself an abominably poor liar. Furthermore, she was the most stubborn woman he knew—even more stubborn than his sister Annie.

He poured two glasses of brandy, returned to the settee, and handed one to her.

She nearly snatched it out of his hands and downed it.

Aidan lowered himself to the cushion next to her, positioning himself where he could see her. "Another assignation with your gentleman?" he asked coolly. "Is he married perhaps? Is that the reason for your stealth?"

"For pity's sake, there was certainly no assignation, no stealth, and there is certainly no gentleman, married or otherwise. Even if there were, what business is it of yours?"

He'd set her to fuming again. It appeared he was rather good at that.

Upstairs, a clock chimed midnight.

"Nonetheless, I should like to know what woman walks about London at this hour of the night."

"And I should like to know what man follows a woman about this hour of the night!"

He made an impatient sound. "I thought we'd established that I was—"

"Yes, yes, I know. Returning from your brother's. So you say. But perhaps it's just a ruse. Perhaps you wish it spread about that you are brother to the duke of Gleneden. Mrs. Chalmers, you know, has never seen the duke call on you here, else we should all know it! So perhaps it's just a ploy."

Aidan began to laugh. "You've a vivid imagination, Fionna."

It appeared she hadn't heard. "Or perhaps I *am* that vampire you thought I was not, and *I* am merely in disguise." She set her glass aside and flung her arms out grandly, sending her fur-trimmed mantle flying upward, so that she did rather resemble that winged creature of which she spoke, and in the very midst of flight . . .

It fleetingly crossed his mind that the brandy was going to her head.

"And," she pronounced, "you've yet to see me in the sunlight, if you recall."

"I saw you inside your bookshop," he reminded her.

"Yes, but never *outside*. In the sunlight."

Aidan said nothing, merely studied her through narrowed eyes. "You've a habit of prowling about at midnight, haven't you?"

Now, it appeared, she had little to say. Her

gaze skipped away, then back. Only this time she didn't quite meet his gaze.

He was deliberately nonchalant. "How often, Fionna?"

"Not very," she said quickly.

Too quickly, Aidan decided.

"Very seldom, actually."

Liar, he almost drawled. "You must stop, Fionna."

She looked at him then, her gaze—her very being—sizzling. "Must I remind you it's none of your affair?"

"I'm making it my affair."

"Oh, for heaven's sake." She glared at him outright. "I . . . it calms me. It's my way of . . . of ending the day."

"By God, I do believe you're mad."

Aidan's mouth compressed. He saw her eyes flare in pure fury, but just now he didn't care. He was determined to query her further, but suddenly she dropped her head into her hands. With her fingertips she rubbed the spot squarely between her brows.

He frowned. "Are you all right?"

"I'm fine." There was a hint of a catch in the words; she was on the verge of tears, he suspected. "I just have a monstrous headache all of a sudden. And I'm tired. So tired."

No wonder, given the hours she kept! But he decided against voicing this particular censure, for something unexpectedly twisted in his chest at the sight of her holding her head in her hands thus. It struck him that she looked . . . rather lonely. Even a little forlorn.

And he knew with every certainty that the brandy had gone to her head when he eased her up against him, tucking them both into the corner of the settee. Her eyes fluttered, then closed. She nestled against him, already limp and relaxed. With a tremulous little sigh, she curled her fist against his chest.

Aidan had to force himself to relax. He held himself very still, tempering the desire that churned and clamored in his chest, twisting and turning restlessly. He was still shocked by it, by its strength, its persistence, for it grew more rousing with every moment spent with her. He discovered himself embroiled in a rare conflict—he, the man who had always prided himself on his decisiveness.

He wanted her. That had already been established. But the point in question was whether or not he should *act* on that desire, potent as it was.

And tantamount to all was the fact that he'd not yet decided whether or not to pursue Miss Fionna Hawkes.

He thought of her mouth. Small. Delectable.

Lord, maybe Alec was right. Maybe a woman was all he needed to cleanse his soul. *This* woman. But maybe he need take it no further than a flirtation. A dalliance. A kiss. She would allow him that. He could be charming when he wished. Perhaps that would suffice.

Well, maybe two kisses. A little seduction . . . perhaps even a forbidden caress . . .

His mind turned. *If* he decided this was what he wanted, instinct warned that he must proceed with careful, cautious precision where the fractious Miss Hawkes was concerned. She would not be stormed. She would not be led onto a path she did not want or share.

Her fingers twitched. She shifted her head ever so slightly, her lips parted, her mouth upturned. Her breath was warm upon his throat.

Aidan swallowed. Desire churned. His heart thundered. Heat raced through his veins. His cock was hard as stone. His body urged him to spread her thighs wide and take her here and now, to seat himself hard and tight and deep inside her and yield to the fire that seared his every nerve.

His arms tightened. Tensed. Her chest was full against his. Her breast was plump and ripe against his chest. She would never even know. All he need do was stretch out his fingers and . . .

She stirred. "I was foolish to scream," she mumbled against his shoulder. "You . . . you just startled me. That's all. That's all it was. Really."

Aidan froze. Christ, what the *hell* was he thinking? What the *hell* was he doing? He could have

groaned aloud his frustration. He'd already decided to pursue the lady—he'd made the decision this instant!

But this was not the time to begin.

Somehow he held himself in check, willing
away the tension strung throughout his form.
Releasing a sigh, he kissed her knuckles, then
rested his chin against her temple, inhaling the
beguiling scent of lilies, aware of the silky little
tendrils of hair that brushed his mouth.

It brought a surprising peace to his soul.

Fionna woke, her eyelids heavy, her vision ad-
justing slowly to the dark. She knew exactly
where she was. In Aidan's house, in Aidan's
arms, tucked against the crook of his shoulder.
His heart beat a rhythmic drum directly beneath
her cheek, steady and reassuring. At some point
she'd been divested of her mantle; it had been
replaced with a warm, fuzzy blanket.

After several minutes came a whisper. "Awake
now?"

She stared into the fading embers of the fire.
"Yes," she whispered back. "It's late, isn't it?"

"Mmmm. Half past three."

Not so very late to her, she thought vaguely. "I
must go." Her limbs felt heavy. Wooden. She
had no desire—no motivation—to move, but she
knew she must.

Nor did he make any move to release her. Instead his arms tightened around her . . . or did she only imagine it?

"You may as well stay. I've several empty bedrooms upstairs."

The sound she made was half-strangled.

He arched a brow. "I was not suggesting that you share mine," he said rather coolly.

He'd given no indication that was what he meant or that he harbored any sort of designs on her. Of course there was his roguish behavior in the shop the other day. But even then—

Fionna pushed herself upright, suddenly wide-awake and incredulous that he would even suggest such a thing. She was too stunned to be indignant.

"Good heavens," she said faintly. "I cannot stay here!" She dropped the blanket. "I must go home. Now. Please, my mantle. My gloves."

"Come now. My staff is asleep. Or do you have a maid or a housekeeper who will miss—"

"A girl who comes in several mornings a week. Tomorrow morning, in fact," she stressed.

He sighed. "Then I suppose we can have you safely home before anyone notices, and with no one the wiser."

Her hair had come undone; she could feel it half-falling down her back. Grabbing a pin, she tried to twist it back up; she succeeded only in stabbing her scalp.

"Here, let me help you." It was Aidan who

tucked it up in a loose coil and pinned it in place. At the feel of his hands sliding lightly through her hair, a peculiar tightness knotted in the pit of her belly.

Settling her mantle over her shoulders, Fionna snatched up her gloves and almost bolted toward the door.

"Oh, no, Fionna! You won't be walking home alone."

"It's only just across the street—"

His drilling stare told her she was going nowhere without him.

"Almost," she finished weakly.

Fionna watched as he procured his greatcoat and shrugged it on. It should have been a simple shift of movement, that rise and fall of his shoulders. And it was, but for the fact that it was more a lithe ripple of muscle.

Fionna swallowed. She was aware of heat flooding her face, her entire body. Was it any wonder she found the man distracting?

Lastly, he put on his hat. Dark brows rose. "Ready?"

Fionna nodded, her cheeks still burning.

In very short order they were crossing the cobbled street. Fionna hauled in a stinging lungful of air, impatient with her behavior. What the devil was wrong with her? Why, she'd acted the panic-stricken schoolgirl, afraid of being ravished! Which she was not. Neither a schoolgirl, nor in danger of being ravished. Not really. Granted, her knowledge of the earthy side of passion far exceeded actual experience—any experience at all, to be sure. Except, perhaps, for her rather erotic imaginings with Raven and Rowan. And, of course, hidden deep in the very bowels of her desk . . .

Her copy of Vatsyayana's *Kama Sutra*.

Chapter Five

A dark, forbidding place are the moors. Evil abounds in the dark of night.

A superstitious lot, the people of the moors. It is said the demon can change his appearance at whim or will, whether it be beast or foul or ghost.

And I knew then. It could be anyone. No matter whom one saw, it might well be the face of death.

The face of a demon.

Demon of Dartmoor, F.J. Sparrow

It was Sunday. The one day that belonged to herself. She did not have Glynis in. And perhaps it wasn't totally to herself, for she never missed visiting her mother in the late morning. But she felt as if it were.

She sat upstairs in the parlor, gazing outside

from her desk. The day was cloudy. Now and again a brisk wind swirled the branches of the tree just outside her bedroom. A fire burned in the fireplace, casting out its warmth. Snow sifted from the scuttling clouds.

She scooped a bit more coal onto the fire. But all at once her mind was filled with the fading embers of another fire . . .

Two days had passed since Aidan had walked her home; rather, two nights.

Memory flooded her. Damn, damn, *damn* the man. Every time she closed her eyes, every time she left her thoughts drift, *he* was there. It made her ache, remembering how it felt to lie against him—no demands, no worries, nothing but the warmth of simply *being* with someone. Being *held* by someone.

There was no lying to herself. By *him.*

She sighed. What a fool she was. She'd hoped to put it from her mind today—put *him* from her mind and immerse herself in *Demon of Dartmoor.* And she would. In just a moment.

So she told herself. But she made no move toward her desk.

Downstairs, someone knocked on the door of the bookshop. The unexpectedness of it made her start. She straightened upright.

Fionna frowned. She knew the sign on the shop was turned to CLOSED. She considered ignoring it.

Impossible, for the knocking continued.

Setting her mouth in a stern line, she headed

downstairs, prepared to let loose a portion of her temper. If a person sought entrance to a bookshop, surely they could read.

She should have known.

Aidan McBride.

He stood at the door, looking decidedly dashing—as if the man could appear otherwise! Now that he saw her, she saw him lock his hands behind his back.

Fionna's knees were suddenly weak. She'd written of such things, why, the very first time Raven had met Rowan, in fact! Rowan had appeared on Raven's doorstep, during—of all things!—a monstrously cold snowstorm. She hesitated, a little uncertain as to Aidan's sudden appearance.

He wasted no time in clarifying it.

"Will you have dinner with me?"

Her lips parted. "What?"

"I said, will you have—"

"I heard what you said." She shifted her weight from one foot to the other, still a little stunned at his appearance—and his unabashed directness.

"Oh, come," he said lightly, "must you always be so wary? You persist in gazing at me as if I am anything but what I am, as if there is more to what I am than you see. I assure you, there is not. I have a very busy day at my office tomorrow. Despite what you may think, I am not a man of idle propensity." He paused. "I must eat. You must eat. Therefore, I propose we eat together.

A relaxing Sunday dinner is all I'm suggesting. I should like a day of peace. A day with *you*, as it were."

Fionna flushed. She could hardly fault the man for being candid, could she?

"Your reluctance does not ease my mind," he remarked, his manner still casually offhand.

Her skin grew warmer still.

"Why do you look at me so, Fionna? Is it a crime to wish to spend time with you?"

She wet her lips. "Why should you want to spend time with me?" she asked, her voice very low.

The merest smile grazed his lips. "Why indeed," he murmured. "Of course, if I were courting you, the answer would be obvious."

Fionna felt her cheeks heat. Somehow she was never quite sure when he was teasing.

At her silence, he laughed. "What, Miss Fionna Hawkes, have you never been courted?"

Fionna stiffened. Was he making light of her? "*Am* I being courted? It certainly doesn't feel like it," she retorted.

A smile flirted at the corner of his mouth. "Well, perhaps we should change that. And perhaps it's because you won't let it."

Perhaps he is right, needled a little voice inside.

"Come," he said softly. "Come with me."

Come with me. It was almost as if it were something else entirely. Not an invitation to Sunday dinner, but something far more intimate. Something that existed—that involved—only the two of them. Something that involved warmth, heat, and overwhelming maleness versus softness and closeness.

Every sense inside her sharpened. Clamored in a way that was entirely new to Fionna. Seeing him thus, so handsome he drove the air from her lungs—why, it made even a single breath a monumental struggle.

She longed to give in. To let herself be swept away by the man and her urges and dash the consequences. Foolishly—stupidly—she found herself overtaken by the urge to touch him, to reach out but a fingertip and trace the squareness of his jaw, to feel the smooth texture of his cleanly shaven skin.

She'd never touched a man, not really. Never felt the nuances of skin and muscle and bone. And the thought of touching Aidan . . .

A fist clutched tightly in her skirt checked the impulse.

"I can't," she heard herself say. Good heavens, she sounded almost desperate. "Aidan, I must work. I've much to do in the shop," she added lamely.

"Oh, come. Do you do nothing but work? Do you allow yourself no time for your own pursuits? For your own enjoyment away from the shop? Though I suppose, being the owner of a bookshop, you must always have your nose buried in a book."

Mercy, if he only knew! Filled with contradictory feelings, Fionna smothered a sound that was half laugh, half sigh. Why did he have to be here? Why couldn't he just let her be?

"I have another proposal for you, then. If you will not have Sunday dinner with me, then let me help you in the shop. That way, at least you need not toil alone. You might even enjoy the pleasure of my company. I know I should enjoy the pleasure of yours."

Well, there was nothing else for it, she decided wryly. The man certainly earned high marks for persistence!

In his arms the other night, she had felt safe and cosseted and shielded from all manner of harm. She certainly couldn't deny that she had liked it. But her life, her world, was too complicated for something like this. For *him*. For any man.

Especially the brother of a duke.

Through the door, a brisk wind wound its way around her ankles. She shivered.

"I would come in," he said, "but if you recall, I've been banished."

She couldn't withhold her smile this time. "That was a rather silly thing to say, wasn't it?" She bit her lip. "A lapse in judgment, I fear. You are hereafter *un*banished."

A lapse in judgment, she thought. Heaven help her, it was true. When he was near, he made her feel as if some other woman inhabited her body and stole her good sense.

There was a decidedly devilish sound to his low chuckle. It should have served as a warning, she decided much later. Moreover, she should have heeded that warning.

"I shall remember that, my dearest Fionna. Now which shall it be? An afternoon's toil or an afternoon's leisure?"

This time there was no hesitation. "Come in, if you please. I just need to get my cloak and bonnet."

He did not remain in the shop, as she had expected, but followed in her wake to the rear of the shop, all the way up the stairway that led to her apartments.

In her parlor, he glanced around in approval at the soft, pastel colors of her furniture, the plump cushions of the sofa, the white wainscoting that set off the pale blue walls. "Lovely, Miss Hawkes. But, of course, I would never have expected otherwise."

Miss Hawkes. My dearest Fionna. There was no doubt, he forced her to maintain her defenses.

There was also no doubt that she liked it when he called her Fionna.

"I'll just be a moment." Indeed, there was far too much to like about Aidan McBride, she thought as she dashed into her bedroom.

She retrieved her best fur-trimmed cloak from the wardrobe, along with her bonnet. As she was tying the strings of her bonnet in front of the mirror, she suddenly remembered . . .

She'd left the pages of her manuscript lying on the desk, in plain sight. Oh, Lord. If he should chance to see them . . . she dare not even consider the possibility.

Chafing at her carelessness, she rushed headlong back into the parlor, nearly tripping over her skirts.

He was in exactly the same spot as she'd left him. Praying she hadn't appeared foolish, she smiled brightly.

"Shall we be off?"

"Excellent idea," he murmured.

Once they were outside, he tucked her gloved fingers into his elbow and glanced over at her. "You don't mind if we walk, do you? I know it's cold, but it's not far. However, if you prefer, we can take a hansom. Or we're close enough that I can summon my carriage—"

Fionna was already shaking her head. "No need," she injected. "I spend far too much time indoors. And this is not cold, but rather, brisk. Besides, my mother always maintained that a little walking, in weather both fair and foul, was good for both the heart *and* the soul."

"Ah, a woman after my own heart, your mother."

Fionna bit her lip. Damn, but she hadn't meant to mention Mama. Indeed, it was her most stringent wish to keep the details of her life private.

All of them.

They strolled along, south toward St. James.

"Stop," Aidan said suddenly.

Fionna blinked, too startled to do anything but obey. She sucked in a breath, discovered she couldn't release it. She held herself very still, for his head was lowering . . . lowering. And suddenly, all she could think was how his eyes were so unexpectedly blue in his dark face. And his mouth . . . he had such a beautiful, masculine mouth . . . Was he going to kiss her? she wondered frantically. She wanted him to, she realized—and it didn't matter a whit that they were on a public street, where anyone might see. A part of her was appalled at the very prospect—at her utter lack of propriety. Nonetheless, her stomach felt most peculiar, as if it had gone suddenly hollow. It was hunger, she told herself, that was responsible for this momentary insanity.

And Aidan . . . he hovered near. His mouth was so close, as if a kiss was his only intent.

He brushed a snowflake from her nose.

Was she relieved? Disappointed? Either way, she reminded herself sternly, she was definitely in need of a meal. Why else would she feel this way?

Before long they reached a small hotel. The dining room was lovely. The wainscoting was painted white, the papered wall above patterned here and there with yellow and gold, the chairs covered in bright chintz, the tables topped with crisp Irish linens.

She must have made some faint sound. Aidan's

fingers squeezed hers as their eyes met. "What do you think?" he asked, his mouth turned up in a smile that was almost lazy.

She spoke with genuine pleasure. "It's just the thing to brighten up a dreary afternoon," she said softly.

He laughed, a low, husky, almost seductive laugh that set her insides to quivering. Hunger again, she assured herself stoutly.

"I'm glad you approve of my choice," he told her, "though I promise, the food's even better."

And it was. There was roasted beef and potatoes, light and airy Yorkshire puddings. Fionna ate almost as heartily as Aidan.

Aidan insisted on ordering sticky toffee pudding for dessert. While they waited, Fionna sipped her tea; Aidan drank coffee.

It struck again, the strange, fluttering feeling in her belly.

And this time she knew it had nothing to do with hunger.

Fionna was unaware that her chin tilted high, as if she was searching the heavens; in truth she envisioned a man. It flashed through her mind that if she were to encounter Rowan in the flesh, he might have appeared . . . well, much like the embodiment of the man who sat so casually across from her. Dark, sturdy, and strong as the rowan tree for which he was named; never had there been a man so striking as he.

But all of that was in Raven's eyes, of course,

Fionna hastily assured herself. That was why Raven forever battled her feelings for Rowan. Rowan could be a bit high-handed, even arrogant. But there was no denying that Raven considered him quite the most handsome man she had ever encountered—or was ever likely *to* encounter.

Aidan leaned forward. "I should very much like to know what is running through your mind just now."

Fionna smiled demurely. "Nothing."

"Nothing? I highly doubt that."

Fionna conceded. "True," she said lightly, "but it's simply an errant thought, nothing of any importance."

"Perhaps you should let me be the judge of that."

"You must trust me, my lord, for I assure you, it's nothing you'd be interested in."

"Trust," he repeated. "I find it interesting you should say that."

Fionna tipped her head to the side, still smiling. "How so?"

"Well," he pretended to consider, "I do believe you're not a very trusting woman."

Fionna's smile faded. "Not a trusting woman? Whatever on earth makes you say that?"

"Ah, you see? You've turned very defensive of a sudden. That but proves it, I think. Which, in turn, makes me wonder *why* you're so defensive."

"I am *not* defensive."

It was his turn to smile. "Aren't you?" Again that lazy smile, which was growing quite infuriating. Again that shrewd consideration. He leaned back in his chair, awaiting her response.

Fionna glared at him. She opened her mouth to deliver a scathing denouncement, then realized it would only serve as confirmation.

"You don't like talking about yourself, do you, Miss Fionna Hawkes?"

It was true. She would much rather keep their conversation confined to things other than herself. Still, she felt compelled to argue. She had the uneasy sensation that he *saw* too much. That he *saw* what was best left hidden.

"I beg to differ. Do you consider me distrustful simply because I am not eager to spill any and everything that enters my mind?"

"If you were a man," said Aidan, "I believe I'd consider you the brooding sort. Which makes me most curious as to why such a thought should even enter my mind."

Placing his chin on the heel of his hand, he studied her.

Disturbingly aware of his scrutiny, Fionna fought the impulse to squirm in her chair. "And I, too, for I am neither a man nor the brooding sort." Her tone was light, yet ironclad. Holding her teacup in both hands, she met his gaze across the top and feigned nonchalance.

One corner of his mouth curled upward. "What say we play a game?"

"A game?"

"For every question I pose and every question you answer, you are free to pose the same. and I promise to answer as well."

Damn the man! She didn't trust him, not for an instant. If she refused, she would appear to be as distrusting as he thought. Why, the wretch!

So much for keeping the details of her life private. "Very well then," she stated coolly. "Your first question?"

He wasted no time. "Where were you born?"

"In Kent."

"Kent is rather vague. Where in Kent?"

"A village named Southbourne. And you?"

"Gleneden. The family seat in Scotland." He finally ceased that disagreeable stare and reached for his coffee. "Do you have brothers? Sisters?"

"None," Fionna replied. "And you? Though I already know about your brother, the duke. *And* the fact that he is unmarried."

He was nodding. "Yes, Alec. And I have a younger sister, Annabel. Or Anne, though everyone close to her calls her Annie. And she *is* married, to a man named Simon Blackwell. They live in Yorkshire."

"And your brother the duke? Would I find him devastatingly handsome?" Fionna now embraced the game with relish, particularly when he revealed his answer almost grudgingly.

"Apparently most women do," he said. "My

sister wrote to me that he's still considered a most eligible bachelor, sometimes called the Black Scotsman. However, with regard to his looks, I cannot speak to your particular fancy—"

"Oh, I shall take your word for it." Fionna clasped her hands together for an instant. "Mmmm, a devastatingly handsome Scottish duke. An *unmarried*, handsome Scottish duke. Would I swoon if I should ever chance to meet Alec McBride, Duke of Gleneden?"

Aidan's smile had long since vanished. Indeed, his brows had drawn together in what could only be perceived as annoyance. "You wouldn't swoon, Fionna. You're too levelheaded."

"Nonetheless, perhaps I should set my cap for him. Could I capture the handsome duke's eye? What do you think?"

It was great fun to turn the tables and watch him scowl.

"I think it is my turn to ask a question. In fact"—she saw him counting in his head—"I believe I'm now entitled to five more before you are entitled another."

Fionna opened her mouth. "Your family," he continued before she could say a word. "Do they reside in Southbourne? Or here in London?"

Her smile froze. "My father died three years ago," she said quietly.

She was unaware of Aidan's eagle-eyed gaze on her profile. "My sympathies," he said softly.

There was a small silence. "I do not wish to pry, but you mentioned your mother earlier. I trust she is well?"

Fionna looked down. She swallowed hard. She stared just as hard at the intricate pattern in the tablecloth, but all she could see was her mother's face when she'd left her this morning, her expression so vague, as if she stared at her through a shroud.

"I—lost my mother sometime ago." It was difficult to say. Difficult to lie, for Fionna abhorred liars. But she was a liar now, she admitted bitterly. Guilt seized hold of her, grabbed at her insides and refused to let go. It was if she were being strangled, little by little. For one horrible moment she truly could not breathe.

She knew Aidan would think her mother was dead. And yet, wasn't it true in some measure? nagged a voice in her mind. At times she felt as if Mama was gone forever. The nature of her affliction—Fionna couldn't bear to call it anything else—had caused Fionna to hold her feelings, along with her alternate identity, close. So very close.

She valued her privacy; her mother deserved it, and it was up to her to preserve it. She didn't want her life or that of her mother inspected; she would not have gossip plague either of them or ruin her career.

Resolve burned within her. She and her mother were the only ones who knew she was F.J. Sparrow. It must remain that way. *She* must remain anonymous. Fionna was aware that a flurry of speculation abounded about the true identity of F.J. Sparrow. And, perhaps it sounded cold, but such mystery and speculation were good for her pocketbook. She could not—*would* not—risk conjecture that *she* was F.J. Sparrow. She could not see her livelihood falter, not now. She would not see her mother in the likes of Bedlam. The thought made her shudder.

No, she couldn't risk Aidan or anyone else discovering that she made her true living as F.J. Sparrow.

Lord, but she was a fool. She should never have come here with him. Her every sense had warned her to keep him distant. She should have heeded it.

"I'm sorry, Fionna. I can see that you must have been very close to your mother. Truly, I didn't mean to distress you."

His quiet sincerity made her throat clog tight. She swallowed, staving off stupid, foolish tears, busying herself by pouring more tea, her eyes downcast.

Finally, she raised them. It was time to close the subject. "What about you? You said you'd spent a number of years in the Punjab. What took you there?"

There was a momentary hesitation before he answered. Fionna had the feeling her choice of question surprised him.

"The Royal Highland Regiment," he said.

"Oh, I knew I was right!" She nearly chortled. "You *are* a military man."

"I *was*," he corrected. "I resigned my commission."

"What rank did you achieve?"

"Colonel."

"I should have known, that confounded air of command you possess. At first I thought it was because you were a duke's brother. Now I doubly understand why you are the way you are."

"That," he said dryly, "did not sound particularly flattering."

Fionna neither confirmed nor denied it.

"How long were you there?"

"Eleven years." He paused. "I was home only twice, the second time when my father was ill. I stayed until he passed on."

So his father was gone too. "That's a dreadfully long time to be away."

"It is," he said quietly. "Too long, I think. But I-I liked the excitement, the feeling of never knowing quite what might happen next."

"Why did you resign your commission then?"

Something flitted across his features. Had she made him uncomfortable?

"Wait, let me guess," she found herself teasing. "You left a woman behind here and could not bear to be away any longer."

He slanted her a smile that made her stomach plummet oddly. "Any woman I might have left behind would have been long married and well on the way to having half a dozen children clinging to her skirts by then."

His smile faded. Silence drifted. When he finally spoke, his tone was very quiet. "When I left, I never expected to be away as long as I was. And when I returned for good . . . well, I discovered I'd been away too long. I discovered how much my family means to me. Deep down, I always knew it, of course.

"Yet there are things a man must learn for himself, see for himself, do for himself, and for me, being in India was one of them. But sometimes, things happen. Things we don't expect. Things we never anticipate. All I knew was that it was something I needed to do."

Fionna listened intently. His answer was vague. Indeed, it really wasn't much of an answer at all. Was he being evasive? She wasn't sure. Yet something inside her understood.

"So what you're saying," she said slowly, "is that it was time."

"Yes. It was time." He hesitated, then tapped a finger beneath his left eye. "There was also this, I suppose. A half-blind soldier isn't much use to anyone."

Fionna looked at him, puzzled.

"Shrapnel lodged inside. You can't see it, but it's there."

It appeared he was prepared to leave it at that. Fionna was not. "What happened?"

"Rifle backfire. The vision's improved but still compromised." He shrugged. "I wore a patch for a time. My poor mother declared me quite piratical."

Fionna eyed him. Why did she have the feeling there was something he was hiding? And why did she have the feeling he wasn't prepared to tell her, no matter how much she queried?

"Yes, I can see how she might." She dropped her napkin in her lap and regarded him. "How do you make your living now?"

"Shipping. Tobacco. Rum, that sort of thing."

"Mmmm. And do you find it fulfilling?"

"Quite."

Fionna was quiet a moment. "I think there is a part of you that still misses it."

He took a sip of coffee. "Do you know what I think?"

"What?" Fionna had noticed the way he avoided her observation. But now she was all at once rather wary. For the space of a heartbeat his gaze sharpened in a way that made her distinctly ill at ease. It was as if they weighed each other, each measuring whatever it was they sought.

"I believe you are a very shrewd woman, Miss Fionna Hawkes."

"And I think you pride yourself on being a perceptive man."

A trace of laughter flickered in his eyes. "And do not forget, an observant one."

Fionna sighed. "Are they not one and the same?"

He chuckled, a low, pleasing sound.

"You do think quite highly of yourself, don't you?"

"I think quite highly of *you*, Miss Hawkes."

Everything in her seemed to melt. If this was an attempt at flirtation, he was succeeding quite well. Yet Fionna felt woefully ill equipped to handle it.

And perhaps he was as perceptive as she said he was, for all he said was, "I think you see things in people that others would not see."

"What would you say about me, if you were speaking of me—say, to your brother the duke?"

He pretended to consider. "I should say you are the scholarly type. Yes, most definitely scholarly—and most beautiful, at that."

"And how would you describe yourself to someone who did not know you?"

He sat back, his pose easy. "I think I should say I am . . . a man of action. A man of decisiveness and determination." One corner of his mouth turned up. "At least, I hope I am."

She was certain he was, but this she kept to herself. "I envy you your time in India."

"Some think it's grand. Some do not. Either way, it's a far different world and way of life than we know here, that's for certain."

"I should like to see India nonetheless," she said softly. "Or the Orient, perhaps. Somewhere exotic. Somewhere far away."

"Perhaps someday you will."

She wouldn't, of course. She must see to her mother.

Still, all at once Fionna couldn't withhold a tiny little smile.

"Why do you look like that?" he asked. "And why do I sense it is not a compliment you will send my way?"

"What, is that what you seek? Are you the sort who must bask in compliments?"

He accorded her a glance that could only be considered rakish. "I seek only *your* approval, miss."

The brash oaf!

"But you've yet to confide what is on your mind."

"I was thinking about the other day, when you first told me you'd been to India for so long. My first thought was that your family had sent you away in exile. And I did think you were a man of idle propensity."

"Not so. Tomorrow afternoon, I'm off to Paris on business for the week."

"Paris?" There, she'd betrayed her wistfulness again. Drat, she must beware the man. She'd confided far too much already. Somehow he seemed to have that effect on her.

"You've never been to Paris?"

Fionna shook her head. "You'll recall, I come from a small village. My father was local gentry, and he preferred to stay close to home. But he knew I should have liked to see the world, so . . ." She gave a tiny little smile. "We were in the midst of planning a trip to the Continent when he died. So the only place I've ever been is . . . well, London."

"A pity. Perhaps, then, I should take you away to Paris with me." The glance he gave her was almost fiendishly wicked.

"Nonsense," she stated primly. "That would be most improper."

"I could spirit you away then. Now. Tonight. Would that assuage your conscience if it were my will pitted against yours?"

His hand stole out to cover hers.

"So tell me, Fionna Hawkes. Will you come with me to Paris?"

He'd discarded his gloves, and hers were still on the plate beside her. His hand engulfed hers in its entirety, his fingers long and lean and distractedly masculine.

He didn't mean it, of course. Her gaze jolted up to his. But there was nothing innocent in his tone, nothing innocent in his expression. She could see it in the upward curl of his mouth, so sensuously defined. But she also felt herself seized by a current of something else, something that seemed to leap between them . . . connecting them in a way that had never happened before. Awareness stabbed at her, squarely in her middle, so that if she'd been standing, she would have surely gasped and bent low.

Beneath thick, black brows, his eyes were

heated. Playful, she might have called that look, if not for the simmering fire she glimpsed. It was desire, she thought in amazement . . . hot, smoldering, smoky. He still maintained that tiny little smile, but this time there was no mistaking the sensual curl of his mouth.

Desire, she thought again, still stunned. She swallowed. She wasn't familiar with it, not really. She hadn't revealed the truth, that no one had ever courted her in the village; what few young men there had been eventually left to make their fortunes, or pledged themselves elsewhere. Certainly no one sought to court her, not after her father had died. And after Mama . . . Little wonder she'd kept to herself.

She eyed him, discomfited—yet thrilled. He looked like a panther, ready to strike, garbed in the trappings of a gentleman.

Will you come with me to Paris?

What would he say if she said yes? He knew she wouldn't; Fionna didn't know how she knew it, but she did. And oh—how there was a part of her that longed to call his bluff!

But there was also a part of her that yearned and wondered what it would be like to do as he said. To allow herself to be spirited away, to cast away her worries and cares—to indulge in the moment, to indulge herself simply for the pleasure of it.

She had thought she could read him, but all at

once Fionna wasn't so sure. He made her feel out of kilter, wholly off-balance. The other night in his arms, it had felt so good to lean on him, if only for a while. To forget the load she had borne for so long now.

And she could see it, God help her, she could, an erotic vision that ran through her mind, filled her world; her hands running over his shoulders— dark and burnished as his face. His form, long and muscular and naked, all fluid masculinity as he raised himself above her.

Heat seemed to gather at the place between her thighs. Her breasts were swelling, as if her nipples sought to stab through every layer of stiff, starched cloth. She knew that if she looked down—if *he* looked down—there would be no hiding the sight of her nipples standing pebbled and hard beneath her gown. She wanted to clamp her hands over them; better still, she wanted *him* to clamp those strong, masculine hands over them both and . . .

Reality weighted her, heavy as stone. In truth, she thought achingly, it had never left.

For it was up to her to see to her mother. There was no one else. There was only her.

And in that instant, Fionna almost hated Aidan for tempting her. For teasing her so. This was no doubt just a game to him. A game for a wealthy gentleman to land a woman in his bed—no matter who that woman was.

Fionna was a woman who did not play games. Levelheaded, he'd called her. And she was. She couldn't afford to play games. Fionna Hawkes was too sensible. Too responsible. And indeed, she decided with a faint twinge of bitterness, Aidan was right about something else as well.

Family was everything.

She snatched her hand away and stood. "I think it's time we left, don't you?" She managed some sort of sound; for the life of her, she couldn't discern what it was. "Goodness, will you look at the time. Why, it's half past four already!" She turned, scrambling for her cloak, scrambling for composure the entire way home.

Once there, she didn't go to the bookshop entrance. Instead, she went to the rear alleyway and fished her key from her reticule. She pushed it into the lock, opened the door wide, and stepped into the small hall in front of the stairs. She pushed back the hood of her mantle and started to turn, a polite good-bye on her lips. To her shock Aidan was already inside, had closed the door, and was stripping off his gloves.

Fionna blinked, then squared her shoulders. "Sir!"

"I was hoping you might ask me in. A spot of tea, perhaps?"

Tipping her chin to accommodate his height, Fionna looked him square in the eye. "Not today."

Not ever.

"Ah," he said.

Before she knew what he was about, he'd peeled off both of her ivory kid gloves, dropped them onto the marble-topped table, and taken both of her hands in his. Fionna was trembling. She thought of wrenching them away, but his grip had tightened ever so subtly, and to do so would make a scene. Better to pretend she hadn't noticed. Better to pretend disinterest.

Yet in shock she watched him lift her hands to his lips, brushing his lips lightly against her knuckles.

"Do I embarrass you?"

At the feel of his mouth on her skin, everything inside seemed to melt.

"No," she said faintly.

"Distress you?"

She stared straight ahead. Her gaze was level with the column of his strong, brown neck, the points of his shirt. "Aidan," she said with a tiny shake of her head, very low. "I . . ."

Her jaw seemed to have locked in place—why, her entire body. She could say no more. She'd certainly lost the power to move.

And Aidan . . . she was heatedly aware of those sapphire eyes roving her features until she longed to scream.

"No need to say more," he said very quietly. "I see I am to take my leave now."

He released her hands. It came then, when she least expected it . . . perhaps when she should have *most* expected it.

His lips were rather cold from the frigid air outside.

His kiss was not.

And it was like nothing she'd ever imagined. She thought immediately of Raven and Rowan, for it was one thing to write about a kiss, having never truly experienced it . . .

And quite another to actually feel it.

And feel it she did, a kiss so heated and intense, it burned clear to the very bottom of her soul. The taste of him was like nothing she'd ever expected; the combination of warmth and cold turned to fire with blistering heat. His kiss sent heat blazing to every part of her.

His hands stole inside her cloak, closing around her waist and pulling her hard against him. She chafed at the burden of his greatcoat. She itched to rip it open, tear at his shirt until she could feel warm, masculine skin and truly know what it was to *feel* a man's flesh.

And when he finally released her mouth, all Fionna could think was that she wished it would never end.

For a woman who had conveyed reluctance, she'd certainly been eager enough, hadn't she?

She buried her nose between the third and fourth buttons of his coat, her eyes squeezed shut. Her emotions lay scattered in all directions.

Yet all she could think was that now she truly *was* embarrassed.

And most surely distressed.

His mouth lingered on the fine hairs of her temple. "Fionna?" he whispered.

"Yes?" A rather incoherent mumble into cold, fuzzy wool.

"I have a confession to make, my mysterious little miss." She could feel him smiling against her forehead. "You would most definitely turn Alec's eye. You've certainly captured mine. But if Alec were ever to display any fancy for you at all, I would simply have to claim all rights. After all, I saw you first."

Fionna's eyes snapped open.

He continued. "If that should chance to occur, I would have no choice but to fight him for you. My dear mother would be most disapproving, to see her sons brawling . . . of course, I would have to try to dissuade Alec some other way, to save face, you see. I love my brother, but I should hate to see him humiliated when I soundly trounce him."

"You're the larger of the two, eh?" Lord, but she sounded weak as a mouse.

"I daresay we're evenly matched in size and height. But it's not a question of strength; rather, strength of will, you see."

Fionna had a very good idea where he was going with this. It was his way of telling her he would not be deterred, no matter her objections.

Little by little, order in her mind began falling into place once more.

"Now come, sweet. Permit me one last kiss before I leave."

"I shall not! Aidan McBride, you've already trespassed where you should not. This is most indecent."

"I don't think either of us really care, Fionna."

Fionna's jaw dropped. "You are quite autocratic, you know. Why, I do believe you are the most arrogant gentleman I have ever met."

"Yes, I believe you've already made your opinion rather clear," he said with the merest thread of laughter in his voice. "And I can well imagine I am. Now come here, love."

Sweet. Love. She ought to have berated him for such familiarity. Then it didn't seem to matter, for already his arms were tightening. He'd never released her, she realized hazily, so where else was there to go?

And with that kiss, every vestige of thought fled her mind. For that was how he made her feel—mindless and breathless and wanting.

Then it was over, and he was gone, with a rush of frozen air.

Fionna sank back onto the stairs. Madness, she thought shakily. It was madness the way he made her burn hot as fire, the way his mouth unraveled all resistance . . . the way all she wanted was to call him back and sink into his arms once more.

Madness, indeed.

Chapter Six

I saw him in my dreams that night. A creature who could not speak. With naught but a gaping hole for a mouth. He stared at me, his eyes ringed by yellow, eyes that belonged to the devil.

I woke, screaming. But Rowan was there. He lay down beside me. My heart quickened, for the whole of his body was warm where it touched me, and I was so very, very cold . . .

I had never needed him quite so much as I needed him that night. In the way I needed him then . . .

Demon of Dartmoor, F.J. Sparrow

If Fionna had thought that memories of Aidan McBride would recede, she was mistaken. In truth, Fionna would have preferred it so. But if she could not banish the man as she once had, well, then . . . she might as well take full advantage of it.

She immersed herself in *Demon of Dartmoor*. Her writing flowed fast and furious over the next few nights. Raven and Rowan kissed—and kissed again, despite the fury of danger into which they had been plunged. For within the pair burned a frenzy of desire that raged in heart and mind and body . . .

The days were just as any others. She visited Mama on Tuesday afternoon, after the shop closed. The next day she waited on the occasional customer, reworking her manuscript in the back when the shop was vacant, plotting and pondering the evening's work. She maintained her routine, walking most every night, ever cautious, varying her route and time a bit. All was quiet. Nothing plagued her, neither footsteps nor that furtive sense of someone near. How silly she had been! Surely it had all been a figment of her imagination.

Wednesday began the same as any other. It proved a slow day in the shop. Early in the afternoon she opened a package of maps a customer had ordered—the battlefields where Napoleon had fought his many engagements, and their history. She had ordered several other copies, which she placed on a shelf in the far corner of the shop, where other accounts of history's generals were housed.

A stack of books remained tucked in the crook of one elbow. Far from the windows, aware that she couldn't be seen by anyone who might chance to pass, she placed one hand on the small of her back, stretching this way and that. Her back ached a bit from bending over and unpacking her latest acquisitions.

There, she decided. Much better.

Humming a merry little tune, she turned.

A tall figure stood directly in her path—nary the span of a hand lay between them.

Fionna jumped. The books in her arm toppled to the floor. How on earth she managed to suppress a shriek she had no idea.

Aidan smiled at her, a lazily engaging smile— one that might have surely thawed the ice from surely the most hard-hearted of women.

Not so with Fionna.

"I'm terribly sorry," he said. "Did I startle you?"

"You know very well you did. Why, I didn't even hear the bell!"

"Ah," he said blithely, "probably because it didn't ring."

The declaration earned him a glare. "And why not?"

He assumed a distinctly thoughtful air. "Well, perhaps because I removed it before it *could* ring. I wanted to surprise you, you see."

"Well, you not only surprised me," Fionna admonished sternly, "you very nearly frightened the life from me!"

He bent and gathered up the books scattered about their feet. "Where shall I put these?"

"On the front counter will do."

Fionna followed in his wake. When he laid the books on the counter and turned his attention back to her once more, she leveled on him a look of utter reprimand. "I thought you were in Paris for the week."

"I was. Now I am returned, as you can see. And here with you."

"Indeed."

"So anxious was I to see you, Fionna, that I returned from Paris early."

She snorted.

"You doubt me?"

Fionna pressed her lips together. He was so smooth, so glib. Despite her resolve to ignore him, she glanced back over her shoulder.

He regarded her, one dark brow slightly aslant—a devilish expression. Oh, yes, that was it, precisely. He was surely the devil in disguise. It wouldn't be the first time it had happened—a woman seduced by a handsome face while beneath lurked the soul of a devil. She'd employed that particular device in *Satan's Path*.

"What!" he exclaimed. "Why do you look at me so? Is there somewhere else I should be? No. I recall quite distinctly. My presence is not required at my office. Indeed, my presence is not required elsewhere—why, anywhere!"

Throughout his speech, he maintained that devil's smile, that air of assured masculinity. No doubt he'd seduced many a woman with that mysterious smile. As it was, Fionna discovered she had to drag her gaze from his mouth. The memory of his kiss still scorched her lips, clear to her very soul. And now, seeing him once more . . . Her body was seized with a near-painful awareness.

She reminded herself rather sternly that Aidan McBride was no devil. And she was hardly in danger of being seduced!

"Your presence is not required here either, sir."

"You are upset that I startled you." He tugged off a glove and took her hand. "Allow me to make amends."

Despite the cold outside, his flesh was warm, his fingers strongly curled around hers. She stared at his hand as if it were an adder—or tried to, anyway.

"There is no need to make amends," she said shortly. "But I will thank you not to do it again."

"Agreed." He squeezed her fingers. "Now come with me. I have something I'd like you to see."

"Aidan—"

"Come now. Must you always be the contrarian?"

She sighed, a sound of frustration or surrender, she didn't know.

"A short walk," he cajoled. "I should imagine your mother would have approved. You told me so yourself."

"Aidan, are you listening? I can't. I have—"

"Work to do," he finished for her. "It's admirable that you take your work so seriously. It's a trait to be commended, you know."

"Why, thank you," she said dryly, finally tugging her hand away. She picked up a small stack of books and turned away. "Yet it's you, my lord"—she was aware of him trailing directly behind her—"who always manages to keep me from my work."

She halted, only to discover she now faced him directly.

The sound she expelled was one of utter impatience. "Aidan McBride, must you forever—"

Her eyes narrowed on a point directly behind one broad shoulder.

Aidan frowned. "What? What is it?"

Even before he turned, she stepped with determined precision around him and insinuated herself between him and the place where the shelves stretched up, nearly to the ceiling.

A dainty finger waggled. "What the devil," she muttered, almost to herself.

Aidan watched as she dragged a book from its berth. Her expression turned from one of puzzlement to an utterly fierce scowl.

He took it from her. "What the devil indeed?" he said with a laugh. "*Demonology* by Elton Spears." Glancing up, he read aloud the other titles on the shelf from where it had been withdrawn. "*Celtic Witchcraft and Spirits* by Sir James O'Malley." He glanced up at the titles beside it. "*Spells and Potions of the Middle Ages,* author anonymous."

Fionna drew a deep breath. "You do not understand. That book does not belong there. It is out of order."

"And?"

"And—it is out of order!"

Aidan shrugged. "No doubt someone looked at it and failed to replace it where it belonged. It must happen all the time."

"That is true. But it is quickly set to rights, by me. I am a woman of regularity, Aidan, a woman of utmost regularity. Furthermore, no one was in this section of the shop today."

Aidan opened his mouth. Before he could say a word, she spoke. Her tone, like her expression, was troubled.

"I am meticulous about such things, Aidan. The shop isn't so large that it is difficult to keep track of things. All is in order when the shop closes, when it opens—every book in its proper place. Naught is amiss. Each day, every day," she stressed. And that volume in particular, she thought to herself, for she had another copy upstairs that she used occasionally for her own works.

To Aidan it was a trifling matter, yet she remained adamant. Distressed, even. And mistaken, no doubt, not that he intended to point it out, not when she was so clearly upset.

He slipped the book back into place—its proper place. "There," he pronounced. "And now naught is amiss in Fionna Hawkes's Every Book and Cranny, so there is no longer any need to fuss."

"Pray do not make light of me," she said quietly.

"Come, love. Cease your fretting and walk with me. I beseech you, do not be miserly with your time."

She flared. "I am *not*," she pointed out, "fretting. I am not being miserly with my time. Moreover, I am certainly not your *love*."

"Ah," he murmured. "Fionna's Law?"

"If you prefer to think of it that way," she said pleasantly.

"Well, then, let me apprise you of Aidan's Rules. You are altogether too serious, Miss Hawkes. Thereby, a breath of air is in order. A brief late-afternoon stroll will revive you, I suspect. Refresh you for whatever plans you have for the evening."

"I have no plans for the eve—"

She stopped short; he grinned outright, his teeth very white in his tanned face. Her pulse was all at once beating like the wings of a bird.

Well, she decided, she'd fallen into his trap rather neatly, hadn't she? This man had a way of making her feel things she would rather not feel; saying things she would rather not say. And when he gazed at her the way he was now, the warmth she saw there made her pulse leap high in her throat.

He offered his arm. "Shall we?" he murmured.

Fionna hesitated but an instant. "Let me fetch my cloak," she said rather breathlessly. "I'll be just a moment."

Upstairs, her emotions were all a-riot. Her step quick, she retrieved her warmest cloak. She was eager, she realized. Tying her bonnet before the mirror, she regarded her image. Color had rushed to her cheeks; her eyes were bright. The incident with the book had disturbed her, and rightly so. It was just as she'd told Aidan—she was very thorough about such things. And yet, perhaps he was right. Perhaps she was mistaken. Heaven knew he'd distracted her thoroughly from the very moment they'd met!

Perhaps he was right in another way. Perhaps she was too serious. She couldn't deny that her mother's plight was ever in her mind.

And she liked him. She liked *being* with him. She enjoyed his wit, his engaging manner. Even—heaven help her—the way he'd begun to tease her. The things he said . . . the *way* he said them . . . the way he gazed at her sometimes. There was no mistaking it for anything but what it was—flirtation. Unsubtle. Unguarded. No, more than that. A smoldering desire—

Oh, she tried to pretend she did not know it for what it was. She pretended she did not like it.

But she did.

No, she could not have called herself an honest woman had she not responded to it. To *him*.

And she was very much afraid he knew it.

They walked south toward St. James, until they came to an area of exclusive shops. Aidan did not hesitate, but walked straight toward a shop with wide, high, elaborately carved double doors. He held one open that Fionna could pass through.

"Good day," greeted the shopkeeper smoothly. He was a short, well-dressed man, and Fionna had the feeling it took him but half a glance to peg Aidan as a man who could afford to spend a goodly sum if he so wished. "I am Mr. Francis. May I direct you to something in particular?"

"Mr. Francis." Aidan shook his hand. "I should like the opportunity to peruse a bit. I've recently returned from India and am still in the process of searching for just the right clock for my entrance hall."

Mr. Francis smiled. "Ah, I hear the heat in India can be quite ravaging. I should imagine you are glad to be back in England."

"I am indeed. Particularly when time has such a tendency to fly while in the company of such a lovely lady." He smiled at Fionna, a glint in his eye, then turned back to Mr. Francis. "Alas, however, one still has need of a timepiece or two, eh?" Before Fionna could blink, Aidan tucked Fionna's hand firmly into the crook of his elbow, anchoring it there with the pressure of his own.

Fionna was too well mannered to make a scene, but the glance she shot Aidan was fulminating. He merely turned slightly, which of course brought her body closer into his own. It was nigh impossible to maintain any distance between them!

Mr. Francis was oblivious. "May I point out, sir, the floor clock behind you. It's a bit different than the usual, but the Earl of Harris has a similar one at one of his estates."

Aidan and Fionna both turned. The clock he referred to was square and almost stocky, gaudily edged with gold.

"A remarkable piece," commented Mr. Francis. "Keeps perfect time."

"You are right, Mr. Francis. It is rather unusual." Aidan slanted a glance at Fionna. "What do you think, Fionna?"

Fionna nearly choked. The clock was hideously gaudy.

And now the rogue was gazing at her with unabashed laughter. "Fionna?" he queried anew.

"It is just as you say"—she had to cough to conceal her mirth—"quite unusual."

Aidan turned to Mr. Francis. "A bit ornate for my tastes, I believe."

Mr. Francis waved a hand. "Well, we have an excellent array. Do you see anything you like, sir?"

"I see much that I like." Aidan's gaze had settled on Fionna's lovely profile while she was busy looking around. She was unaware of the way his eyes slid hungrily over her profile, sliding down to the frogs that held her cloak in place, as if he longed to slip each one from its berth and delve beneath to discover what lay beneath.

Mr. Francis had bowed low. "If you are in need of my assistance, you have only to call," he said cheerfully.

After a moment, Aidan released her hand. "A bit of browsing perhaps?" he suggested.

Fionna nodded, all at once feeling uncharacteristically shy.

Aidan sauntered down the aisle in front of them, while Fionna turned and roamed down the next, quite enjoying herself, actually. Other than her lovely rosewood writing desk and some small accessories now and again, she'd never had the opportunity to properly choose her own furnishings. The furniture in her present apartments was lovely, but it had belonged to her mother. When they had moved to London, not only had they sold off the land and house, but much of the furniture, for there simply wasn't room. Fionna had taken what she needed for her apartments.

At the end of the third aisle, she paused. Almost lovingly she ran a hand over the smooth, gentle curves of the clock before her. Memories flooded her, ones she hadn't recalled for years now. There had been a similar clock in the entryway of their home. She used to play endlessly in front of it, lining up her dolls, watching her father sitting in his study on one side, her mother busily stitching at her embroidery on the other side. And at night, it was the sound of those low, mellow chimes that oft were the last she remembered just before drifting off to sleep.

"That's it. The one with the slim, elegant lines. That's the one I want."

Fionna looked up in surprise.

Aidan stood less than an arm's length away. Lost in her musing, she hadn't heard his approach.

Mr. Francis stood just behind him, beaming. "A classic piece, wouldn't you say? Classic and lovely . . ."

"Aye," said Aidan.

It wasn't the clock he was staring at, she realized in shock. It was her. And hearing that low vibration in his tone . . . seeing him, an unmistakable thrill shot through her. And . . . just for an instant . . . it was as if the world ceased to turn.

Neither of them appeared to hear Mr. Francis going on. "An excellent choice, my lord. Solid English oak, through and through. Very fluid, very elegant, simple, lovely lines."

Fionna's heart clamored hard in her throat. She couldn't move. She couldn't speak, even if she'd wanted to.

"And your lady, sir? Does she approve?"

Aidan reached for her hand. He brought her gloved fingertips to his lips.

"She adores it, don't you, my sweet?"

Fionna's eyes rounded with shock. It was clear

Mr. Francis believed they were wed. "I . . . I . . ." was all she could manage.

"I believe," Aidan said with laughter brimming in his tone, "the lady is quite speechless with delight."

Moments later, Fionna was off admiring a beautiful mantel clock while Aidan handed Mr. Francis his card and completed the transaction.

When he was finished, he stepped near. "Another?" he whispered in her ear. "For my bedroom, perhaps."

Fionna bit her lip, struggling not to laugh. What a rogue! And he made no secret of it, which somehow made her laugh. Once they emerged onto the street, she couldn't hold back. "That was quite wretched of you to let him think I was your wife! What if I'd said I adored that ghastly gold horror in the corner?"

"Then I should have been obliged to buy the most ghastly, horrid clock in all London."

Crossing the cobbled street, she slipped a little on a patch of frost that covered the uneven surface. Lightly he cupped her elbow, bringing her upright. Even through the smooth kid of his gloves, the layers of cloak and gown, it was as if he laid his hand on her bare skin. The feel of him was stimulating in ways she'd never imagined. Oh, and it made no sense, but . . . even while those very thoughts were stimulating to her imagination with regard to Raven and Rowan, she was very much afraid those very same thoughts of him might waylay her creativity as surely as the man himself. He was altogether too handsome. Altogether too distracting.

As if to remind her, heat flashed through her.

"Are you overly warm, Fionna?"

"No," she said quickly. "Why do you ask?"

"Your cheeks are quite flushed."

And no wonder. Heat radiated from her face. Her entire body, despite the frigid temperatures.

"I rather expect it's the cold." She knew she flushed even more, and sought to focus on the lamppost towering on the street corner. She had no idea her pace had quickened.

Aidan had no trouble keeping up with her stride. But at the corner he stepped in front of her. Fionna had to stop abruptly else plow directly into his chest.

"Well, then, perhaps you're in need of some tea." He gestured to the doorway beside them. "I know I am."

"Tea?" He stood so close, too close. Fionna swallowed with difficulty. "Tea sounds just the thing," she said hastily.

Moments later they were installed at a table near the stove in the corner. Aidan's knee bumped hers as he shifted his chair a little. It spun through her mind he was too big for it.

And he was still altogether too close for her peace of mind.

Fionna ignored him, glancing toward the window. Sunlight sparkled through the frost, spinning in a whirl of color. Very deliberately, she shifted her thoughts away from this wretchedly handsome man to *Demon of Dartmoor*. To the scene she planned to write later. Dartmoor's demon had stalked Raven to a small, abandoned house, while Rowan had stalked him, stealing inside to find Raven. The details of the chase eluded her, but she could fill those in later.

And now a new thought took hold. The pair would manage to elude the creature, but to do so, they would need to duck into a tiny closet. She envisioned it in her mind, conscious of the feelings building inside Raven. Fionna could feel the budding heat of awareness that pulsed through Raven, as Fionna pictured her pinned between Rowan's thighs, shrinking back against him, for she had no choice. And Rowan's arm lay banded about her waist, as if to protect her. As if to draw her closer still . . .

Aidan sighed.

"Are you angry, Fionna?"

"No. Of course not."

"You've barely said a word since we left the shop. Do I bore you?"

Fionna blinked. "What! Of course you don't. Why ever would you ask such a thing?"

His gaze was direct. "Well, I thought we were having quite a lovely afternoon. But before we came inside, I almost had the feeling you were trying to get away."

Running away was more like it.

"That's ridiculous! You do not bore me. And I am having a lovely afternoon."

He slowly stirred a lump of sugar into his tea. "Really?"

"Really."

"Then why did you have that distant look in your eyes a moment ago? Your expression was quite pensive. As if you were far, far away." He laid his spoon on the saucer. He took a sip of tea, then lowered the cup again. All the while his gaze held hers. "It's not particularly flattering, you know." A gleam had appeared in those vivid blue eyes.

Fionna's heart clamored. "Well, I was thinking." "Of?"

"Of . . . a rather novel idea," she said weakly.

"Ah. And can you share this rather novel idea?"

Mercy, if he only knew. "Not at present." Pasting on a smile, she changed the subject.

If he noticed anything amiss, he said nothing. An amicable silence drifted between them as they started toward home a short while later. A splinter of afternoon sunlight wavered across the street.

Across from Hyde Park, a Gypsy woman sat inside a curtained stall, her face scored by lines and the texture of leather. When she spied them, she turned and offered a sly smile.

The old woman beckoned, stretching out a bony, veined hand, gleaming with rings, bracelets dangling on both arms. She wore gaudy red and yellow clothing, her hair covered with an equally bright scarf.

"Mistress! Gent!" she called, her voice rough and thickly accented. "Lend me your palm! Allow a poor woman to tell yer fortune."

Even before the old woman spoke, Fionna's step had slowed ever so little. Fionna cast her a look from the corner of her eye. She'd been thinking of using a Gypsy in her next book, *The Scourge of Scotland*.

Aidan had noticed as well. Fionna glanced at Aidan, her eyes full of mirth. He gave a slight nod, then flipped the woman a coin.

The Gypsy caught it, bit it, then grinned at him, revealing a gummy, wide gap where her upper front tooth should have been.

"Sit, mistress. Sit." With a dramatic whirl of brightly colored red skirts and noisy jangle of bracelets, she made a grand gesture and indicated the table before her.

Aidan held the seat out for Fionna. Unable to smother a smile, Fionna glanced at the woman.

"Your hand, lady. Let me see your hand."

Fionna uncurled her fingers. The woman pored over it for a long time, tracing the lines with rough fingertips. She studied Fionna's face for a moment.

"You have not lived in the city long, have you, my dear?"

"I should say I have lived here quite some time," Fionna said lightly.

The Gypsy threw back her head and gave a cackling laugh—as if she knew Fionna was lying.

The woman ran a finger over the lines of her wrist. "You are alone in this world, no?"

Fionna raised a brow, neither confirming nor denying it. This, she knew, was how they worked. Drawing bits and pieces from their patrons, dispensing vague notions yet molding it that it might fit any number of people. Gleaning reactions, reading expressions in order to twist it to their advantage.

"Ah, yes," the Gypsy said almost slyly. "A pity a beauty such as you should be so alone in this world."

"Oh, come," Aidan interjected. "As you can see she is hardly alone."

The Gypsy ignored him. Her eyes gleamed as she raised her head to regard Fionna. Then she returned to studying her palm. She made great pretense of studying it as if she could see every mystery of the world written there.

It was all a game, Fionna knew.

"I see that you were very happy as a child, mistress."

True. But Fionna was aware that the woman had already assessed her clothing, her demeanor—and probably Aidan's as well. Clearly she had not grown up in poverty, so it was an easy deduction

that yes, her childhood had been one of contentment.

"I should imagine many are," she murmured.
"And just as many are not."

"You were," said the Gypsy with such empha-
sis that Fionna was taken a little aback. Black
eyes narrowed. "But much has changed since
then, lady, for you harbor a great secret."

Good God! Somehow Fionna maintained her
smile.

The woman closed her eyes, swayed. Her eyes
opened, black and fathomless. She peered up at
Fionna once more. "I believe you will not always
be alone. You have the chance at great happiness
once more, mistress. But your journey will not be
easy. Many trials await you. I see . . . much heart-
ache. You must take care lest happiness elude
you forever."

The old woman shook her head. She bent low,
so low that Fionna felt the rush of breath on her
skin.

"Guard yourself," the gypsy said suddenly.
Sharply. "Someone near you is cursed. For all
eternity. Guard your heart—and guard your
life, for evil awaits you." Her gaze encompassed
Aidan, narrowed, then she appeared to dismiss
him. Black eyes returned to Fionna; the Gypsy
regarded her intently. "I sense danger," she
warned. "I sense darkness. Yes, darkness follows you—danger awaits you!"

Despite herself, Fionna gave a little jerk. She

could not help it. Her mind veered straight to those nights when she had felt as if she was being followed.

Her smile froze, even as Fionna chided herself. What was this? She'd written of things far more graphic. Her characters were exposed to things that were far more frightening than a . . . a woman who pretended at seeing what mysteries lay in the future.

"I—"

She was allowed no chance to continue.

Gnarled, bony fingers clutched hers. Her voice was a raspy whisper. Fionna sought to drag her hand away. The old woman's nails dug into her palm.

"You must heed me, mistress! Heed me lest danger consume you!"

Fionna struggled to rise. Still the Gypsy refused to release her.

Aidan stepped close. "Enough!" he told the old woman sharply. A hand in Fionna's elbow, he tugged her to her feet. Together they began to walk away.

The Gypsy's voice followed. "Hear me, lady!" she called shrilly. "Beware! Beware the dark! Beware the night!"

Chapter Seven

Again I dreamed. He walked toward me, an unearthly shroud, for his tread gave no sound. He
was heavily cloaked, from head to toe . . . this
demon. Within those folds was no form or features, yet the shape of him was that of a man . . .

Demon of Dartmoor, F.J. Sparrow

Fionna's heart was pounding, hard and almost
painfully. Her mind was screaming. How could
the Gypsy know? How? Had she somehow divulged the feeling of sometimes being plagued?
Aidan hadn't noticed—and there was an observant man—so how had the Gypsy? Unaware of
it, her pace quickened until she was almost running. The cold, frozen air seemed to burn her
lungs.

Beware the dark. Beware the night.

At the corner, Aidan caught her and whirled her around. "Fionna! Don't be frightened. There's nothing to it. She's just an old woman; it's all in fun. Nothing she says will come true. Nothing she says is real."

"Of course it's not. I'm not frightened." Brave words, breathless words. It wasn't so much that she sought to assure him but herself. She didn't believe in such nonsense. It made no sense, yet she had the eerie sensation the woman had seen something.

"I think I should like to go home now." To her horror, her voice wasn't as steady as she wished.

"Of course."

She shivered. From the cold, she told herself when they arrived at her apartment. He helped her out of her cloak and stripped off his great-coat. Fionna didn't stop him. She was secretly glad of Aidan's presence, not that she needed a man to watch over her. It was rather like Raven and Rowan, she decided vaguely . . . it wasn't so much that Raven was always in need of a res-cuer, but Rowan was usually there should the need arise.

And now Aidan was here. With her. Here when she had no one else.

He caught both of her hands in his, then swore. "Your skin is like ice!"

"I forgot my gloves."

Aidan scooped coal into the fire, then guided her onto the overstuffed chair nearest the stove.

Dropping to one knee, he rubbed her hands between his. Fionna was aware of him searching her features.

She struggled to summon a smile. "I'm sorry. I played the fool rather brilliantly, didn't I? How silly of me."

"Not so silly," he said grimly. "But how the devil does she expect to make her living telling fortunes when she frightens everyone half to death?"

Fionna said nothing. The Gypsy had been right about so many things. Her childhood was a happy one. She was new to London—well, at least fairly new. She was alone. Of course there was Mama, but, in all honesty, until Mama was well, she was alone.

If Mama was ever well again, whispered a niggling little voice that she hated. No, she thought. No. She had to believe that someday Mama would be better.

Despite herself, she shivered. She knew Aidan was aware of it when he delivered a firm admonishment. "Do not dwell on the old witch, Fionna. Darkness? Danger? And beware the night?" He made a scoffing sound. "My God, I've never heard such nonsense—"

All at once he broke off. His regard narrowed.

Beneath thick, black brows, his eyes were unwavering. Blue as sapphires. But most of all, unsettling in a way that made her want to long to throw up an invisible shield between them.

It was as if he saw everything inside her, everything she hid.

"Fionna," he said again, his tone utterly calm. "Is there something I should know?"

"Of course not!"

A most lengthy silence. A most lengthy stare. Then he asked, "Did you walk alone last night?"

"No," she said quickly. It was true. She hadn't walked. Not last night.

His lips compressed impatiently. "It will do no good to lie to me, Fionna."

Her jaw thrust out. "Do you accuse me of being a liar? How dare you, my lord!"

And how childish that sounded. But if she was defensive, she assured herself, it was because she resented his intrusion.

He remained quiet, so long she fought the urge to squirm and fidget. Then he said softly, "You begin to frighten me."

"What . . . why?" She was genuinely puzzled.

"These nocturnal sojourns of yours. This business about it calming you, your way of ending the day . . . I dislike it."

Fionna's chin came up. "I do what I wish. I go where I wish, when I wish. It is my custom to walk—"

"It was your custom."

"Meaning?"

"Meaning I don't think it's wise to continue it."

"I don't recall asking you, sir!" Who the devil did he think he was? Her temper was about to boil over. "And when I walk, I prefer to walk alone," she stressed. "That is precisely the point."

He appeared totally unimpressed.

Fionna took a breath. "I am six-and-twenty, my lord. I have been responsible for myself for a number of years now."

He studied her. "You take offense. You think I interfere where I should not?"

"I do."

"You consider yourself an independent woman then."

Her mouth drew into a thin, straight line. "Call it what you will. As for you, sir, well, you may call yourself protector of the Crown, protector of the Empire. But I am in no need of a protector, either you or otherwise."

He tipped his head to the side, his gaze never leaving hers. "Why," he said softly, "do I have the feeling there is something you are not telling me?"

"You have no right to question me, Aidan," she said flatly. "And may I remind you we've known each other but a short time. Why should you be privy to my every thought?"

"Why indeed," he murmured. "Nonetheless, I dislike the idea of leaving you alone tonight when you are so distressed. Is there someone you could stay with? A relative, perhaps?"

"There's no need." She was adamant. "Yes, I was thrown a bit out of kilter by the Gypsy, but I am fine. It was silly to react the way I did, so no need to worry. Now, may I show you to the door?"

He was tempted to argue; she saw it in the flash of those incredibly blue eyes. Instead, he got slowly to his feet, retrieved his greatcoat, and shrugged it on. "Very well then. Escort me to the door if you wish."

Manners dictated precisely that. A polite farewell hovered on her lips. But before she could issue a word, he turned suddenly.

The entrance hall was small. To her dismay, she found herself squarely between Aidan, the wall at her back and side, the stairs on the other side.

Trapped, as surely as if she'd been caught in a snare—his snare.

He did not gloat—she'd have surely slapped his cheek if he did! Instead, he smiled slowly, as if he had all the time in the world. Very deliberately, he took her chin between thumb and forefinger.

"I ought to take you home with me," he said almost lazily.

"That should give Mrs. Chalmers a great deal to talk about." Rats! The declaration was not entirely steady. Did he hear it? Fionna held her breath and waited.

"Then I've half a mind to stay here."

"That," she said breathlessly, "should give Mrs. Chalmers even more to talk about!"

"At least then I should be sure you don't go out tonight."

Fionna's temper flared. Her lips compressed. Aidan directed his eyes heavenward, as if indeed he prayed for patience.

"Very well then. I think I shall post a man outside this door."

"I shall send him away!"

His eyes probed into hers, his intent clear. "Then I'll send another. As many as it takes."

He did not jest.

"Very well then. I-I shall not leave home tonight."

He smiled. "Excellent choice, sweet."

"Pray desist from calling me that!"

"Why, my love?"

Lord, but he was maddening. "You know very well why!"

"Ah," he almost purred. "Darling, then."

"Only a rake would dispense such endearments so often—and in a manner no less than cavalier!"

"I am not cavalier, I assure you."

Fionna expelled a breath of sheer frustration. "You think you know me, Aidan. But you don't."

"I know all I need to know." If it was a rash declaration, she could have laughed. She could have played along. As it was, the expression she glimpsed on his face . . . Playful, she might have called it were it not for the simmering light burning in his gaze.

Her jaw thrust out. "This is just a game to you, isn't it?"

"A game? Hardly. I know what I want, Fionna."

He eased closer, shifting so that his coat brushed the thrust of her breasts. His touch was not accidental, she realized. His nearness was not accidental. "Shall I tell you what I want, Fionna?"

Fionna longed to bolt up the stairs.

Alas, he made it impossible. And—oh, mother of God—a tingle of excitement shot through her. A tingle of anticipation. For what, she wasn't sure . . .

She licked her lips. What to do . . . what to do?

His gaze had drifted to her mouth. He stood very still. "I want you, Fionna Hawkes," he said very deliberately. "And by heaven, I will have you."

Fionna was stunned. His eyes glittered with purpose. His air was bold-as-can-be. This was no flirtation. Gone was the engaging, jaunty stranger who had sauntered into her shop the day after they met. This was an outright declaration of . . . of a conqueror!

"Just like that?" she said faintly.

"Just like that."

Logical thought was a process that suddenly proved almost impossible. "We are strangers, Aidan. Truly we are."

"We were never strangers, Fionna. Not even from the first. I know all I need to know. And I would know far more if you would let me close."

"You are close!"

"You're well aware what I mean."

His look was censure itself. Damn him, she thought in icy fury. Damn him for making her feel guilty when she had no reason to!

She quashed it down. The breath she drew was uneven. "Do not toy with me, Aidan."

"I do not toy with you, nor will I tarry. I said I am not a man for games, Fionna. Rules, yes. Games, no. So perhaps it's time I made myself clear."

His gaze fixed intently on her mouth, pinning her. Without words. Without touch. All at once she was neither furious nor cold. Instead, he was melting her inside.

Her mouth went dry. He did that to her. A mere man. A mere look. She flattened her spine against the paneled wall, as if he could not reach her there. She fought to maintain her distance from him, both physically and emotionally. Now her back was literally against the wall.

She made a faint sound. "Please do not do this." Her tone was very low. "Do not—"

"What? Kiss you again?"

Already his head was lowering, his mouth so close their breath mingled, his and hers . . . together. As if they were one . . .

Hers caught, then became ragged. She made a small sound, almost a whimper.

"Shh, it's all right. No touching. Only kissing."

"Kissing? What is this? Aidan's Rules again?"

His lips were against hers now, molding and warm and coaxing. His kiss was long and leisurely and made her insides melt to butter. She reveled in the texture and heat and pressure of his mouth. His mouth was warm, his lips softer than she had realized before. She sensed his absolute control—she envied him his control!—along with his restraint. Yet she could also feel his slight smile as he ended the kiss.

"I won't have you say I'm a bounder," he whispered. "Remember . . . kissing only. No touching. My mouth against yours. Yours against mine. And the next time, the next time, sweet . . . touching only."

He kissed her again. And indeed they touched nowhere but their lips. Sensation exploded inside her. Everywhere. Yes, everywhere. It was as if he touched her all over. Her nipples, tingling as if he stroked them. Between her thighs, warm as if he stroked there. She would have blushed—but it felt so good. It felt too good. That it seemed almost forbidden was the last thought in her mind.

"Perfect, Fionna. Yes, right there. I can feel the tip of your tongue pressed there, at the corner of my mouth. Shall you see for yourself? Here, let me show you."

She didn't possess the restraint he did. She couldn't help it. Her hands moved of their own volition. She lifted them to twine around his neck.

He stopped her with a sound deep in his throat. "No, love," he reminded her. "Not yet. The next time, I promise. The next time . . ."

"No, Aidan." She tried to sound stern. To stand firm. "There will not be a next time."

"Hush, Fionna. Hush."

She opened her mouth, but his was already there. She knew what he was doing. Making her want . . . this. Making her want him.

And she did. God help her, she did.

On and on he kissed her, turning his mouth this way and that, his tongue twining with hers, long and deep. Then drawing back, his mouth almost flirting with hers.

From the moment they'd met, she thought vaguely, he made her feel quite irrational. Not only that, she was acting irrationally.

Fionna Hawkes would never have spent half the night in a man's arms, a man she barely knew. Fionna Hawkes would never have allowed that man to kiss her. Not once. Not twice. Not thrice. And certainly not like this.

To her shock, she still fought the urge to grab his head and keep his mouth welded to hers. The only way she could stop herself from flattening her entire body to his was to flatten her palms against the wall at her back. Indeed, she was almost clawing the wall. That alone prevented her fingers from burrowing into the dark hair that grew on his nape.

When she was with him, she felt giddy. Inundated. Filled with everything about him. The warm scent of him. His size. The width of his chest. It was as if he'd invaded every part of her. Her senses, her emotions, her heart.

She was half-mad with need when at last he released her mouth.

Fionna opened her eyes. "Aidan," she said when she was able to catch her breath. "I mean it. This is the last time I will allow you to—"

Her reprimand was cut short by the feel of his finger trailing a path down her jaw. She might as well have never spoken.

"Sleep well, Fionna. And lock the door."

Fionna stood mutely while he let himself out. The instant the door was closed, she turned the lock. Still in a daze, she mounted the stairs.

Upstairs in her parlor, she pushed aside the curtain and watched him walk down the street. She leaned her forehead against the freezing pane, hoping it would cool the heat raging inside her, praying it would end the twisting, aching need still climbing within her.

For Fionna recognized it for what it was. She could deny it no longer.

It was desire. Reckless. Foolish.

For that's exactly what she was. A fool. A fool to wish for something that could never be.

She stared out into the night until her eyes began to blur. Visions of the Gypsy filled her mind. She shuddered, willing them away.

Beware the dark. Beware the night.

She should work. But she needed to walk, to gather her scrambled thoughts together in some semblance of order that she might.

But she couldn't. Not tonight. Resentment rose like a tide inside her. She hated feeling so confined. Almost stifled.

Most of all she hated feeling as if . . . as if the night was no longer her own.

Beware the dark. Beware the night.

For it haunted her, that warning. Raven and Rowan would have to wait, she realized. Her shoulders slumped. She stepped away from the window.

And she did something she had never done before, not once in her life.

Throughout the night, she slept with the bedside lamp burning low.

At home once more, Aidan strode into his study. Sinking into the chair nearest the fire, he released the studs of his collar, unbuttoned his shirt, and stared at the play of the fire.

Christ, he was still burning inside, his veins blistering with desire.

Did the chit have any idea of the way she turned him completely upside down? And him! What a fool he was! What on earth had possessed him to think a mere kiss with the lady might satisfy him? A kiss!

He wanted more. Much more. He wanted Miss Fionna Hawkes beneath him, around him, above him, her slim, naked limbs twined with his. He ached with the need to feel himself rooted deep and hard, all the way to her womb.

He would be satisfied with nothing less.

I want you, Fionna Hawkes. And by heaven, I will have you.

And now she knew it too.

Well, he thought with a self-derisive smile, so much for subtle finesse.

He had the feeling he'd rattled his little miss right down to the very tips of her toes.

He'd told himself she couldn't be stormed.

But that was exactly how Aidan felt.

Did she have any idea of the way she tempted him? How much she stirred him? How she tasted like rain upon dry, parched earth—God, he could still taste her! What sweet, delicious torture it was to kiss her. To taste every sleek little hollow of her mouth, every damp, tiny crevice of her tongue, and touch her nowhere but her lips.

Yet he didn't regret it. Not for an instant.

The reward was too great. Feeling her trapped against him, the sweet, hungry clinging of her lips no less than his, the surging rise of hot, innocent passion . . .

It was like dying and being reborn.

He'd convinced himself he knew the meaning of discipline, understood each and every boundary. He'd wanted her breathless and waiting and wanting. Yet when she had reached for him, stretched herself up to wind slender arms around his neck, for one perilous instant, he didn't think he could stop her.

His limits had nearly burst. The explosion of desire inside him nearly pushed him over the edge.

All that stopped him was tasting the truth of her desire in her lips—the truth of a desire that met and equaled his.

Unfortunately, the lady had already warned him he'd not find such welcome again! Her will was as strong as his. He disliked the possibility that she might choose to deny him again—even worse, that she probably would.

But that wasn't the only thing on Aidan's mind. Fionna's reaction to the Gypsy bothered him. Though she tried to hide it, she had been frightened. Why? A woman's reaction?

No. No. For one, Fionna wasn't just any woman. She was certainly not a timid mouse to cry and weep at anything she might fear.

He sought to assure himself that such a warning might prey on anyone.

There was no question—oh, she'd tried to pretend otherwise, but Aidan was quite certain Fionna had been well and truly shaken.

He also disliked the fact that she walked alone at night. He'd stopped her for tonight, but she was right. Who was he to interfere with her life. She had every right to go where she wanted, wherever she wanted.

A faint bitterness crept inside him. Perhaps it was good that she was independent. He didn't want anyone looking to him for guidance, for protection. Not anymore . . .

After all, he might well fail her, too . . .

But she was still very much on his mind later that evening when Alec strolled into his drawing room. On the side table, he dropped a satchel.

Aidan raised his brows curiously.

"My set of *Monthly Chronicles*," Alec said. "The ones with *Demon of Dartmoor* by F.J. Sparrow."

Aidan rolled his eyes. "You'll hound me until I've read every damned one of his books, won't you?"

Alec gave a low chuckle. "Whenever the opportunity presents itself."

They settled in with cigars and whisky. There was a bit of small talk, then Alec suddenly frowned.

"You are preoccupied," he stated bluntly.

Aidan stretched out a booted leg. "I simply have matters of concern on my mind."

"Clearly." Unsmiling, Alec reached for his glass. "What matters of concern?"

"Things you need not know about, Your Grace."

Dark brows drew together. Alec scoured Aidan's features. "Pride be damned, Aidan! I know your secrets and I don't give a damn. You're my brother. You did what had to be done. I simply want to assure you that you should never hesitate if you feel the need to discuss—"

"Alec, I told you. It's not that."

"What then?" Alec leaned forward, studying Aidan, his glass suspended halfway to his lips. All at once he lowered it slowly.

"Dammit, tell me! What is the reason for this black mood?"

Aidan shot him a withering glance. "My mood is not black. I'm merely pondering."

"Pondering what?"

"Lord, but you are a nag," Aidan muttered.

"Retribution," was all Alec would say.

"Very well then. There is a woman on my mind, if you must know." Aidan twisted the glowing end of his cigar into his ashtray. "You do recall advising me that a pair of tender arms might offer contentment for my troubles."

"And now this woman plagues you? Has she disdained you then?"

Aidan briefly lifted his eyes heavenward. "Am I a monster then? There are many who say I look like you, you know. And if I chose to take your advice, well, then, why do you look at me so? Is it so improbable that I should be interested in a woman?"

Alec released a laugh. "Interested? Interested hardly warrants such worry on your part. And you're growling at me!" Leisurely Alec crossed his legs and studied his brother. Lean fingers curled with unstudied ease around the crystal glass; the one that held the cigar rested lightly on his knee.

Aidan's mouth compressed. "I am not growling!"

"Very well then. I will not debate the point." Alec continued to regard his brother, a faint smile on his lips. All at once he broke into a laugh. "But since we've established that this has to do with a woman, well, if I had to guess, I should say that you are enamored."

Aidan said nothing, merely raised his glass to his lips. "Sheer speculation," he stated coolly.

Alec chuckled. "I'm worrying for nothing then. She is a coquette, eh?"

Aidan didn't hide his annoyance. "She is definitely not a coquette. She is a lady, through and through."

Alec grinned. "Ah, and therein lies the problem, methinks. The lady has disdained you, hasn't she? She fails to return your ardor."

Aidan glared. "Alec, have I ever told you that there are times you should keep your opinions to yourself?"

"Never," Alec said smoothly. "And before you say that I should, let me say this: there are remedies when a woman proves reluctant, shall we say. And I happen to know an immensely charming, willing lady who specializes in, let us say . . . unburdening a man's distress . . ."

"My, but you are the expert when it comes to the female sex, are you not?"

"Expert, connoisseur, yes, I claim them all."

Alec blew a puff of smoke into the air. "Modest tonight, aren't we?"

"Cease your complaining, Aidan. Now, as I said—"

"It's not a mistress or a courtesan I need or want," Aidan stated bluntly. "I already know a woman who could without doubt ease my distress. Now, please cease your prying, Your Grace."

"Your Grace! Oh, my, Aidan, this is serious!" teased Alec. "And you fool no one, least of all me. I understand perfectly well the reason for your moodiness. I assure you, you're hardly the first man to be rebuffed—"

"Alec, did you hear me say I had been rebuffed?"

"Ah, my apologies," Alec said glibly. "Dare I presume then that the lady is proving herself a trifle . . . difficult?"

"Did I say she was difficult? I don't believe I did," Aidan returned gruffly. He mulled. "Though I admit that may well prove the case."

Alec grinned. "Console yourself, then. There's no fun to it when a woman falls plumb into your hand."

Hardly a chance of that, Aidan decided.

Alec, in the meantime, continued, "You've never been one to waste a moment of life, have you, Aidan? You've been home . . . what? A mere

three months? And already you've been captivated. Honestly, that truly surprises me. Will you
at least tell me the identity of this woman who
has taken your fancy?"

Aidan set aside his glass. "Alec, you are a gossip. Has anyone ever told you that?"

"No one but you." Alec grinned.

Aidan glowered. "You do this only to torment
me."

"I fear I cannot deny it," Alec said lightly.

"Need I remind you that you are nearly three-
and-thirty, and—as far as I know—have never
even come close to choosing a bride."

"What of it? I am of the belief that I will know
I am ready when my future bride makes her appearance. Thus far in my life, she has not."

"Well, I am glad you find this so very amusing.
I only hope that one day this lady leads you a
heartily merry chase, and then I shall be the one
to laugh."

"Oh, but you are cruel to wish me thus!" said
Alec. "But you mistake my intent, Aidan. Perhaps I can be of assistance."

"You?" Aidan snorted. "How?"

"Well, you will recall I am hosting a dinner
party the end of next week."

"A dinner party?" Aidan frowned, his expression blank.

Alec sighed. "I sent you the invitation several
weeks ago, Aidan. But clearly you have other

things to occupy your mind—things other than an engagement with your brother, the rest of your family, and a few friends."

Aidan glared. "You needn't insinuate I am feebleminded."

"Nothing of the sort, man. I'm simply curious as to the name of this woman."

Aidan regarded him through narrowed eyes. "Her name is Fionna Hawkes. She has the bookshop across the street on the corner. Why?"

Alec's smile widened. "You shall see soon enough, Aidan. You shall see."

He and Alec enjoyed another whisky and cigar. By the time he saw Alec to the door, his moody demeanor was gone.

Whistling a little, he returned to the drawing room and his favorite chair. His gaze chanced to alight on the books he'd bought at Fionna's shop—*Satan's Path* and *Howls at Midnight*. He'd yet to read a single page.

He bent and picked up *Satan's Path*. Weighing the leather-bound book in one hand, he fanned the pages with the other, then sighed and lowered himself onto the chair, stretching out his long legs and crossing them at the ankle.

Perhaps Alec was right, he decided. Perhaps it was time he became acquainted with F.J. Sparrow.

Chapter Eight

There is nothing. Nothing. It is as if he has disappeared. I pray that he has. Yet it was Rowan who guessed how the creature always managed to escape so easily . . . By some trickery . . .

Through the body of his latest victim.

Demon of Dartmoor, F.J. Sparrow

The following morning, a glance at the clock sent Fionna scampering down the stairs to open the shop. She was late, by nearly ten minutes, a rare occurrence. Usually she turned the sign to OPEN promptly at ten o'clock.

Five minutes later, she heard a knock. From behind the counter, she glanced up. What was this? Her patrons seldom knocked.

Her step light, she hurried across the floor. From the corner of her eye, she spied a glossy black coach, the doors trimmed with bright blue and red. What the devil . . . ?

The door squeaked as she opened it. On the threshold stood a blue-and-red-liveried footman.

"Miss Hawkes?"

Fionna nodded.

The man gave a bow. He held out a small silver tray; in the center was a small ivory envelope.

Dumbfounded, Fionna stared at it, glanced at the coach, then back at the tray.

The man bowed again. "For you, Miss Hawkes," he said with a thick Scottish burr.

Fionna lifted it gingerly.

The footman grinned and tipped his hat. "Good day, miss."

"Good day to you, too, sir."

Fionna closed the door slowly, still staring at the envelope. The oddest notion fluttered through her mind. *No*, she thought vaguely. It couldn't possibly be . . . She broke the seal and read:

> *The pleasure of your company*
> *is requested at a dinner party*
> *to be given by His Grace,*
> *Duke of Gleneden,*
> *at eight o'clock, 29 January 1852.*

She was still rather stupefied when she finally lifted her head. A man was strolling directly across from the shop. She knew that carelessly fluid pace, that jauntily perched top hat, the rhythmic swing of his walking stick.

Before she knew what she was about, she threw open the shop door and hailed him. "Aidan! *Aidan!*"

He came to a halt and glanced over. Too late Fionna saw Mrs. Chalmers coming down her steps, her wiry gray hair tucked beneath a frilly woolen bonnet, her rotund body hidden beneath a voluminous cloak. At her feet were her two little terriers, yapping shrilly and tugging madly at their leads—and tugging Mrs. Chalmers along with them.

But not before Fionna saw the woman's little cherry mouth form a startled little "o."

Fionna groaned. Wonderful. Now surely all the neighbors would know that she was on a familiar basis with Lord Aidan McBride. It spun through her mind that Mrs. Chalmers's little creatures were as noisy as their mistress was nosy.

The woman gave a wave to Fionna and Aidan. She saw Aidan toss out a greeting to the woman. He stopped to chat a moment with her—no doubt the woman was all agog. But thankfully, it wasn't long before Mrs. Chalmers turned, her dogs leading the way.

Aidan watched until she was around the corner, then ventured across the street toward the shop.

Fionna had ducked back inside. If she could have recanted her outburst, she would have. Now she had no choice but to admit him entrance.

"Well," Aidan teased as he stepped inside, "miracles do indeed occur. I am honored that you seek me out."

Fionna waved the invitation madly. "This—this," she sputtered, "is your doing, isn't it?"

"Begging your pardon, Fionna, but I haven't the foggiest notion what you mean." He doffed his hat and laid it on the counter, along with the umbrella and gloves, then plucked the card from her hand and read. His brows shot high.

"So Alec has invited you to his dinner party."

Fionna was still sputtering. "That's all you have to say? How the devil does your brother even know that I exist?"

"I suppose it might have something to do with the fact that he visited last night. A pity Mrs. Chalmers was not out to see him call on me," he added blithely.

Fionna merely glared at him heatedly.

His tone was as bland as his expression. "You'll attend, won't you?"

"I will not!"

"What, sweet? You've nothing to wear?" He took out his looking glass, appraising her from head to toe. Fionna went hot all over. "I should enjoy helping you choose a gown. Or if you like, I'm certain my cousin Caro or my sister Annie would be happy to assist you."

"I am not a country bumpkin, Aidan McBride.

I'm perfectly aware of the proper attire and the proper behavior."

His smile faded. "I do not imply that you would not," he said quietly.

"Aidan! I simply cannot go!"

"Give me one reason why not, Fionna."

"I . . . I . . . " She floundered. She, the woman who made her living as F.J. Sparrow, who had never lacked for words before, who prided herself for her eloquence! Why, then, did words elude her now?

The light was back in his eyes, eyes so blue they made her melt inside. "You cannot snub a duke, my lovely. It just isn't done."

Must he sound so cheerful? So sensible? And how did he always manage to make her feel like mush inside and out?

"Come," he said softly.

His tone made her heart turn upside down. Their eyes held. Fionna swallowed, unable to tear her gaze from his. She was trembling inside. This was madness. She had allowed him far too close already.

"Very well then. I *dare* you to attend. I *challenge* you to attend."

"That is not fair!" Her protest could have been no more vehement. Damn him! He knew that she would not back down from a challenge.

"I will use whatever means are at my disposal in order to convince you," he said with a shrug of indolent ease. He paused, as if to consider. "Ah, I have it! Perhaps I should kidnap you, Fionna. Oh, but I fear that would defeat the purpose, wouldn't it? If I should spirit you away, neither of us would be able to attend Alec's affair. If I should kidnap you, why, we would not be seen for many days and many nights." His expression turned almost smoldering. "I admit, though, I find the prospect quite fascinating. I'd take you to Gleneden, I think, where we would be far, far away from everyone. Hmmm . . . Alec and my mother are here in London. We would be quite alone, you and I. Or perhaps we could go where no one would find us . . ."

Fionna caught her breath. The image conjured up by the mere suggestion of being totally alone with Aidan made heat fan wide in her belly, the points of her breasts swell and stab hard and tall into her chemise. She suppressed the urge to clamp her arms across her chest to banish the tingle of sensation that flashed like lightning.

"I can think of many things the two of us could do . . . alone, with no else watching. With no one else near. With no one else the wiser."

"Aidan." Shakily, she spoke his name.

"So, my sweet. What do you think? Is it off to Gleneden? Or off to Alec's dinner party?" He paused, then went on. "Damn," he said with a sigh, "but I suppose it must be Alec's dinner party. Otherwise, we should cause quite the scandal. What do you say?"

Aidan's voice seemed to come through a fog. Fionna was still imagining what it would be like to be alone with such a man. She'd never allowed herself to think what it might be like to be with a man in that manner. But now she did. To make love with Aidan, to lie naked and warm against him . . . all of him . . . oh, Lord, but this was getting quite out of hand!

"It's a simple enough request, Fionna. Will you attend with me?"

"Aidan—" Helplessly she spoke his name.

His eyes darkened. "Please, Fionna," he said in that tone that made her insides quiver and heat rush like a tide all through her body. "You will prick me sorely if you don't."

He caught at her hand. "It's nothing terribly formal. My family. A few friends."

As he spoke, he rubbed his thumb up and down the skin inside her wrist, back and forth, back and forth. He was wooing her. Soothing her with his voice. Seducing her with his touch. Swaying her with tenderness.

"If I go," she heard herself whisper, "you must promise to be a gentleman."

"It's a dinner party," he said with a faint laugh. "I can hardly ravish you in front of friends and family."

Fionna bit her lip. "There! You see? You shouldn't say such things as ravishing me or running off to Gleneden. You shouldn't even think such things. You certainly shouldn't say them!"

"I do not see the harm in it. There are only the two of us here. And I ask—when have I ever been anything but gentlemanly?"

Fionna blinked, then tugged her hand away. "And what of last night? You know what you did. Or have you forgotten so quickly?" She felt her cheeks go scalding, just thinking of it.

She should have known! Beneath his polished exterior lurked the heart of a rogue. His slow-growing smile was utterly wicked. "I forget nothing, my dear Fionna. In fact, quite the opposite. I know precisely what I did, what we did. We kissed. No more. Indeed, I believe you should be aware I exercised a great deal of restraint, for it was but a hint of all I long for—"

Fionna threw up both hands. "Stop! Cease! This is precisely what I mean! Aidan, if I agree to attend your brother's dinner party . . . You must promise. You must promise your behavior will be impeccable."

"Agreed. But I will exact a promise in return."

The statement sent warning bells clanging through her breast. Her guard went up immediately.

"You must promise not to set your cap for Alec." He laid his hand over his heart. "If you did, you would deal me a mortal wound."

It appeared she worried for nothing. Releasing a sigh, she struggled to frown. Impossible! His seductive charm—that devilish smile that made her heart pound and her senses swim—was irresistible.

"Is it a promise, sweet?"

"Y-es."

He cocked a brow. "That didn't sound particularly convincing."

"Yes, then. Yes!"

His eyes sparked. He captured her hand and brought it to his lips once more.

"And I promise you a night you'll never forget. *Adieu*, my love."

Precisely at three o'clock, Fionna flipped the sign to CLOSED. Within minutes, she walked up the cobbled walkway that led to the asylum.

Inside, her mother sat where she usually sat—in the middle of the sofa.

"Hello, Mama!" Fionna spared no gaiety in her greeting to her mother. Her chest burned when Mama said nothing. Her eyes merely followed her as Fionna sat beside her.

She enfolded her mother's hand tight within hers. Lord, but she was more feeble with each and every visit! Her skin was like parchment; so frail was she that Fionna feared that with the slightest pressure of her fingers, the bones of her mother's hands might surely snap.

Despair dragged at her heart, heavy as the weight of the earth and all in it. Was there nothing they could do? She must speak with Dr. Colson—

again. Yet what was the use? Inwardly she raged. She was well aware of what he would say—that these things took time, sometimes months, before there was any sign of improvement.

She began to fear Time.

Fionna longed for just one sign—*any* sign—for then she might take hope. Then she might take heart.

As it was, she felt naught but helplessness. Hopelessness.

For Fionna, it was a bitter pill to swallow.

"Mama," she cajoled. "Nurse says you barely eat. Can you try, dearest? For me?"

Her mother regarded her vaguely.

Fionna slipped a small tin from her bag. "Look, Mama. I've brought you some of those ginger biscuits you love. They're your favorite, remember? You always said no one could bake better ginger biscuits than I."

Her mother still stared at her, her features without expression.

Fionna tried again. "Please, Mama. Try just one." She gave a shaky laugh. "Then you can tell me if I've lost my touch."

Her mother turned her eyes aside. She tugged her hand free.

Fionna refused to give up. "I'm going to a party next week, Mama. At the Duke of Gleneden's London town house. Can you imagine, a duke?" She laughed. "I haven't met him yet—I won't until then—but his brother . . . you'd like Aidan, I think."

Despite her mother's silence, Fionna continued. "Do you remember the year we went to Sir Archibald's party? You and Papa danced until you declared your feet would surely fall off." Fionna smiled wistfully. "You so loved dancing and singing and music."

Her mother stared at her with dull eyes. "Essie?" she whispered, her voice so paper-thin Fionna almost had to strain to hear.

Essie was her mother's sister. Dead for at least ten years. Fionna wanted to cry aloud. Instead she pressed her mother's hand against her cheek. "No, Mama, I'm not Essie. I'm Fionna. Your daughter, Mama. Your daughter Fionna."

"You look so young, Essie. And I'm so old." Her voice trailed away.

Fionna tried again. "Listen to me, Mama. I'm not Essie. Essie is not here—"

Her mother's face crumpled. "Essie!" she cried. "You're not Essie? Where is she? I want Essie! And where is William? He did not come to tea today. Only on Fridays. Otherwise, he forgets," she fretted, "and I miss him so dreadfully! I've scolded him soundly, but it does no use. Still he does not come . . ." She began to cry. "Is he angry at me? Is everyone angry?"

"Mama, please do not cry! No one is angry. Look at me, Mama. I am here. I will always be here!"

But when at last Mama raised her head, Fionna knew then that she was gone. Her tears had dried, but she had retreated to that place so far, far away. That place where nothing or no one could reach her.

Not even her daughter.

And then it was Fionna who wept. She who felt so very, very lost and alone. She dashed the tears away so that no one would see as she left Mama's room.

Several blocks away, she passed a group of well-dressed men and women standing in front of a hotel. They spoke among themselves. Even before Fionna passed by, she was aware of sharp disapproval, though they were not overly vociferous. They kept glancing over their shoulders.

Bits and pieces of their conversation drifted on the air. Fionna could not help but hear.

"We must speak to the clerk immediately, Bartholomew," clucked a buxom woman. "I refuse to stay in this establishment another night. I did not come here to be exposed to this! Why, he is demented! Deranged!"

Fionna glanced up sharply. On the opposite corner stood a man. His clothing was torn and ragged. He wore neither coat nor hat. "It's doomed we are! All of us, doomed!" he was crying. A gentleman strode by, stepping into the street to avoid him. "Can you not see them, the Romans with their swords and spears? We must hide, all of us. Everyone must hide!"

He lunged toward the gentleman, grasping his elbow. The gentleman thrust him away harshly. "Away from me, you lunatic!"

"To the hills!" the man screeched. "To the hills! They come! They come for us! Flee. Flee now!" An earth-shattering scream pierced the air. "I am fallen . . . fallen!" He fell to his knees and covered his head. "Mercy, Caesar. Mercy!" He began to weep uncontrollably.

Fionna passed the foursome just as a beak-nosed woman thrust her chin high. "Touched in the head, he is!"

"Why is this horrid creature here on the streets?" sniffed the first. "Why is he not in Bedlam with the rest of his kind, locked up where he belongs?"

Fionna walked more quickly, her throat clogged tight. She was desperate to be away. But inside she was screaming. How could they be so cruel? They would consign him to Bedlam. Were they aware of conditions there? Dr. Colson had gently made her aware of that wretched place. Those poor souls consigned there were treated like animals. Their care consisted of being put into restraints—manacled and chained to the floor or wall.

She shuddered. Guilt swelled. Her stomach twisted; she felt sick inside, sick to the depths of her soul. Fionna felt helpless, sad and angry at the poor man's plight. Yet when she thought of her own dear mama, so very lucky. She hated that Mama must be confined to Dr. Colson's institution, yet if it were not for her ability to maintain finances, Mama might well have ended up in a place such as Bedlam.

The thought plagued her to no end. And so there was no help for it . . .

Fionna walked that night, for it seemed it had been forever since she had done so. It was not in defiance of Aidan. She felt . . . caged. Indeed, it was almost just as the Gypsy predicted . . . she felt as if *she* was the one who had been cursed, and this was the only thing that could free her. The air was dense, heavy with mist. But the darkness cradled her like the warmest of shrouds, melting into her, comforting her, calming her, cleansing her of the demons of the day.

Fionna whirled. Her head cocked to the side as her ears strained. Strained mightily.

She was mistaken. There was no one here. No one but her. Little wonder she was spooked, she told herself, when she wrote of beasts and monsters. It was simply her imagination running wild again.

She lifted her face to the gleaming disk of the moon, paused, then spun around in a little circle, her arms lifted high. Aidan needn't worry, she decided. *She* needn't worry. Her gaze encompassed all within sight. She was free at last. And certain that the night belonged to her alone—that *she* was alone.

* * *

She was not alone.

His form melted into the shadow of a tree, hiding him from view. He did not dare follow, for he'd not seen her for many a night. Granted, he was not always able to watch, or follow . . . but he had begun to wonder if she'd discovered his presence, a thought he disliked intensely. He did not want to frighten her.

He wanted only to watch her.

For now, at least. For now he was content to bide his time. Ah, but when she discovered the truth, he knew she would find his little game as delightful as he did. What had she thought when she discovered his little foray into her bookshop? What would she think of the little present he'd left her only tonight?

No doubt she'd be filled with as much amusement as he. After all, she did love a good mystery.

He laughed softly, recalling her mother's confession when he visited.

She had beckoned him close.

"My Fionna is famous, you know," she had said.

He'd merely smiled.

"She is! She is a novelist!"

"A novelist?" he'd said. *"Pray tell me, which novelist?"*

She had beckoned him still closer.

"My Fionna is F.J. Sparrow. But it's a secret. You will not tell, will you?"

He hadn't believed her, not at first. The woman had delusions, after all—he'd seen them for himself, many times. But there was the occasional period of complete sanity.

And somehow he couldn't quite dismiss her insistence that day. He'd queried her, of course, probing gently. In the course of his work, he fancied himself quite good at discerning truth during his patients' insane ravings.

He'd been rather shocked to learn it was true. The woman simply knew too many details for it *not* to be true.

The lovely Fionna Hawkes was indeed F.J. Sparrow.

He'd been utterly beguiled even before he knew her other identity. Suddenly it all made such perfect sense, for she understood the ways in which a soul could turn dark and twisted and tormented. Why, she was just like *him*. She would understand him, he was sure of it. And now, his little games of cat and mouse were his way of paying homage to her. Oh, but what a pair they would make!

Ah, yes, it was destiny that called them together. They both loved the dark. It was part of their world—the night, the mystery, the shadows and the demons she created.

It was too soon to reveal himself, he decided. He liked this game. And soon enough they would be together. Soon.

The wind swirled, parting the mist, as if heed-ing his call. He watched her swirl . . . Beautiful. So beautiful, the merest hint of her form outlined in the glow of the gaslights.

For now, it was enough to see her like this from time to time.

For now, he could wait.

Very quietly Fionna walked toward the shop, straight to the rear entrance. Removing her hands from the warm, furry muff, she retrieved the key snuggled deep in the pocket of her cloak.

Stepping forward, she bent slightly to push the key into the lock. As she did, her foot kicked against something.

She glanced down. The gaslight on the corner cast out a feeble light, yet she was able to see a bow wrapped around a dozen stems. She made a sound of pleasure. She hadn't been gone long, but while she was, Aidan had left her flowers! Hothouse, to be sure, but flowers nonetheless. Of course, she expected his censure for going out at night the next time she saw him.

But Fionna was touched beyond measure. No one had ever sent her flowers before. Happy, she scooped them up, opened the door, stepped into the tiny entrance hall and turned up the lamp that burned on the wall. Smiling, she started to lift them, to press her nose against them, expecting the aroma of sweet perfume and velvety soft petals.

In shock she dropped them to the floor; there

was a faint, scratchy sound. Stunned, she stared at the lifeless petals now scattered about her feet.

Dead. All of them. Wilted and shriveled and lifeless.

Her mouth went dry. It was as if she'd been plunged into a river of ice.

She practically dove for the door, fumbling for the lock, making sure it was latched tight. She did the same for the shop, then ran up the stairs, straight into her bedroom, where she slammed the door.

She was still shaking when she sank onto the bed.

This was no accident, she realized numbly. Someone had done this deliberately. Someone had left dead roses on her doorstep. On purpose. *On purpose.*

Her gaze slid to the window next to the bed. Despite her fear, despite every instinct that warned against it, with nervous fingers she pushed aside the delicate lace and peered into the night.

Mist lay thick and heavy, obliterating all.

Her breathing rapid, she drew the curtains tight and fast, as if to close out the night.

There had been no footsteps tonight, either behind her or ahead of her. The other times she thought she'd been followed . . . she'd been plagued by an eerie certainty.

Not so tonight.

And somehow that terrified her more than

anything else. *Had* she been alone tonight? Had someone followed? *Watched* her? And why? Why would someone follow her? Why would someone watch *her*?

Was she being watched even now?

Everything inside her was churning. Had she been able to see something—*anything*—that she could confront . . . But to confront what she could not see . . .

She cringed at the thought that crept in, that she failed to keep at bay.

Was she losing her mind? Like poor Mama?

No. *No.* By God, she could not give in to such weakness. She would not give in to this—this interloper! She would not be cowed.

Yet for the second night in a row, she crawled into bed, aware of a bone-deep iciness. Bravado was a lonely companion. For the life of her, she could not warm herself. She huddled beneath the quilts, trembling and shivering.

And once again, when at last she slept, it was with the lamp burning low all through the night.

Chapter Nine

I dreamed that night. But not of demons. Of Rowan. He lay beside me. It is as if we are at the ends of the earth, where nothing can reach us. His mouth so near . . . His legs so close, all tangled up with mine.

Demon of Dartmoor, F.J. Sparrow

Fionna threw herself into preparations for the duke of Gleneden's dinner party, for several reasons. One, it allowed her to put the incident with the dead roses from her mind—or at least, far from the forefront. Two, in all honesty, Fionna was filled with excitement about attending. She'd never been to such an affair—she'd never met a duke! And though Aidan said it was to be an informal evening, Fionna was determined to make a good impression.

She spent the week going from shop to shop, searching for just the right gown, precisely the right accessories, from her hat to silk stockings, from the velvet ribbon bracelet to the French three-button kid gloves.

She had Glynis in to help her into her gown that night and dress her hair, drawn back into a simple but elegant twist. With the aid of a little pomade that Glynis produced, even the tiny errant wisps of hair at her temples and nape were whisked into place.

Her gown . . . well, Fionna had never indulged in such a gown before. There had been no need before now. Her practical side scoffed at the purchase of something she neither needed nor would not use. She did not attend balls or parties, or anything of the like.

But this was different. Now, she wanted to look pretty. Not for herself, but for Aidan. She browsed many a shop for just the right gown. The dressmaker had started it for another woman, who had decided she did not want it after all. A few alterations were all it needed.

And it was exquisite, made of pale green silk that brought out tiny gold flecks in her eyes. The neckline was *à la grecque*, deep and off the shoulders, giving way to a deep vee that made her waist look unbelievably tiny.

Glynis shook her head when Fionna held up a teardrop necklace. "Oh, no jewelry, miss," she objected. "You've no need of it, not with such smooth, creamy skin. It would take away from it, I think."

When at last they were finished, Fionna moved to the beveled full-length mirror in the corner. Glynis gave a dreamy sigh and clasped her hands. "Oh, miss, you're lovely. Quite the loveliest lady I've ever seen."

Fionna turned and gave her a hug. "That's exactly how I feel," she said with a laugh. "Thank you, Glynis."

And that was certainly how she felt a short time later when she opened the door downstairs and Aidan stepped inside.

He stomped the snow from his boots and glanced over at her.

"*Good God!*"

Fionna half-raised an arm self-consciously. "What?" she queried. "What is it?" Anxious dismay shot through her. Had her coiffure come undone? Was she underdressed for the occasion? *Over*dressed? What? she wondered. *What?*

"A moment," was all he said. "Allow me a moment."

His eyes wandered over her, at least twice over. His regard was long and undeniably appreciative. When at length those incredibly blue eyes fused with hers, Fionna's heart gave a little leap, then began to beat with a frenzy she could not control at what she read there. Oh, bother! Whom did she fool? Why should she hide it? Everything inside her glowed. Her heart sang, and she didn't care a whit.

Lean fingers caught hers. He lifted her hand to his mouth and kissed her fingertips, never breaking the hold of their eyes. "You're truly stunning," he said simply.

"Actually I feel—" Fionna broke off breathlessly.

Aidan raised both brows. "Yes?"

"I feel rather drafty," she said with a laugh. Lightly, she touched the skin just below her throat.

It was there that Aidan's gaze lingered. Finally he cleared his throat. "Let me just say that . . . it becomes you."

Fionna laughed up at him.

"Don't move," he said suddenly.

Fionna blinked.

"The way you look right now. Your eyes . . . . they're sparkling. You"—he seemed to be searching for the right thing to say —"*you* sparkle. I like seeing you like this. I like seeing you so carefree, in a way I've never seen you before."

And she was.

Almost a week had passed since she'd seen him. Only a week, yet it seemed like forever. She couldn't lie to herself. She'd missed him, she realized, missed him dreadfully. Perhaps more than she should admit.

He helped her into a long, black velvet mantle.

The inside was lined with the same silky green material as her gown, the hood trimmed with fur.

Strong hands remained settled on her shoulders. "Ready?" he murmured.

Fionna nodded, her pulse still racing from his expression when he'd first caught sight of her.

"Let us be off then." He opened the door.

Fionna was just about to pass through when she suddenly remembered. "Oh, wait! I've left something!" Catching up her skirts and mantle in one hand, she raced up the stairs as fast as she was able. When she returned, she carried a small, tissue-wrapped package tied with a pretty little bow.

Aidan helped her into his carriage. Fionna eased back into the soft cushions. Aidan swung in next to her, then rapped on the window.

The carriage rolled forward.

Aidan eyed the little bundle in her lap.

"Is that for me, love?"

Fionna shook her head.

Both brows shot high. "No?"

"No," she said firmly.

"Fionna!" he said with mock hurt. "You wound me to the quick."

Several seconds passed, and then he asked, "Is it a gift?"

"It is." A secret little smile curled her lips at his curiosity.

"For whom?"

She wrinkled her nose. "Why do you wish to know?"

"Well, if it's not for me, I cannot help but wonder who it could possibly be for?"

"You're very full of yourself, my lord!" she protested. "Very well then. It's a gift for your brother."

"Alec?" He was stupefied.

"Mmmm. Why are you so surprised?"

"I am not so surprised as I am jealous, sweet."

"Well," she demurred, "I've not forgotten how you once told me that most women find the Black Scotsman devastatingly handsome."

"Yes, I recall precisely what I said. I asked if you would swoon if you should ever chance to meet him."

Fionna placed the back of her hand on her forehead, closed her eyes, and pretended to sway.

Aidan lowered his head. Her breath fluttered like a leaf in the wind when his lips touched her ear. "Dazzle me with a smile again, and I'll say no more."

She did, flashing one that made him feel as if he'd been kicked in the gut.

The carriage rounded a corner, rocking her against him. Aidan slipped an arm around her, pleased that she didn't draw away.

He studied her unobtrusively. She was gazing through the window, her shoulder tucked beneath his. Faith, but she was beautiful, and she didn't even know it—which to him made her all the more so.

At times she appeared so sedate. But the lady was ever keen-eyed, often sharp-tongued . . . and vibrant. *Always.*

And tonight there was a new element, one he took immense pleasure in observing. She was sensual. Ripe. Her eyes brimmed with emotion. *She* brimmed.

A stab of undisguised desire shot through him. He wanted her. He wanted her quite badly. Fionna was incredibly strong-willed, but so was he. For now, he told himself, he would not rush her. He would bide his time, though it cost him dearly, and play it her way. Trust, he had learned, was not something that came easily to Miss Fionna Hawkes.

But in time the lovely lady *would* be his—for a will of iron was a particular trait that the McBrides had long possessed. What they wanted, they would have. Obstinate and stubborn, some might have called them. "Determined" and "decisive" were terms he suspected all of the McBrides would prefer to be called.

Fionna leaned forward, peering toward a town house where several footmen stood. The house was ablaze with lights.

"You're not nervous, are you?"

"A little perhaps," she admitted. "When we lived in the country, we attended numerous parties with nearby country squires. But I've never before met a duke. Especially a devastatingly handsome duke," she teased.

He lifted his eyes heavenward. "Who could have known she could be so cruel? She but drives the knife deeper!"

The carriage rolled to a halt. The door swung open and they alighted from the carriage. Aidan pulled her hand into the crook of his elbow.

A white-gloved butler swung the door wide. "Good evening, my lord . . . Miss." The man inclined his head politely.

"Good evening, Carlton. Where is Alec?"

A footman had stepped up to take their wraps.

"His Grace is in the drawing room, my lord. You are the first guests to arrive." He withdrew with a low bow.

Aidan captured her fingers once more and strode forward, covering her hand with his own. Yes, Fionna decided, she was definitely a trifle nervous.

As they entered the drawing room, a tall darkhaired man rose from a wing chair before a roaring fire.

Aidan lowered his head. "Remember," he warned, his whisper for her ears alone, "if you dare to swoon, I swear I shall not catch you."

Fionna bit her lip, smothering a laugh.

"Aidan! The two of you are the first to arrive."

"Yes, so Carlton informed us," he said, as Alec

stepped up. "Alec, I should like to present Miss Fionna Hawkes. Fionna, my brother, Alec Mc-Bride, Duke of Gleneden."

"Miss Hawkes, welcome. I'm so very pleased you accepted my invitation. My brother speaks very highly of you." His greeting was gracious.

The duke was also every bit as handsome as Aidan said, his hair the glossiest black she had ever seen. He was the taller of the pair, but Aidan was broader. Dressed entirely in black but for his snowy white shirt, the duke was, she decided, truly a Black Scotsman. Only his eyes were like pale blue crystal—warm and sparkling now, but Fionna suspected they could be icy indeed. She could well imagine that when he chose, he could be a formidable man.

As could Aidan, advised a little voice in her head. She simply had yet to see that side of him. It would not be wise, she suspected, to cross either of them.

She studied them covertly. Yes, the duke was most attractive indeed. The resemblance between them was strong; there was no mistaking them as brothers. But in her eyes, the duke wasn't nearly so attractive as Aidan. In formal attire, the points of his collar so very white against the bronze of his skin, Aidan was . . . well, quite the most breathtaking man she'd ever seen.

"Come," the duke invited. "Sit and be comfortable."

The duke indicated a sofa angled directly next

to his wing chair. Both men waited until Fionna had lowered herself to the sofa before seating themselves. Aidan placed himself directly next to her.

"Fionna has a gift for you, Alec," he said easily. "Though I pleaded mightily, she insisted it must go to you."

"A gift! For me?"

"Yes, Your Grace." Fionna extended the tissue-wrapped bundle. "A measure of my thanks for your invitation."

The duke pushed aside the layers of paper to reveal a leather-bound book.

"The Devil's Way!" He flipped open the cover to the first pages. His eyes widened. "A first edition!" he marveled. "And signed by F.J. Sparrow!" He laughed delightedly. "Thank you, Miss Hawkes. Words can hardly convey my gratitude."

Fionna smiled. "You just have, Your Grace."

"Aidan must have told you how much I coveted this novel, didn't he?" Fionna had no chance to respond. "And a first edition, almost impossible to find now. My word, how on earth did you manage to procure it? And signed by F.J. Sparrow—why, I still cannot believe it!"

"Secrets of the trade," Fionna murmured. "After all, books are my livelihood."

The duke looked at Aidan. "You failed to tell me the lovely Miss Hawkes was a magician!"

Aidan snared a glass of champagne from a footman. He passed it to Fionna, then took another for himself. "I've discovered the lovely Miss Hawkes is a woman of many surprises." He cast Fionna a sidelong glance. "I cannot help but wonder what other secrets she holds."

Fionna looked down, somehow managing to maintain her smile. Her chest ached. Her fingers clutched hard on the stem of the champagne glass. Oh, if he only knew!

There was a sudden clatter at the front door. "Hellooo!" called a bubbly female voice.

"Ah," said the duke, "I believe Caro and John have arrived."

Caro, Fionna discovered, was cousin to Aidan, Alec, and Anne, their sister. John was Caro's husband. In very short order, she met Anne—or Annie as her family called her—and her husband Simon, visiting from Yorkshire for the month. Both couples clearly doted on each other. It was there in every look they exchanged, though they touched but rarely; wordless endearments Fionna couldn't help but envy.

Firmly she reprimanded herself. Her duty was to her mother, for anything less was nothing but a betrayal—a betrayal she could not live with.

She would never desert her mother.

Vivian McBride was the next to arrive. All three of her children had inherited her vivid blue eyes, though all in varying shades. Fionna was stunned that such a tiny woman had produced such towering sons as Aidan and Alec. Also present was Simon's aunt, Leticia Gardner, Dowager

Countess of Hopewell. A dozen other guests as well had been invited.

Fionna's head was spinning by the time they sat down to dinner, but she managed to remember every one of their names.

Somehow the conversation turned to ancient Scottish curses and hidden treasures. Vivian McBride ran a fingertip around the rim of her wine goblet. "I believe Gleneden has one," she announced. "Something to do with a family pirate."

"What?" Alec laid down his fork. "Mother! A curse? A treasure? A pirate? Why have I not heard of it before now?"

"Well, I expect because it's been so long I barely remember it! Indeed, your father used to tell you and Aidan tales of pirates and an ancient curse. He frightened the two of you so, I insisted he stop. As for treasure, why, it was all nonsense. Everyone knew it. Why, I scarcely remember what it was about!"

Aidan and Alec looked at each other. "Well," said Alec, "all children look for hidden treasure."

Aidan tipped his head to the side. "Wait," he said slowly. "I seem to remember something about a curse—"

"Rubbish!" Alec declared before he could finish. "I am the eldest. How could you possibly recall such a thing if I do not?"

"Now see here, Alec," Aidan began.

"Children, children! Must I remind you that you are well past the age of bickering?" Vivian's gaze then swung straight to her daughter. "And Annie, cease your snickering!"

Everyone laughed. Indeed, much more laughter and lighthearted banter followed when the group trooped into the drawing room.

Anne linked arms with Fionna. "So you are Aidan's lady! I am so very, very pleased you are here tonight. He's been remarkably close-mouthed about you, you know."

Fionna was flabbergasted. She hardly would have called herself Aidan's lady, but to refute Anne's assumption would have been . . . well, no less than rude.

Perhaps it was the dinner conversation with regard to curses . . . perhaps it was her gift to the duke . . . perhaps it was inevitable that the subject eventually turned to F.J. Sparrow and *Demon of Dartmoor.*

"Miss Hawkes, have you read F.J. Sparrow? He authors *Demon of Dartmoor*," piped the Dowager Countess of Hopewell. "Oh, but of course you have. How silly of me! I should imagine the entire city is beating down the door of your establishment vying to obtain his books."

Once again Fionna had no chance to speak.

"Well, to the devil with the demon," declared Vivian McBride stoutly. "It's Raven and Rowan I want to know about." She leaned forward, her delicate blue eyes all agleam. "Did everyone read last week's chapter? The two of them kissing wildly on the tower? His hand on her . . . " She gave a trill of delighted laughter. "I vow I nearly expired then and there—why, I hated for such a kiss to end! And I wonder . . . the two of them . . . do you think they will ever become lovers?"

The eyes of the three McBride children swung to their mother. Anne's mouth fell open. "Mama!"

"Oh, come, dear," Vivian said crisply. "I am your mother, after all. Do you think I do not know of such things? How on earth do you think you and Alec and Aidan came into this world?"

"Yes, Raven and Rowan have quite captured everyone's fancy," Alec finally interjected. "I suspect F.J. Sparrow will keep us guessing."

A lively discussion ensued. Fionna lowered her eyes, a faint smile on her lips. It was vastly amusing. No, more than amusing that everyone was so convinced F.J. Sparrow was a man. At times like this, it was downright fun to keep such secrets, with no one the wiser. No one but her . . . and Mama.

Something inside her twisted. But she would not let it ruin the evening, which slipped away far too quickly. Almost before she knew it, Aidan was handing her into the carriage.

Aidan's gaze settled on her. The warmth reflected there made her heart skip a beat.

"So," he murmured as it lurched into motion. "What did you think? Did my family frighten you away?"

"Hardly." Fionna had particularly liked Anne, who was outspoken and gay. She and Aidan were among the last to leave, and Anne had thrown her arms around her.

"You must come see us before we return to Yorkshire! I should regret it forever if you do not. We are staying at Mama's. Perhaps you and Caro and I could go shopping. Or—no, wait!—come to tea instead. We would all love it!"

Aidan was still gauging her reaction. "I had a lovely time, Aidan. Truly."

"I'm glad." His regard was steady on her face. "But your secret has been revealed."

Fionna nearly choked.

"You're trying to worm your way into the good graces of my brother, aren't you?" He gave a low chuckle. "Aye, you've succeeded in winning him over. He shall worship you evermore for gifting him with a copy of *The Devil's Way*."

"It was the least I could do," Fionna managed.

"I always thought I was possessed of a keen perceptiveness. That I could read others, through their actions, their movements. But you, Fionna . . ."

"What?"

"Do not be coy. I saw you tonight. Listening to those women gossip about F.J. Sparrow. Smiling, your head cocked slightly to the side, your expression . . . amused. I'm not sure what else to call it. And I wondered then what was in your mind. Indeed, I remember thinking that you looked like a child who'd hidden away some secret from all the world . . ."

His voice trailed away. Something flashed across his features.

Her smile faded. The intensity on his face made her uneasy.

The silence was never-ending. Filled with trepidation, she endured it as long as she could. "Aidan? Why—" her throat had gone bone-dry. Her heart was thudding wildly. That she was able to speak even a word was a miracle. "Why do you look at me so?"

He had yet to relieve her of that unnerving stare. "Good God," he said slowly. And then again: "*Good God.*"

The carriage rolled to a halt.

Aidan did not move. His eyes bored into hers until she could have screamed. He leaned forward just a hair, and now the merest smile creased his lips.

"I know," he said softly. "Fionna . . . *I know.*"

Chapter Ten

I knew then. The danger lies not only with the demon we seek. The danger lies within me. Rowan beckons. Nay, not with words. But with his mouth. With his touch. I vow to resist him. But I can see his want. Feel his desire. He tempts me, heart and soul. I want him to touch me. I want . . .

Demon of Dartmoor, F.J. Sparrow

Fionna's heart foundered, then began to thud madly. No, she thought vaguely. It couldn't possibly be . . .

The carriage door swung wide.

Fionna waited no longer, but hurtled herself down the steps, nearly tripping over the footman in her haste to be away. At least, she tried to get away. Aidan's hand closed firmly about her elbow. Oh, the wretch. He was beside her, matching her, step for step, as if they marched in formation.

Her thoughts were scrambled so that she could barely think. She fumbled in the pretty little handbag she carried. The contents were few. A little coin purse—why ever had she brought it in the first place? A handkerchief embroidered by her mother. At last! Her fingers closed around the key and brought it up. She tried to thrust in the lock and missed; Aidan's shadow blocked the light from the moon—on purpose, she was certain of it!

The key fell to the ground. Aidan scooped it up, neatly pushed the key in the lock, and opened the door.

Fuming, Fionna stepped into the entryway and spun around quickly . . . alas, not quickly enough. He'd already closed the portal.

Her chin tipped high. "Good night, my lord," she said calmly, "and thank you for a most charming evening."

He was having none of it. "Shall we continue our discussion upstairs?"

"I wasn't aware we were having a discussion!"

"We are," he said firmly. "Or at least we will be soon."

Fionna stood her ground, her back to the stairway.

He gave a mock sigh. "Oh, come, Fionna. Aren't you curious what I was going to say? Or could it be that you already know?"

She glared at him.

Aidan placed his hands at his waist and widened his stance. His stance managed to infuriate her even more.

"Oh, dear," he said smoothly. "Forgive me for being so inconsiderate. The hour is late. You must surely be tired. Perhaps I should carry you instead." His eyes were alight with a gleam most wicked. "I should quite enjoy that, I think."

Fionna whirled and stalked up the stairs.

Once they were in her apartments, she faced him squarely. Oh, but his smile was so smug, his tone so mild.

"Your expression leads me to believe you'd like to deliver me a blow squarely in the belly. Or perhaps slap me soundly on the cheek."

"I should like to do both," Fionna said from between her teeth.

"I fear you'd inflict little damage, my love."

"Really?"

"Really."

"Then I must remind you of the night we met, Aidan. The night you enlightened me as to the . . . vulnerable areas of a man's anatomy. My memory is quite vivid," she said sweetly. "The face, you said. The eyes, if one is able. The chest or belly or"—she emulated perfectly the swirl of his finger as he had done that night—"parts thereunder. A knee, I believe you said, was particularly effective at bringing a man down. Yes, that was it—precisely."

His grin was wiped clean. It was Fionna's turn to smile smugly.

Fionna swung off her cloak and hung it from one of the hooks beside the door. Aidan then removed his greatcoat—he persisted in making himself quite at home!—and hung it next to hers.

She strode into the parlor and seated herself in the silk-striped damask chair adjacent to the sofa. There! If he chose to sit, he'd have to do it on the sofa.

Which was precisely what he did, at the very end nearest Fionna. But first he shrugged off his formal jacket and draped it on the dining room chair. As he seated himself, he casually arranged his legs so that mere inches separated their knees. His forearm lay placed on the armrest so that if he chose, he had only to lift a hand to touch her. A not particularly subtle strategy, she decided furiously.

As he had once before, despite his evening attire, he reminded her of a wild animal ready to strike. Beneath the brilliant white of his shirt she glimpsed the shadow of dark hair on his chest and belly. An odd thrill shot through her. Her fingers curled and uncurled. There looked to be . . . well, rather more than she expected. She wondered at its texture, how it might feel. Fleecy? Bristly?

She was appalled at the direction of her

thoughts. She wrenched her mind back to the matter at hand.

Which, unfortunately, was at the forefront of his as well.

"I find myself in a bit of a dilemma."

"How so?" Her tone was prim, her fingertips perched lightly on her knees.

His long, slow scrutiny made her ill at ease, while he was totally at ease! It was maddening. Aidan, however, found himself enjoying the moment.

"I am at a loss as to your true name. I introduced you tonight as Miss Hawkes. But should it have been Miss Sparrow?"

Her chin tipped high. "I've no idea what you mean."

"Pray, let us dispense with the pretense. I've finally figured out that Fionna Hawkes and F.J. Sparrow are one and the same."

She licked her lips. "You're mistaken."

He tapped his fingertips together. "Am I? If I should hazard a guess . . . What is your second name, Fionna? I am curious."

Fionna glared.

He pressed on. "Your second name, love."

She set her teeth again. "When will you desist in calling me that?"

"I won't. Because you will be my love," he stated with such certainty that she was rendered momentarily speechless. No, not just certainty— sheer arrogance!

Before she could argue, he raised his brows. "You avoid the question, Fionna. It is Fionna, is it not?"

"It is," she said tightly.

"Fionna . . . ?" He waited expectantly.

"Josephine," she said even more tightly.

"Fionna . . . Josephine . . . Hawkes. F.J. Sparrow. The master of murder and monsters and mayhem is really the *mistress* of murder and monsters and mayhem."

Oh, Lord, it was true. Her instincts had been right. She had been a fool to let him get so close to her! She stared down at her hands, flattened now against her silk-covered thighs.

"Was it so obvious then?" Her tone was very low.

"Heavens, no! I only just realized it tonight. I consider myself a bumbling idiot for failing to recognize it earlier."

"How did you know then?" At least she raised her head.

Aidan paused. "'*I'm quite able to take care of myself, thank you very much,*'" he quoted. "Raven said it to Rowan in one of your books. An exact quote, I believe Alec said, why, the night we met. And you said it to me, Fionna, that very same night. And all of a sudden in the carriage . . . it simply came together, like pieces of a puzzle. Books are your livelihood, you told Alec tonight. The fact that you own a bookshop. The book you gave Alec, *The Devil's Way*, a first edition that you said was nigh impossible to find—a *signed* first edition. The names . . . Hawkes. Raven. Sparrow. All at once it just made perfect sense. All at once I suddenly *knew*."

Fionna kept silent. She'd thought herself so clever. And to think how she and Mama and Papa had once laughed over it . . .

Her heart twisted. How much her life had changed since then. So much, yet in so little time.

"You are truly mistress of the dark. It's why you walk at night, isn't it?" he queried. "To think. To mull."

"Yes." A shiver went through her as she remembered the dead flowers that awaited her return the other night. Should she tell Aidan? No. It had been such a perfect evening, even though Aidan had discovered her secret. She wanted nothing to ruin it. Besides, in all truth, to this day, she had never actually seen anyone. Even the flowers—well, perhaps it was just a rather nasty joke. A prank. Perhaps they were meant for someone else.

Aidan had tipped his head to the side. "What is it?" He reached for her hand, barely stroking his fingertips across her knuckles, a gesture that somehow made a huge lump rise in her throat.

"It's nothing," she said quickly.

His gaze narrowed. "Are you certain? Suddenly you looked as if you were hundreds of miles away."

"Of course I'm certain."

"Well"—a faint twinkle appeared in his eyes—"now that I know the truth, I concede that you are entitled to a few eccentricities."

Fionna yanked her hand back, bristling. "I hope you're aware that if I'd wanted you to know I was F.J. Sparrow, I would have told you."

He arched one brow. "Meaning?"

"Meaning that you can't tell anyone, Aidan." He had learned she was F.J. Sparrow, yes. Now three of them knew—her, Aidan, and Mama. A pang shot through her. Perhaps Mama no longer even remembered. She ached inside, recalling how Mama had thought Fionna was her dead sister Essie.

No one beyond the three of them could ever know. And she couldn't risk Aidan's knowing the rest. She hated herself for telling him her mother was dead. She despised herself for such deceit. It was as if she'd betrayed not only him, but her mother. She hated that she must conceal it from everyone, even Aidan. *Especially* Aidan. Yet she could not gamble with something so vital. She couldn't chance anyone finding out her mother was alive.

In an asylum for the insane.

She could accord no blame for her mother's malady. But—she despised herself even more—there were times an abiding shame crept in. She despised herself for it. She wanted it not, yet was no escaping it. And then it wasn't about regret. It wasn't about F.J. Sparrow, or finances; at times it wasn't about protecting Mama, or anything of the like.

It was about her—Fionna Josephine Hawkes. Protecting herself. The burning shame hidden deep inside, that someone might discover and *know* that her mother was mad.

Insane.

Guilt, bitter and bittersweet, poured over her.

It seemed she wasn't always so righteous as she pretended.

Yet no matter the reason, she had to save Mama. She had to save *both* of them.

She lifted her head, regarding Aidan. "You cannot tell anyone I am F.J. Sparrow," she repeated. "Not your brother. Not your mother. Not friend nor foe nor any acquaint—"

"Yes," he said dryly. "I quite grasp your point. You are quite famous, though, you realize. Didn't you hear everyone at the party tonight? Everyone wants more of Raven and Rowan. More of demons and devils and—"

"It's not just some grand joke. If anyone should find out—*anyone*," she stressed, "it could mean the end of my career. The fact that no one is aware of F.J. Sparrow's identity adds to the mystery. It adds to the fascination. Do you think I don't know that? If people knew who he is—who *I* am—it would all be gone. Poof! And it's my work, Aidan. It's my life. I can't jeopardize that."

"I'm well aware of your reasons, Fionna." His

tone held a faint censure, almost curt. He leaned forward, his gaze oddly penetrating. "This is why you won't let anyone close, isn't it? Why you won't let *me* close? But something tells me there is more. Why is that, Fionna?"

She made no reply. Inside, Fionna cursed a silent oath, followed by another. This was no idle guess on his part. Aidan made no idle guesses. He was shrewd to the bone! She'd grown accustomed to hiding her feelings; she'd made a most stringent effort to do so, and she'd been convinced she'd been successful. So how the devil did he know her so well?

Her lips compressed. She would neither confirm nor deny it, by heaven. Tucking her feet beneath her, she prepared to rise.

He stopped her with a lift of his hand, a shake of his hand, already uncoiling his body. "No, sweet. Remain where you are. And know that your secret is safe with me." He stood looking down at her.

"There is just one thing I would ask of you, Fionna." He paused. "A small price, if you will."

Fionna was astounded. The rogue! "What—what price?" she sputtered furiously. "How dare you hold this over me after all!"

She would have surged upright if not for the fact that he stood directly over her, her slippers aligned squarely between his booted feet.

"No," he commanded. "Sit! Do not move! That, dearest Fionna, is the only price I ask."

Warily Fionna watched as he made a half circle around her chair.

He was directly behind her. What the blazes was he about? She'd seen the faint laughter lurking in his eyes. The urge to twist around and confront him was overwhelming. Yet somehow she stopped herself.

"You become tedious, Aidan." And she sounded almost petulant.

"And you are but more intriguing," came his whisper. "Shall I tell you how much you intrigue me?"

Her mouth had gone utterly dry. Fionna gripped the arms of the chair. He planted his hands directly over hers, holding her in place. It dawned on her that she was trapped. Dragging in a breath, she tipped her head back to discover her eyes sighted directly on his mouth, tipped up at the corners in a glimmer of a smile.

His gaze trickled slowly down . . . to the hollow between her breasts, which were surely . . . well, amply displayed.

And avidly surveyed.

Fionna swallowed. Her nipples pricked high.

"Do I embarrass you, love?"

She nearly choked on her tongue. "You know very well that you do!"

His smile widened slightly. She knew then he was well aware of her body's reaction to his riveting regard.

Time hung unending. He remained unmoving.

Behind her. Above her. And then . . . and then . . .

Angling his head just so, he kissed her—kissed her upside down.

Chaos raged inside her. He wound his fingers through hers, this time angling his head the other way.

It was strange being kissed like this, a sort of tender entrapment. Strange, yet incredibly provocative.

Still, a vague remembrance surfaced. "You said no kissing this time," she admonished rather weakly. "Your rules, remember? Aidan's Rules."

"The rules have changed." No apology. She was reminded of how he'd once referred to himself as a man of decisiveness. A man of action.

A long time later, he released her mouth, only to run his lips down the pulsing vein of her throat, dipping and swirling, tasting her with his tongue. She was aware of the slight roughness of his cheek against her own.

"Aidan." His name was the merest wisp, her protest no protest at all. "Aidan, I can't think when you—"

"Don't think," he uttered, his tone almost rough.

"I can't help it! I—"

"Feel, Fionna. Just *feel*. Feel—" His mouth closed over hers, his tongue circling around hers. He made a sound deep in his throat; it resounded in hers. "Feel this," he said into her mouth.

His head lifted, but there was no time for regret. Almost before the strings of her corset were freed, his palms slid into the bodice of her gown, closing around her breasts, filling his hands with soft, overflowing flesh, for her breasts seemed to swell of their own volition. His palms rubbed tiny circles around the points of her nipples, first one way, then the other.

She'd written about this, with Raven and Rowan. She recalled moving restlessly in her chair as she'd written the scene, pressing her hands against her bosom in order to quell the sensation that gathered there.

But this was so much better than she could have ever imagined. This, then, was what he meant by touching, she realized hazily.

Tiny needlelike pinpricks centered there, in the very peaks. He tantalized. He tormented. Yet she longed for it to go on and on, for she sensed there was more. Her lips parted. She panted softly, aware that he watched his hands lift her breasts, his thumbs whisking across her nipples, then circling slowly. Yes, he watched . . . and *she* watched, and it was arousing beyond belief.

Her heart was skipping madly. She discovered herself wondering what his mouth would feel like there, at the very crest of her breast. At the very same instant, her face seared. She was aghast at the direction in which her mind had veered . . . aghast at *his* next move.

With fluid ease, he lifted her, shifting their bodies so that he sat in the chair instead—while *she* sat in his lap.

His feet were planted wide—and she was planted snugly between the vise of his thighs. Her body jerked, shock splintering through her. Her bottom was snuggled against the part of his physique she had stunned herself by mentioning earlier.

His thighs were bands of iron. As for what lay between . . . A blatant hardness. She tried to squirm away, only to feel that part of him surge. Surge high and . . . swell, unless she was mistaken. And Fionna was quite sure she was not. Dear Lord, how was it possible that he—

"Aidan," she managed. "Aidan, please. This is not . . . we should not—"

"Hold, Fionna. Don't think. Don't speak."

The hooks at the back of her gown were released with a dexterity that left her stunned. He spared her no modesty, no apology. The bodice of her gown was dragged down to her hips, leaving her naked. Fire trailed in the wake of his fingertips. Her hair had come undone, falling around one shoulder and trailing down the length of her arm. The skirt of her gown had somehow become tangled about her knees, revealing a scandalous length of silk-covered leg.

His gaze still dwelled on her chest. His head lowered slowly. His target was clear . . . Anticipation swelled. Expectation surged.

Her heart stopped when his tongue touched the point of one nipple. Dipping and swirling, he licked a slow, circling stroke around and around.

Sensation lit like a flame, sensation that was almost painful. She wasn't quite sure why . . . and when her nipple disappeared into his mouth, she did. She clutched at him, arching into him. When at last he began to suck long and hard and strong, the bottom dropped out of her belly; she was granted her first glimpse of heaven. The next came when he commenced the same, taunting play on the other nipple, leaving the first dark and shiny and wet.

Her lips parted. Her breath hissed in, but she hadn't a prayer of saying a word.

Aidan pressed his face between the mounds of her breasts. "God," he said gratingly, and then again: "God above, but you stir me!"

He raised his head, his turquoise eyes glittering, his breathing ragged. His mouth returned, fiercely this time, his tongue swirling and mating with hers.

Tentatively, a trifle awkwardly, she slipped her fingertips between the buttons of his shirt. His hand joined hers, as anxious as she. The instant she was able, she twined her fingers through the crisp dark hair on his chest.

She could concentrate on nothing but the feel of his mouth taking hers again and again, the pressure of his arm locked possessively around her waist, as if he feared she would bolt at any second.

Deep in the recesses of her mind, she knew she

should have. Yet nothing was further from her mind.

His kiss was like ambrosia. Delicious. And touching . . she'd never dreamed it would be like this. There was so much more to touching than she had ever imagined. She was allowing him liberties she should never have allowed, but it felt so wondrously good she didn't care. She couldn't stop the pleasure she felt . . . she certainly couldn't stop him.

And she was about to discover how much *more* there could be.

With unerring determination, unwavering deliberation, their mouths clinging wildly, Aidan's hand strayed inevitably lower. Skimming the silken folds of her skirts, drifting beneath the hem, his fingertips caressed a silk-clad thigh, clear to where it ended—and beyond.

No, he did not stop there, nor did he give even a thought to it. Without pause, he continued his journey, strong male fingers slipping into the slit in her drawers. With no hesitation, he clamped every inch of her mound.

Fionna gasped, dragging her mouth away. Her legs stiffened and slammed shut. She didn't realize that in so doing, she'd trapped his hand.

Not that Aidan was wont to remind her. Alas, though, he was now almost fully erect, driven to bone-stiff hardness.

Her face and breasts were suffused with color, her eyes huge and wary. He'd felt her jolt of shock, interpreted the confusion on her face, the unmistakable awareness of what and where he touched.

"Aidan," she choked, "I cannot . . . You cannot mean to—"

"And I won't. I won't have you despise me, Fionna. When I make you mine, I want no doubts. When I make you mine, you'll want me as much as I want you."

He kissed her anew, kissed her until he felt her resistance wane, initiating a slow, dancing rhythm on the satin plane of her thighs. Soft curls brushed his knuckles, sending him half-way to madness. Feeling her go damp and wet against him nearly tumbled him over the edge. He laid his thumb directly against the sensitive peak hidden deep within her nest. A tremor shot through her; he swallowed the stifled little sound she made.

"It's all right," he muttered hoarsely, feasting now on the tantalizing spot where her shoulder met her neck. "It's just another way to pleasure you. Let me, love. Let me please you."

With two fingers he traced the valley beside her chasm; her flesh was hot and slick, plump and swollen, almost weeping beneath his gentle exploration. Heat blasted through his body, a heat that rivaled that of India; he was steaming along with her.

"I want," she panted. "I need . . . Damn you, you're torturing me."

He eased a finger inside her, retreating, then easing forward again. He couldn't dismiss the tender flesh clamped tight around him, for her virginal state rendered her tight and small. "Wait, Fionna. Wait. I don't want to hurt you." Sweat popped out on his brow. Little by little he advanced. Higher. Deeper. Her flesh yielding beneath his gentle but inevitable penetration.

She moaned. "It's not enough. Dammit, it's not enough!"

His laugh was triumphant. "Patience, love. Patience."

She buried her head against his shoulder.

He buried his finger inside her cleft, as far as he could. His thumb slowly circled her velvety pearl, pressed, then circled anew, faster and faster, gaining a tempo he knew would drive her wild.

Her hands came up, clenching and unclenching against his chest. He felt the tension strung throughout her body and knew precisely what caused it.

Knew precisely how to ease it.

"Don't fight it." The words were a low, silken whisper, yet his tone was almost gritty with self-control. "Just let it happen, darling. Just let it happen."

She couldn't stop it. He knew that pure sensa-

tion burned inside her. She writhed around his
finger, her hips seeking, stark and wanton.

He knew precisely when the spasms of release
seized hold. She cried aloud. Her body contracted around him, again and again. She col-
lapsed against him, spent and satiated, his finger
still deep inside her.

Aidan, however, was more aroused than he
had ever been in his life. Every part of his body,
every muscle, every nerve, was taut and on edge,
almost to the breaking point. A crimson haze of
desire scorched his insides, for though Fionna
had gained release, he had not. He could barely
think.

Powerful arms lifted her, catching her so that
she faced him, her bare legs bracketed around
his. A long arm swept around her back. "You
pleased me, love. And I am glad that I pleased
you so much. But the next time we are together
like this, it will be a different part of me that will
be inside you. The next time it will be *this*."

Reaching between them, he fumbled with his
trousers, freeing his rigid erection, curling her
fingers around thick, swollen flesh and sealing
it there with the pressure of his own. "And there
will be nothing between us, sweet. No barriers
of clothing. No barriers of words. Do you understand what I am saying?"

Fionna gaped at him, stunned at what he'd
said. Stunned at what he was doing. She could

feel that rigidly masculine part of him . . . good heavens, her palm was *filled* with that rigidly masculine part of him. And therein lay but more shock . . . it was truly only part of him.

His expression was tense and unsmiling, his eyes glittering with a desire so fierce and intense, she was struck dumb.

Realization was slow to return. When it did, shame roiled over her. She would never be able to look at herself in the mirror again. She would never be able to look at *him*.

"Let me go!" she cried.

He released her. She scrambled to her feet and surged away, turning her back on him. From the corner of her eye, she was aware of him shrugging into his jacket. How the blazes could he be so calm when her hands were trembling so that she had yet to cover herself properly?

Behind her, she heard him sigh.

Before she knew what he was about, he'd whisked the gown up so that it covered her breasts, then turned her to face him.

Fionna jerked away. Amber-flecked eyes blazed up at him.

"I will thank you to leave," she told him tightly.

He cocked a brow. "As a matter of fact, I *was* leaving." Mercifully, he'd regained his control. However, it appeared Fionna had progressed to a radically different emotion.

He frowned. "You're angry."

"Of course I'm angry! How dare you," she sputtered. "How dare you say such a thing. How dare you *do* . . . "

"Yes?" he prompted. "How dare I do what?"

He knew she would not say it, the wretch. She tipped her chin high. "You should not have . . . you should not have done what you did!"

"I see my bluntness has offended your sensibilities. However, I fear I must continue to be blunt. I heard no protests, Fionna. All I heard were sounds of pleasure. Of passion. And the ones I heard," he finished with such calm that she was all the more outraged, "were unmistakably yours, love."

This time the sound she made was one of pure rage. This time she was certain there was no mistaking it for anything else but what it was.

"What, will you accuse me of seducing you then?"

If she could have made such a claim, she would have. But it wasn't true. Nonetheless, she was compelled to respond.

"What I think," she said very deliberately, "is that you maneuvered me to your own end."

"If that were true, I assure you the *end,* as you call it, would have been much different. And the means to that end, as well, might have been, well . . . a little different as well."

Fionna went scarlet to the marrow of her bones.

"Or perhaps not," he added thoughtfully.

Fionna stiffened.

Aidan, meanwhile, gave her a long, slow look as he retrieved his greatcoat. "Think what you wish, Fionna. Say what you will. But if you cannot be honest to me, then at least be true to yourself." His gaze bored into hers. He did not gloat, he did not crow. "You, my lovely, desire me every bit as much as I desire you. You just proved it. The difference between us is simply that I refuse to hide from it."

Chapter Eleven

We followed the creature that night, followed so closely that in the end we had no choice but to hide.

Hide as if we were one, Rowan and I. Our mouths together. My body wedded to his. My body wedged between his...

Demon of Dartmoor, F.J. Sparrow

He spoke of passion. He spoke of pleasure.

Somewhere in the depths of Fionna's soul whispered a voice that told her he was right. That she hid from it. From him.

From herself.

She could not forget what Aidan had done. The pleasure and passion that had coursed throughout her body. And so she put those emotions to good use, made the most of it. She let fly her imagination. She let herself be swept away.

Her writing that night was of a decidedly erotic bent. She dared more than she had ever dared before. Raven dared more than she had ever dared before . . . and so did Rowan.

It was late when she fell exhausted into bed. Nonetheless, sleep did not come readily. Her mind was racing around and around. She groaned when the light began to peep through the curtains. A raging headache throbbed in her temples. She'd barely staggered from the bed when Glynis knocked.

She opened the door, still clad in her nightgown, her robe tied hastily.

Glynis blinked. "Would you prefer I come back tomorrow, miss?"

"No. No, it's not necessary, Glynis."

"P'rhaps a nice warm bath would be to your liking," the little red-haired maid declared cheerily. "Shall I prepare one, miss?"

Amazingly, Fionna smiled. "Oh, that sounds divine. What on earth would I do without you?"

Indeed, it did much to ease the pounding in her head. Glynis fluttered to and fro, chattering as only she could chatter. Fionna languished as long as she dared, then climbed from the tub. Glynis helped her dress. The maid had already prepared a small repast. While Fionna ate her meal, she pondered increasing the girl's salary. Glynis completed her chores, then went on her way.

It was nearly ten when Fionna flung her cloak over her shoulders, hastily tied her bonnet, and ran down the stairs. In the shop, she seized the broom and fairly flew out the door to sweep the smattering of the night's snowfall from the steps.

There! Done, and just in time to open the shop.

It was such a lovely winter day, she paused for just one more moment. Others complained about the cold, but Fionna didn't mind. It was better than endless days of dismal rain.

The sun was framed against a vivid blue sky, reminding her of the village in winter. Once, when she was young, Mama and Papa had taken her for a sleigh ride through the forest, across snow-covered hills. The sun sparkled brightly. Nestled protectively between her parents, layers of blankets draped across all of them to shut out the cold, Fionna couldn't remember when she'd ever felt so loved—when she'd ever been so happy. It was beautiful; how she loved winter! She'd watched as the wind blew snow off the branches of the trees. They'd stopped to warm themselves at Vicar Tomlinson's cozy little house near the church.

A huge lump rose in her throat. Reluctant to give up the memory so quickly, she lifted her face to the brilliant arc of the sun, tipping it ever so slightly to avoid the reflection on brilliant crystals of snow. She turned for one last look. Mrs. Chalmers was just climbing from her carriage; they each gave a wave. Just as Fionna prepared to turn away, a shadow darkened the walk. She recognized that fluid stride, the tilt of his hat, the swing of his cane. Here was the man who had kept her awake long into the night. She gathered her courage and her tongue.

Aidan had ceased his walk not three feet away. She longed to emit a groan, but she decided it would be best to take her cues from the man. Within limits, of course.

Silence prevailed.

"Well," Aidan said at last. "This is proving to be rather awkward. I, for one, should prefer that it not be the case."

"You are right, of course." Fionna let out an uneven breath. "Perhaps it would be best," she said slowly, "if we had another—discussion." She didn't know what else to call it.

"Excellent idea. However, I have business scheduled for the rest of the day. May I suggest this evening?"

Fionna's pulse leaped. Evening. A calculated move?

Oh, heavens. She was being much, much too paranoid. Yet how she envied him his composure, his aplomb, for she felt as if she were flying out of control. But somehow she managed to maintain a pleasant countenance when Aidan said, "Shall we say seven o'clock?"

Fionna nodded. "Good day to you then."

He swept her a bow. "Until this evening."

As it was, the day seemed endless. Only two customers entered the shop, shortly before noon. Finally, she retreated to the back office to write. She was anxious to finish up *Demon of Dartmoor.* Then it would be on to *The Scourge of Scotland.*

She hadn't worked out the plot yet, but a vague idea lurked in the back of her mind—it was how she worked best. Perhaps she could write of some ancient beast, some evil spirit come to life. Aidan's face fixed securely in her mind—the Scourge of Scotland indeed!

Alas, there was little point in trying to write. The words simply would not come. How she hated it when that happened. And it had been happening all too much of late—she'd never encountered such difficulty before. Why, it had been difficult ever since she'd met Aidan McBride!

She was admittedly apprehensive about meeting with him this evening. She fixed a light supper, of which she could barely eat a scant bite.

At a quarter of seven, she began to prepare tea.

Promptly at seven she heard his knock. A most polite greeting, and she ushered him upstairs.

Fionna went to fetch the tray of tea. The scoundrel! He had taken a place in *that* chair, the one where they had . . . ! She couldn't finish the thought. She had the distinct feeling he did it solely on purpose, as if to goad her.

She wouldn't allow it. She wouldn't allow him to discomfit her.

She poured for both of them. "I trust you had a pleasant day." She handed him cup and saucer and directed her attention to her own, eyes downcast, taking far longer than was necessary to drop in milk and sugar and stir—stir—stir.

Aidan lowered his cup. His mouth thinned. "Egad, Fionna! Can't you even look at me? You make me feel an utter blackguard."

And he made her feel like a fallen angel. She focused on his hands, so undeniably strong and male, curled around the delicate china cup. The memory of his hands—his fingers—sliding beneath her skirt suddenly revived all too keenly. A single finger penetrating her. *Breaching* her, so daringly bold she went hot all over, *especially* that place that he had claimed. It was all she could do to keep herself from squirming.

He made no effort to hide his impatience. "It is not," he stated grimly, "particularly flattering that you find this so unpalatable."

Fionna set aside her cup. She pinched the bridge of her nose until it hurt, relishing the ache, for it enabled her to gather her thoughts and her courage. Finally, she raised her head and placed her hands primly in her lap.

"Very well then. What happened last night . . .

well, it can't happen again, Aidan. It mustn't."

There was a brooding silence. Nay, a brewing silence.

Not once did he take his eyes from her face. It was unnerving.

"It mustn't happen again," she repeated, this time even more nervously.

"I beg your pardon?"

His tone was so calm. She envied him his composure, even as she hated his unruffled manner. Oh, the wretch, he *was* a blackguard. He knew full well how difficult this was for her! He would make her say it aloud.

Her lips compressed. "You know very well of what I speak."

"Tell me."

"You . . . kissing me." She had to swallow in order to continue. "The way you touched me. I-it can't happen again," she finished all in a rush.

He sat back, drumming his fingers on the arm of the chair. "You kissed me back, Fionna. Quite . . . feverishly, as I recall. I should say that all was quite . . . feverish."

"It's quite unfair of you to remind me," she said, her voice very low.

He reached for his cup, sipped, then replaced it on the saucer. "May I be blunt, Fionna?" He gave her no chance to respond. "You enjoyed it as much as I."

"That is hardly the point—"

"That is exactly the point."

"I am trying to make you understand," she told him unevenly. "I enjoy your company, Aidan. Truly. My life has been lonely of late. My life has been solitary. It's been a choice I've had to make." She held her breath, afraid to divulge too much, yet striving for honesty. "I freely admit, I should miss your company, for I've enjoyed the times we've been together—"

"Especially last night." There was a devilish slant to the tilt of his head, his mouth . . . oh, but he was outrageous.

"Aidan! Pray let me finish. I think it would be best if we were simply friends, as it were."

"Friends?" he mused. "Friends don't kiss like we did, sweet. Friends don't *touch* like we did."

"Precisely what I am trying to say. Precisely why it can't happen again! Isn't it possible that we could simply be comrades of sorts?"

"Comrades?" He released a laugh.

"Do not amuse yourself at my expense," she snapped. "We are friends, Aidan. Nothing more."

"In your eyes, Fionna. The word is subjective. Friends can be lovers. Lovers can be friends— and should be."

Lovers? Fionna suppressed a gasp. The conversation had taken the very direction she'd hoped to avoid. Tried desperately to avoid. But even she knew that what they shared last night had gone far beyond the bounds of friendship.

"Don't say such things." The heat of a blush crept up her neck.

He laced his fingertips together, letting them rest on his waistcoat.

"We both know it, Fionna. Last night proved it. It could have easily progressed to—"

"No! Don't say such things, Aidan."

The makings of a smile tipped his mouth. "I could carry you into your chamber right now," he said softly, "and make love to you and you know it. Concede the point."

Her heart leaped in panic. "You are wrong! You think much of yourself, my lord. I concede nothing, certainly not such a ridiculous assertion."

His smile widened. "Ah, Fionna. That is a challenge a woman should never issue a man. It only makes him want to prove otherwise."

Dismay flooded all through her. "Aidan. I beg of you, do not."

Again that silence. She could have screamed.

"Friends, Aidan. Friends," she stressed.

"And if I do not agree?" He stretched his legs out.

"Please do not make this harder for me."

"So you think to leave it like this?"

"Yes." There was nothing more to say.

"Nothing has been resolved, Fionna."

"Everything has been resolved."

"In your eyes, perhaps. Not mine. You proposed this discussion. Therefore, I suggest that we come to a mutually agreeable solution . . . even if it takes all night," he said mildly.

Fionna was aghast. "You cannot stay here all night!"

"I'm quite adept at slipping in and out of places unheard and unseen," he murmured, "compliments of my time in the Punjab."

Fionna glared at him.

"You do realize," he said very softly, "that I find this conversation immensely revealing."

She stiffened. "How so?"

"You deny yourself what you truly want, Fionna. In spite of your feelings. In spite of your desire."

"You do not know me as well as you think, my lord."

He tapped a finger against his temple, a steady rhythm, as if she'd not spoken at all. "I wonder why that is, Fionna. A choice, you said, to lead a solitary existence. Your choice, I believe, were your exact words."

Her chin came up. "I like my life as it is."

"You live it like a recluse," he stated baldly. "I continue to ask why, yet you continually evade an answer."

The truth was brutal, she thought with a wince. Outwardly she held his gaze. To her credit, it never faltered.

"You stray from the subject, Aidan, the subject of friendship."

"And lovers."

"No." She gazed at him unflinchingly. "We are not lovers. We will never be lovers."

For the longest time he said nothing. He got to his feet and stood there, that odd smile still playing about his mouth. "We already are, sweet."

"The devil we are!" Her objection was stormy and heated.

"Calm yourself, my buzzing little bee." He laughed, in a way that would have made her catch her breath if her heart hadn't been pounding so desperately.

"You do know your lack of experience betrays you, don't you, sweet? There are other ways of making love than . . . well, I shall spare your modesty . . . the one *you* are thinking of. Ours was but one way. Indeed, there are others as well."

Her face seared, but she didn't back down.

"Then I vow that either way—*any* way—shall never take place between us, Aidan."

He studied her, his eyes slightly narrowed, his head tipped to the side. To her utter vexation, she discovered his expression most confounding. She hadn't the slightest notion what was going through his mind.

Then he said, "Escort me to the door, will you, love?"

With the greatest of pleasure. Fionna longed to bare her teeth and growl.

The other half of her had a far different view. He shrugged on his greatcoat and turned.

He stood perilously close. And being so near to him, so very close to him again . . . was perilously sweet.

But that maddening smile had once more returned. Fionna longed to gnash her teeth.

"You will not sway me, Aidan. We are not lovers."

"Not yet perhaps."

"Friends cannot be lovers."

"Ah. Fionna's Law?"

"If you prefer to think of it that way, then yes."

"This is my preference, Fionna. I agree that not all friends should be lovers. But as I stated before, all lovers should surely be friends, don't you think?"

"Aidan's Rules?" Her tone was a bit caustic.

"If you prefer to think of it that way, then yes." He borrowed her statement of the moment before.

"And this is my preference, Aidan. Regardless of your conclusion, we are not lovers. We will never be lovers."

He stepped even closer. His gaze roved every inch of her features.

"Have you ever been in battle, Fionna?"

She frowned. What was he about? "You know that I have not," she said almost crossly.

He trailed a fingertip down her nose.

"Well," he said with a hint of brogue, "now you are."

Chapter Twelve

He was near. I felt his cold breath on the nape of
my neck, like a hand of ice closing tight about
my flesh.

Demon of Dartmoor, F.J. Sparrow

Fionna did not sleep well that night.

She tossed and turned, unable to put him from
her mind.

Still tired, she visited her mother in the morning. It was Sunday and she would not forsake
her visit. Mama was napping already. She did
not rise, but remained where she was, lying on
the sofa. She was groggy, still half-asleep, wak-
ing occasionally to stare at her.

Nonetheless, Fionna sat beside her, taking her
hand between hers.

"Mama," she whispered, "I've met a man, Mama." She smiled slightly. "His name is Aidan. Aidan McBride." She smiled slightly. "His brother is a duke. Can you believe it, Mama? Ah, but he has me so muddled I'm hardly able to write my stories! Difficult to believe, isn't it? Do you remember when you and Papa could scarcely pry me away from my desk to eat supper?

"It's all very strange, you see, how much Aidan and I are like Raven and Rowan. I know you haven't read about them—why, you might be rather shocked if you did! But Raven had never been tempted by any man until Rowan came into her life. And, I know this may sound silly, especially coming from your daughter, but that's how it is with Aidan. Rowan, you see, persists in prodding his way into Raven's life. That's exactly why it's so uncanny, I think. No matter how hard she tries, Raven cannot ignore Rowan. No matter how *I* try, I can't stop myself from . . . from wanting him. From wanting to be with him."

Mama stared at her vaguely. Fionna drew a sharp painful breath. Like a blade it was, clear to her heart, for it all seemed so fruitless. Her mother's state continued to worsen; all Dr. Colson ever said was that these things took time.

Part of her was screaming inside. Why was she talking to a woman who didn't even know she was here? Who probably hadn't the foggiest notion who she was or what she was saying.

It was all Fionna could do not to give in to an overwhelming despair.

Yet she couldn't. If Mama couldn't fight, then she must fight for her, for who else was there? She couldn't give up. Mama was lost, somewhere in the darkness of her mind. Wandering again. If anyone could find her, it was she, her only child.

She had to believe it. She prayed with all her heart that deep down, some part of Mama was still there. That she could reach her. That Mama could *hear* her.

That Mama would come back.

"You'd like him, I think, Mama. He's a bit rakish at times, yet that's part of his charm. He's not a philanderer, not a frivolous man. When I'm with him, at times I'm overwhelmed. At times I feel out of control. And when he leaves, oh, Lord, I feel . . . so alone!"

Tears stung her eyes. She plucked at her skirt, then glanced at Mama. Her eyes were closed.

"He wants me, Mama. *Me.* He-he's told me so! Can you believe it? Why, I hardly can! I feel giddy with happiness, knowing that a man like Aidan McBride wants me, Fionna Hawkes. It's because I've never experienced anything like this before, I know. And he fascinates me so that I can barely think sometimes. Why, sometimes *he's* all I can think of."

Mama's eyes half closed. Her pretty blue eyes stared at the wall, vague and distant.

"I have a confession to make, Mama. When I write about Raven, I pretend that I'm Raven. Raven is adventurous. Relentless in her fight against evil creatures, beasts and demons. For Raven, there's always a way out.

"But there's no way out for me, Mama." Fionna's throat grew thick with tears. Her voice was low and choked. "And I'm so afraid I'll fall in love with him, but I know I shouldn't. Not with—with things the way they are." The truth rent her clearly in two, as if cleaved by a blade. "I want to let him in, as close as he wants to be. He wonders why I deny him. And I don't know how much longer I *can* deny him. He's so determined. He persists and persists . . . and I'm so afraid I'll yield!"

She swallowed. "Is this what love is like, Mama? Is this how you felt with Papa?"

Her mother's face seemed to crumple. Tears filled her eyes.

"William!" she cried out. "Take me home, William. Take me home!"

Fionna bit her lips until they nearly bled. A single tear trickled from the corner of one eye. She dashed it away.

Still, she thought achingly. Still, her mother asked for Papa.

Her step was slow, as if it hurt to walk, as she left the hospital for home.

The day was cloudy, laden with dark, grayish skies, the air thick and heavy and cold. Fionna shivered as she went upstairs and shoveled more coal into the stove. She disdained tea for an early supper, then walked into the parlor to sit for a while before beginning to work. From the corner of her eye, she glanced at her favorite chair. She still couldn't bring herself to sit in it, for that was the very spot where Aidan had explored her body with such shockingly intimate expertise.

And she'd relished every thrill, every shiver of delight.

But it was just as she'd told Mama. For Raven there was always a way out. But this was a man, flesh and blood, Fionna reflected silently. Aidan. And in spite of her arguments against it, she wanted him.

And that was something Fionna didn't know how to fight.

If only it was so easy. If only she could let him in, as close as he wanted to be. As close as *she* wanted him. Perhaps someday, she reflected wistfully, when her life wasn't so complicated.

But by then she would be too old.

By then Aidan would be gone.

She was reminded of everything she'd confided to her mother, things she hadn't even dared to admit to herself.

No, it wasn't fair to encourage him. It wasn't fair to either of them.

He was brother to a duke.

And her mother was mad.

It was an impossible situation.

Nothing could ever come of it.

She was right. They'd resolved nothing. And Aidan wanted everything.

More than she could ever give.

* * *

In the evening, she began work on the current chapter of *Demon of Dartmoor*. But first she glanced over the last chapter, the one she'd just turned in—the one that was most suggestive. Nay, more than suggestive. The one she was certain would have readers gasping for air and clamoring for the next, or heaving it across the room.

She was betting on the former. Sales had improved most profitably since she'd heightened the allure between Raven and Rowan in *Demon of Dartmoor*. And surely enough, not long after she began to write, it wasn't long before the tip of *her* hand touched the tip of one breast. Touched and pressed . . . and circled.

The pen slipped from her fingers. The other hand joined the first, the pressures strengthening, the pleasure intensifying ever more . . . Shocked, she shoved her chair back from her writing desk. A trifle dismayed with herself, she fanned the pages and set them aside.

Aidan McBride was proving most detrimental to her completion of *Demon of Dartmoor*. He continued to stifle her creativity! She spared a quick glance at the clock ticking on the mantel, then hesitated but an instant. Snatching her mantle from its berth, she ventured outside. She needed to think.

She needed to walk.

She loved the dark. She loved the night. And she would not be robbed of her inspiration.

The temperature was much the same as it had been throughout the day. She lifted her face, hunching her shoulders against the chill, aware of a sifting fall of snowflakes drifting from the skies. While some might not have considered it a particularly welcoming environment, Fionna scarcely gave it a second thought. She'd trudged through snow. She'd braved rain and wind and, occasionally, a bit of thunder. Nothing stopped her. Nothing gave her pause—nothing but that blasted uncanny feeling of being surreptitiously surveyed.

Heaven help her, she felt it now.

Disquietude plagued her. Then a shiver slid the length of her spine, why, her entire body. She halted just around the corner from her home, her ears straining. Unbidden, she recalled those other nights when she'd heard footsteps behind her. At the same instant, she recalled not just that, but the day she'd found her book of spells shelved in the wrong spot. And those dead, accursed flowers laid on her doorstep.

She could not say with absolute certainty that she was not being watched. She whirled, searching every scrap of land, between every tree. Had she been able to see something—anything!—then she could fight it. But to confront what she could not see . . .

She whirled and walked straight into a broad, wool-covered chest. Like a wall, it was. With a cry, she actually reeled backward.

Strong hands caught her elbows and brought her upright.

She recognized his scent even before she recognized *him*.

"Aidan!" A plea or a curse? "What the devil are you doing about at this hour? Must you startle me so?"

"The better question, my love, is what are *you* doing about at this hour?"

Drat the man! Must he dog her every step?

"I am concerned for you, Fionna," he said quietly. "If you insist on these nightly jaunts, let me at least accompany you. I promise, it will be as if I am a ghost."

That was exactly how it felt. As if a *ghost* followed her. She sought to suppress a shudder.

"May I accompany you home?"

She released a jagged breath. "If you must."

It was but a short distance to her door. He gave a slight bow. "Good night," he said softly.

She hesitated. "Good night, Aidan."

How on earth she stayed herself from calling him back, she never knew.

* * *

Somewhere in the depths of his being, Aidan knew that Fionna sensed what *he* already knew.

In time they *would* be lovers.

The tactician in him had long ago decided his plan of attack. Impatient though he was, he must continue to persuade her. Woo her. Court her. Strip away her defenses little by little.

He had not been a master strategist for nothing.

Yet thus far she had proved herself vastly elusive. Elusive and aloof. Fionna was not a woman to yield oh-so-sweetly. To be swayed from a course she did not want.

It only made him want her all the more. But he could not go to her, *make* her want him. She must come to him. And it must be of her own free will. Her decision.

Not his.

Else all would be lost. *She* would be lost.

He had judged long ago that she was a woman of remarkably strong will. She girded herself. Guarded herself with a will of iron, the will of a soldier.

The challenge was to make her want him as much as he wanted her.

To help her recognize that in yielding to the passion she held deep in check—to yield to her desires—was not defeat at all. Not surrender, but victory.

Victory for both of them.

And oh, but the lady was proving quite the challenge indeed!

But Aidan was ever up to a challenge; he relished the parry and retreat.

But the choice must be hers. The next approach must be hers. Difficult as it was, he must force himself to wait, to let her come to him. He had forced as much as he dared.

Saints be praised, it did not take long, else he'd have been at his wit's end. His butler Alfred admitted her early the very next evening.

He strode into the marbled foyer, his expression warm. After Alfred took her cloak, Aidan clasped both her hands in his, keeping them close, though he sensed she fought to snatch them away. Must she always fight him? And herself as well?

Yet he felt the way she trembled, the way she fought to control it. "Fionna! A pleasure to see you."

He could almost see the way her heart lurched. His smile was hardly guileless, and he knew she saw it by the tilt of her chin.

"Come." He led her into the drawing room. "Sit." He did not release her fingertips until she'd eased herself onto the very edge of the sofa, poised as if she sought to flee at any instant. He smothered a laugh and sat close to her, as close as he dared without inciting her ire.

"Tea?" he inquired politely.

"No, thank you."

"Wine?"

"Certainly not."

After Alfred exited the room, she wasted no time in announcing the reason for the visit.

"I believe we should come to an accord," she declared. "There are treaties in battle, are there not?"

"But of course. Those in opposition may agree to negotiate treaties . . . or negotiate surrender."

She did not like that. She maintained a pleasant enough countenance, but he could have sworn he could hear the gnashing of her teeth.

"Naturally, however, there must be willingness by both parties to enter into discussion first," he said.

"And you refuse?"

"I did not say that. But clearly you are not happy with the status quo, else you would not have come to propose a treaty." There was a most gratifying satisfaction in reminding her of that.

"I am not interested in surrender." It was a flat denouncement. "A treaty, yes."

"A treaty under what terms?"

"That we remain friends!"

He gave a low chuckle. "If no terms of agreement are reached, Fionna, then it is simply a return to the battlefield."

"So we're back to that again, are we? You won't agree that we can be friends?"

"Friends? No more than that?"

"I believe that is what I just said."

"Well then . . . No."

"Then it is no battle we engage in, my lord, it is an outright declaration of war."

She desired him. Every bit as much as he desired her. Aidan had already recognized long ago that his feelings were not lust. His emotions were too engaged. His heart was too engaged.

But Fionna fought it. She fought both her feelings and his, and every instinct in him clamored to prove what she refused to acknowledge. Yet he feared it would only drive her away.

She would not give in. By God, he would not give up.

"Not so," he told her smoothly. "You have set out your terms. I have yet to set out mine. I have but one, Fionna—that you leave open the possibility that there can be something . . . more between us."

Her eyes were snapping, her mouth pinched tight. "You are the most disagreeable man I have ever met."

"And yet here you are, having presented yourself at my doorstep. You continue to bewitch me, Fionna. To amaze me. A perfect match, are we not?"

"Do not make light of me, Aidan."

He regarded her with a smile that barely tipped his lips as he tugged her to her feet. "Do you know what I think? You push me away, Fionna. With words. With those beautiful, flashing eyes of amber and gold. But you want me." Leaning forward, he pressed a fingertip into the soft flesh of her lower lip. "Nay, do not argue. You fight it, Fionna. I feel it. I see it. And yet you are here," he said again.

Fionna decided then and there it had been a horrendous mistake to approach him. The man simply could not be reasoned with! The only question was whether to run—or whether to remain.

She would not, she decided staunchly, be a coward.

His eyes had grown dark and smoky. A silky undertone crept into his voice. "Never tempted by any man, Fionna. Never tempted by any man . . . before me. Never tempted by desire. Untouched by any man . . . before me." Lightly he molded the shape of her breast in his palm, his thumb traced the outline of her nipple. Bending low, his lips pressed a tiny kiss at the corner of her mouth, his breath warming her cheek as he whispered, "Are you tempted, sweet?"

Fionna slapped his hand away.

Drat the man! He was damnably—remarkably— observant. "You are perceptive, I'll give you that, Aidan McBride. But so am I."

"Tell me then," he said with that same lazy little smile. "What do you see in my eyes?"

"I see a man who is tremendously self-assured, incredibly arrogant, a man who believes very little escapes his notice."

"You evade the question, my dearest Fionna. What do you see in *my* eyes?"

Fionna was unexpectedly flustered. He had a tendency to do that; she wished she employed the same command over him! Fionna swore a silent, rather unsatisfying oath to herself. Damn that perceptive mind again!

"What do you see, love? Or perhaps, what do I see in *yours*?"

He pretended to consider, his mouth pursed, a dark brow arched high. "Ah, perhaps that you want me to kiss you."

Fionna sizzled. "Perhaps you should look again," she said tartly.

He snared her chin in one hand. The sudden movement caught her by surprise, but in the time between one instant and the next she screwed her eyes tightly shut. "Not much to see, eh, my lord?"

His low laugh of pleasure did strange things to her insides. Her pulse fluttered. Every nerve seemed to quiver. "You never cease to delight me, Fionna. Do you understand now why I am so enraptured?"

She opened her eyes and glowered at him. Why could she never control herself with him?

"If it's friends you wish, then friends it is."

Fionna eyed him dubiously. Somehow she wasn't so convinced.

"You doubt me?"

Her mouth pursed. "You know very well I do."

"Very well then. Must I say it aloud? I agree to your terms as laid out the other night. But I have one condition."

The rogue, she should have known! "What condition?" she asked tautly.

"That we celebrate, dear Fionna. I propose we attend tomorrow night's opera-ballet at the theatre . . . as friends, of course," he added smoothly.

Bedamned, she had played right into his hands! Perhaps she'd wanted to all along.

"Have you ever been to an opera-ballet?"

Fionna shook her head.

"An excellent time to experience your first then."

Her eyes narrowed dangerously.

"The first time is the best, or so it's said," he said lightly. "You'll love it, I promise."

Alfred fetched her cloak. Aidan disdained his inquiry that a footman escort the lady home.

During the time she'd been at his home, a dense layer of mist had draped a heavy curtain over all. Fionna strained to see the way. Even the trees that filled the square were invisible. She stumbled a little. Aidan caught her elbow and brought her upright. He took her hand snug in his, delivering her safely to the back of the shop. Fionna's heart was hammering, her pulse suddenly clamoring.

If he insisted on coming inside, would she deny him? *Could* she deny him?

Mercy, that she could even ask herself such a thing served as a warning!

"I have one request," Aidan said with no preamble at all.

"One condition, one request. What, shall I expect a list then, my lord?"

His low, seductive laugh made her go weak in the knees.

Strong, black-gloved hands closed around her shoulders; she could feel the strength in them. Half a step closed what little distance separated them. So close were they that Fionna was forced to turn her face up to his.

His gaze settled for a breath-stealing instant on her mouth. Despite the chill, the air was suddenly heated and intense. Inside, Fionna felt intoxicated.

The devil himself couldn't have resisted him. How could she? Yet somehow she should have.

The mist swirled, clearing a little. Fionna pretended not to see the desire banked in his expression. "What request?" she heard herself say.

"Wear that lovely green gown you wore to Alec's party."

Her lips parted in surprise; her breath fogged heavy in the mist. He swallowed it in the heat of his kiss.

Fionna was utterly adrift. Her lips clung helplessly. Whatever protest—whatever she might have said—was wiped away as if it had never been. For when he kissed her . . . ah, when he kissed her!

Her mind never listened.

And neither did her heart.

It is as I feared.

The quill scratched madly as he wrote in his diary. He likened it to the way his lovely Fionna wrote in her novels.

Yet he'd known something was amiss. She did not walk nightly with such regularity as she usually did.

And tonight . . . he'd seen her with another man. He'd seen the possessive way the man's hands came down on her shoulders.

But then the mist shifted, layer upon layer, and he could see nothing!

The man she'd been with . . . Had he kissed her? Had she kissed him?

A surge of such jealousy as he'd never known before pooled in every pore of his vitals, until he was consumed by a violent storm of blackness.

Little by little, it passed.

In his profession it was a necessity to keep one's feelings—one's emotions—hidden from others. When he thought of the times he'd longed to throw back his head and jeer at the stupid, stupid confessions he was forced to hear . . .

Yet still a fist coiled tight in his belly, coiled like

the serpent in the Garden of Eden. He'd cherished her from afar for much too long. They were spirits, spirits who belonged together and must remain forever one.

But the time was not yet right for him to reveal himself, he decided with a sly little smile, sitting back in his chair. He liked his game too much to end it now.

Yet she belonged to him. She was *his* prize. His and no other's.

But perhaps a reminder was in order.

Chapter Thirteen

It is the spawn of Satan we seek. I have fought him before. But always with Rowan. My eyes squeeze shut, for his mouth is warm upon mine. I am terrified, really.

Terrified of the demon, I wonder? Or terrified that in my weakness I shall yield to my desire? Yield to Rowan, who ever protects me, though I swear I need it not.

Demon of Dartmoor, F.J. Sparrow

They shared a bit of small talk on the way to the opera-ballet. Once inside the theatre, Fionna's eyes widened. Diamonds and jewels glittered everywhere, and once they were seated in the box, she laughingly declared herself half-blind.

She stole a glance at Aidan. Only then did she realize his smile was a bit pained.

Too late she realized her mistake. Until then she'd forgotten that his vision was compromised. "I'm so sorry. I didn't mean anything by it, truly."

He squeezed her hand. "I know, Fionna. I know."

Then the music began. A busty soprano appeared, along with a tenor with a voice from heaven. But it was the dancers who held her entranced, who captured her and transported her to another place and time.

To Fionna, the music was expressive, the dancing even more so. Amazed, she watched performer after performer dance *en pointe,* then proceed to defy gravity, seeming to float through the air, then flying across the stage as the music rose to a crashing crescendo.

When it was over, Aidan handed her into his carriage.

"I vow I am in love," she announced once they were in his carriage, snuggled deep within velvet cushions. Her eyes were still shining.

Aidan pulled a velvety blanket over her lap, for the night was bitterly cold, most probably the coldest of the season. "You enjoyed yourself then?"

"Yes, yes, yes!" Fionna was practically bursting, her mind still full of melody and song and dancers dipping and twirling. "Did you see the Russian dancer who caught his partner seemingly in midflight?"

"The one whose costume left little to the imagination when it came to his—"

"Yes, yes!" she cried, laughing and laughing. "You read my mind. The very one!"

Aidan's tone was wry. "You, Fionna Hawkes, are a very naughty woman."

Fionna sighed. "Truly, Aidan, it was lovely. Thank you for asking me."

"It was my pleasure," he murmured.

The horses clopped along.

Aidan watched her lean back. All at once he traced her smile with the pads of his fingers. "What does this sly, secretive smile disguise?"

She cast a glance at him through her lashes. "Well, I was merely wondering if I could insert a similarly dazzling ballet into my next novel."

"Prancing, dancing demons? Whirling, naked monsters perched on tiptoe?" He laughed as hard as she had.

"Oh, stop. Have you no vision of—"

"Frolicking demons and maidens fair? I think not!"

"Yes, I suppose you're right," she said with a dramatic sigh. "I shall have to discard the idea of frisky, frolicking demons performing pirouettes beneath the light of a full moon."

"Yes," he affirmed, "I suspect your readers would be quite aghast."

The carriage turned the corner. They were almost home now, But they passed hers, trotting on to stop before his.

She half-turned. "Aidan—"

"A nightcap," he said softly. "A glass of wine to end a very perfect evening."

It was that very smoothness that proceeded to speed her pulse to skittering.

In wild excitement.

"This is most improper." Her heart beat high in her throat. It was but a token denial. Fionna was honest enough to recognize it for what it was.

Aidan's low laugh sent shivers of delight over her skin, throughout her entire body. "Most improper? Fionna, it is most improper for a genteel young woman to write of rather erotic encounters between two lovers."

"I prefer the word earthy," she stated primly, "and I would remind you, Raven and Rowan are not lovers."

"But I suspect they will be. Soon, I predict."

"And what would you know about it?"

"What would I know about it? Well, love, I've read *Demon of Dartmoor*. At least, every installment published thus far. And like everyone else, I await the next."

"Perhaps they will be lovers," she said lightly, that same, secret little smile flirting at the corners of her mouth. "Perhaps they will not."

"What, you will not tell me? You can trust me not to reveal it. A secret between friends, remember."

"No, I won't tell." She frowned at him good-naturedly. "That is half the fun. To keep everyone guessing to the end."

"You won't even tell *me* what happens to the demon?"

"Well, his fate is sealed. Need I say more?"

Aidan chuckled again, a sound that made her heart turn over.

In the entrance hall, he removed her gloves, her cloak, her hat. All was done with great deliberation.

Fionna's eyes were huge. She nearly gulped. "Where is Alfred?"

"No doubt snoring in his bed." Lean fingertips caught at hers. "Come," he said softly.

Their footsteps echoed across the tiled, polished floor.

In the drawing room, on the table before the sofa, sat a tray with a decanter of ruby red wine and a pair of delicately stemmed glasses. At the far end sat a beveled glass vase of fragrant red roses. Fionna seated herself, while Aidan settled himself comfortably beside her.

Pouring for each of them, he handed her a glass, then leaned back with his own, turning the stem around and around. He did not drink. Instead, there was the devil's own gleam in his eye. "Confess, Fionna. Are you angry at me?"

Fionna tipped her head to the side. "Why, my lord, would I be angry?"

"I've kept you from your night's work."

Fionna pretended to consider. "This, my lord, is true. However, thanks to the help of a . . . friend, shall we say . . . I am learning that one should not always be a slave to one's work." There was an unmistakable gleam in her eyes. "One is permitted to make an allowance now and again."

He chuckled and held a glass high. "Touché."

There was the clinking sound of crystal. Fionna took a sip of wine. It was excellent, smooth and rich on the tongue, but her mind—to say nothing of her heart!—was running a-riot.

Had Aidan done this on purpose? A planned seduction? Should she be furious? Outraged?

Heaven above, she wasn't.

Aidan lowered his glass. His smile faded. In that keenly perceptive way he had, it was as if he saw into each and every corner of her mind and heart.

His gaze roved her features, one by one. Very softly, he said, "Do you have any idea how very lovely you are?"

Fionna lowered her gaze to the clear ruby liquid. She couldn't look at him as she spoke. "Aidan," she said, her tone very low, "did you bring me here to seduce me?"

He parried her question with one of his own. "Do you want to be seduced?"

Her tongue was suddenly thick. "All I know is this"—her voice wasn't entirely steady—"if I did want to be seduced, I . . . I would only want to be seduced by you."

His eyes darkened. "You shouldn't say things like that, sweet. Not to a man who is on the verge of discarding every ounce of good breeding instilled in him. Not to a man who holds back his desire as I have done. As I *do*. No, you shouldn't say such things to a man who is just a hair away from giving in to such need." A hint of a smile reappeared on his lips. "But what would you say if I told you that *I* wanted to be seduced?"

That brought her gaze back to his in a heartbeat. She swallowed. Then, God above, she couldn't tear her gaze away.

Was it possible . . . ? She wet her lips. "Do *you* want to be seduced?" The question was little more than air.

His regard was solemn, his expression intent. "Only," he said very quietly, "if I can be seduced by you."

Half-dazed, Fionna watched as he set his glass aside; hers was plucked away and joined his.

"I mean it, Fionna. Tonight . . . *this* night . . . can be as much as you like. As little as you like. I've made no secret of my desire. No secret of what I want from you."

Fionna wet her lips. "Yes, but—"

"Did you think I did not mean it?"

Mutely she stared at him, still a little stunned at what unfurled this instant. Somehow until now, it had never seemed real. It was like—like some imaginary scene plucked from one of her novels. Somehow she had never dared to think that it would come to pass. How could there be reason when coherent thought could barely take hold! To yield such control to another . . . to yield control of her heart . . .

It was unthinkable.

Oh, Lord, it was all she wanted.

"If that's what you think, Fionna, you've much to learn. I told you once that I want you. I told you that I would have you. My desire has not waned. My determination has not faltered. If anything, it only grows stronger, for I want you more than I've ever desired anything—anyone— in my life."

All the while he spoke, he toyed with her hand. Tracing the back of her hand, the outline of her thumb, swirling across the base of her wrist, testing its fragility, circling its span. Catching her knuckles, he lifted her hand between them.

She tingled everywhere. In places she'd never even known of.

He'd said there were many ways of making love. Oh, God, it was as if he was making love to her now. With only the feel of his hand against hers. If there could be such pleasure in this, what more awaited?

Fionna was trembling from head to toe.

"You hold the advantage, Fionna. *You.* The terms of surrender are yours to dictate, sweet. Do you understand what I am saying?"

Fingertips touched. Drifted. Threaded together and clung. Opened. Splaying wide, fingertip to fingertip.

Everything inside her went weak.

"Look at me, sweet."

Her eyes strayed helplessly away, only to return. Her mind was full of doubts and fears, her body full of need and chaos and desire. It was more than she could stand. Her throat clogged tight. Speech was impossible.

"This night will be whatever you make it," Aidan said gravely. "No more, no less. Leave now if you wish."

There was something tugging on her heart. *He* was tugging on her heart.

Running through her mind were all the reasons this shouldn't be happening. Everything inside her urged caution.

She shouldn't want him the way she did. But she did. Heaven help her, she longed for him with every fiber of her body, every beat of her heart. It was dangerous to let him close. Foolish—oh, so foolish!

But she was tired of fighting him. So tired of fighting herself.

A dawning realization crept over her.

She could be with him, for now. But it could

never be more, she reminded herself. It could never be forever. She must accept that.

For to do otherwise would be foolish.

But she wanted to be his woman. His lady. His love, if only for tonight.

Leaning over, he kissed her mouth. Long, lingering, and tempting. So unbearably sweet she wanted to cry out. At last he raised his head. Waiting. His eyes were a glimmer of light.

Her lips parted. She touched his mouth, a fingertip at the center of his lower lip. "I-I think I want to stay."

He shook his head. "It needs to be more than that, love." The softness of his tone belied his deliberation. "I have always considered myself a patient man, but I need more than that. My decisions are not rash, and I would ask the same of you. Once your choice is made, there's no going back. No recanting, no renouncement. I am a man, love, a man as any other, and there is only so much *this* man can take."

There was a ragged rush of breath. Her own, she realized hazily. He was right, she thought dizzily. This was more than a treaty. This was surrender in its entirety.

And when he captured her face between his palms, she could contain it no more. She claimed her life was her own—in truth it was not. She shouldn't want him like this, but she did.

Yet suddenly it was all so very crystal clear. She saw her emotions with such clarity, it was almost as if she'd been blind. Everything . . . from the very instant she'd met Aidan, had been building to this.

This moment.

This night.

Perhaps she'd known all along.

She'd simply failed to accept it.

There was so little she did for herself, she acknowledged almost painfully. She had denied herself so much. Given up so much.

But she could do this.

Yield what he sought.

Admit to what she wanted.

One night. She wanted to be Aidan's lady at least one night. *This* night.

It had been so magical . . .

And Fionna wanted more magic.

Capturing her chin between thumb and forefinger, he raised her face to his. "What do you want, Fionna? *What* do you want?"

A pulse beat almost violently at the base of her throat. His eyes were like sizzling blue fire. The burning hunger she glimpsed there made her heart thunder in her ears.

She gave a tiny shake of her head, her gaze riveted to his. "You know what I want." Desire bled through to her voice.

Now it was Aidan who shook his head. "Tell me, sweet."

Tears stood high and bright in her eyes. Her face was scalding hot.

Her arms crept around his neck. Slowly, ever so slowly, as if in fear. But there *was* no fear. She could never be afraid with Aidan.

"I want to stay. And—I want you to kiss me again."

So close to him like this, the heat in his body was almost palpable. She felt it all through her. Hers was no less intense. There was no denying the passion that flared high and bright in her veins and turned her utterly boneless. She longed for him to kiss her until the world faded to oblivion, longed for it as never before.

Yet still he made no move to touch her. He had gone absolutely still, his gaze roving hers, as if he wanted to hoard her in his eyes.

Everything inside her seemed to burst, welling forth with no hope of containing it.

She buried her face against his shoulder, her face hot. "I want you, Aidan," she said again. This time it was a helpless cry. "I want to be yours."

A low growl erupted from his throat. "Then *be* mine."

Fiercely, he caught her up against him, his arms like bands of iron around her back, almost crushing her. It was exactly what she wanted, what she needed. He kissed her with fiery greed, almost wild, his tongue twining around hers. He allowed no room for reticence; there was none. She returned in equal measure precisely what he demanded and reveled in it.

She was only half-aware of being divested

of her gown. Deftly he released the hooks, tugging it to her hips. She had a vague sense of her corset being tugged away. The backs of his fingers skimmed the valley of her breasts. Stockings were unpeeled. But her gown and petticoats were caught beneath her.

"Lift your hips," came an urgent whisper.

A tug, a twist, and she was naked.

She felt herself borne backward on the sofa. Swamped with arousal, Fionna laid her palms against his cheeks, loving the texture, the beauty of his mouth.

"Kiss me again," she pleaded.

Even before she had finished, his mouth came down on hers. The hot seal of their lips unbroken, he shrugged off his jacket, then fumbled with his shirt, almost ripping it off. A part of her wanted to laugh at his eagerness.

With a groan he dragged his mouth away, pushed himself to his feet, then tore off his boots and his trousers.

Fionna half raised herself on an elbow. One glimpse of him quelled the impulse to laugh.

The only light in the room came from the fire burning in the fireplace, the glow of a small lamp. For the space of a single heartbeat, he stood above her, his body in silhouette, his frame reflected in shades of amber and gold. Yet in that instant that time could scarcely measure, she saw so much. Firelight flickered over his frame, playing over the sculpted tightness of muscle and skin. All she saw was a sheer, primitive beauty and grace and power.

And then she caught sight of his face. His eyes, bright and blazing, locked fiercely with hers. Fionna had written of desire such as this, the greedy, almost desperate longing that Rowan harbored for Raven. But she had never seen it on a man's face.

Never until now. And now that she did, it stole the breath from her lungs.

His cheekbones flushed with passion. There was something almost feral about the possessive need in his expression, and she was nearly moved to tears. Her throat tightened oddly. Never had she dared dream that a man might look at her thus, simmering with want.

She wished she could brand the memory of his face and body in her mind and heart and savor it forever.

But he moved too swiftly.

One glimpse of a wide, hair-matted chest, the merest hint of jutting arousal was all she had before he planted his hands very deliberately alongside her body. Fionna smothered a sound of disappointment. Maidenly modesty be damned, she'd wanted to see for herself the part of him that—

The thought was cut abruptly short when he stretched out above her. Skin against skin. Breasts against chest. Belly to belly. There was not an inch of her body that wasn't engulfed by his. Had he not propped himself up on his elbows, his weight would have been intolerable. He kissed her again, and she sensed his struggle to keep his desire in check.

A little playfully—no, perhaps naughtily—she ran her toe up and down the knotted muscles of his calf.

Aidan lifted his head. Now he was the one who gave a hoarse laugh. "Do you toy with me, you little witch?"

The shift in her leg had also made her breathtakingly aware of the steely erection that lay thick and hard against her belly . . . as well as the twin fullness that lay below. And—though the powers above might strike her down here and now—she felt even more of that ample fullness when he laughed . . .

She pretended great consideration. "I may not be experienced," she found herself teasing, "but I should like to think that I am . . . well, perhaps just a bit learned."

He gave an odd little laugh. "An interesting supposition," was all he said.

And then he proceeded to prove to her that he was quite learned indeed.

His mouth on the arch of her throat, the wicked lash of his tongue. By the time he reached her breasts, her blood was surging. And her breasts . . . It was as if they swelled before her eyes— before his—her nipples tight and aching. He sucked hard; Fionna's breath sucked in as well. For all that she proclaimed herself learned, she was stunned to find that secret place between her thighs feeling just as swollen . . .

And already wet.

He played at her breasts until she thought she would go mad. The sight of his head there, the feel of his tongue tracing damp, lazily sensuous circles around one nipple while his hand indulged in the very same play on the other drove her wild.

"I shall have to remember how much you like this," he whispered huskily, raising his head to gaze at her.

"Mmmm." She caught his head and brought it back down so that his mouth hovered just above the very point of her nipple.

There was no question as to her desire.

A low chuckle preceded the moist heat of his breath upon that erect, straining peak. He touched the very tip, then tugged the whole of it into his mouth . . . the sound she emitted was half moan, half sigh.

And all pleasure.

Unbidden, her hands slid over his shoulders, skimming taut muscle sheathed in sleek, hard skin, testing its strength with the press of her fingertips. Her touch pleased him; a low sound vibrated in his throat.

Drawing back, Aidan eased back on one el-

bow and gazed the length of her. There was just
enough room on the sofa to accommodate his
height and the width of both their bodies.

Fionna's hand lodged on the center of his chest,
looking rather small and pale against the thick
forest of hair there. All at once she swallowed.
Memory resurrected. The night he had pleasured
her so thoroughly with nothing but his fingers
returned in full force. He had promised then that
the next time they were together like this, there
would be nothing between them. No barriers of
clothing, no barrier of words.

But most of all she remembered how he had
promised it would be a different part of him inside her.

She had thought herself eager. She had thought
herself fearless. Now she wished she hadn't been
so rash!

Her heart was pounding. She could scarcely
breathe. His body was wondrously formed; it
made her heart quaver and her throat constrict.

And she couldn't deny her curiosity, nor could
she dispel her shyness. Oh, yes, it took far more
will than skill to dredge up the courage to look at
him—really *look* at him.

Her mouth dry, her gaze ventured inevitably
down, past the curls on his chest and belly, clear
to where his rod thrust high and hard against the
white of one bare thigh.

Her recall was instantaneous—as if she'd ever
forgotten. As if she ever could! With stark, unre-

mitting clarity, she remembered precisely how it had felt to touch him there, her knuckles buried in the coarse nest of curls that thickened and surrounded the base of his erection.

Oh, yes, she remembered exactly how it felt. And seeing it now . . .

It wasn't quite what she'd remembered, she thought in awe. It was so much *more* than she remembered.

And Aidan had noticed as well. His eyes were dark, hued like the deepest of sapphires, cleaving directly into hers. The fist on his chest uncurled. A finger began to stray, tracing the line of hair down toward his navel. It was a slow, tentative movement, for this was all too new. Passion unchained. Not just her own nakedness, but his. *Especially* his. She was still half-afraid to touch him. Then all at once he caught her hand, as if he could stand it no longer, and guided it down the tight grid of his belly, between the ridge of his hips.

Straight to the heart of him.

She gasped in shock when he dragged her hand up and down, up and down. Her eyes flew wide. It was a caress as outrageously shocking as when he'd slid his fingers inside her; as bold and daring as the man himself.

"Aid—Aidan!" She stuttered his name, part-question, part jarringly shocked.

"No, it's all right. Touch me, sweet, just like that . . . Oh, yes, just like that."

His whisper compelled surrender. Watching him, the glint of his eyes, half-closed now, her reserve slipped away.

His mouth captured hers, almost ravenous. The bulk of his chest pressed her back into the cushions. With his knees, he stretched her thighs wide open.

She felt the velvet crown of his rod pushing through her nest of curls. Ah, he was there, breaching the outer folds of her channel, pushing steadily forward.

She clutched at Aidan's forearms. Her nails dug in. She did not resist, but she felt her inner muscles tighten against his invasion.

She flinched. She expected pain, but the pressure was so intense. *Too* intense, she realized. He was hurting her, not intentionally she knew. It was simply happening too fast. She tried to relax, yet her flesh did not yield; her inner muscles sought to close out the invader.

She inhaled sharply. "Aidan."

He didn't seem to hear.

"Aidan. Aidan, stop!"

His eyes opened, smoky and dazed.

She struggled to smile. "Remember what you said earlier? That there is only so much a man can take?"

She had the sensation he saw her through a haze, if indeed he saw her at all.

"Aye," he said at last.

Her smile was but a wisp. "Well, there is only so much that this *woman* can take."

She knew the exact instant he understood. His arms tightened to the point where she feared he might crush her. Then he went utterly still.

"Christ," he said grittily. "Christ!"

He withdrew himself very slowly.

Her smile faltered. Strangely enough, she felt . . . empty somehow. His expression was unsmiling, almost grim. Seeing it, her throat constricted. Her mouth trembled.

"Fionna. Oh, God, Fionna, don't look like that! I'm sorry. It's just that I want you so damned much. Too damned much . . ."

He kissed her nose, her eyelids, her tremulous lips, so achingly tender she nearly cried out. Drawing back, he braced himself above her.

Fionna was still almost unbearably conscious of the point of his erection hard and thick at the apex of her thighs.

"Do you trust me, sweet?"

Her eyes clung to his, trapped by something she couldn't name. Endlessly she searched his features. He remained unsmiling, but he wasn't so very grim now. And she sensed a curious tenderness that allowed her the courage to nod.

"Most excellent," he murmured, brushing one last kiss against her lips.

Fionna had thought he could shock her no more.

But what he did next . . .

Pleasantly rough fingertips skimmed the sensitive skin behind her knees, then lifted them high. With the breadth of his shoulders, he braced her wide apart. Wide apart . . . and open.

She gasped, for now she was vulnerable in a way she'd never dreamed might happen.

"You said you trusted me," he reminded her, one side of his mouth curling up. "Do you trust me, Fionna?"

Fionna let out a ragged breath. Acknowledgment came in the merest rise and fall of her chin.

Yet her body jerked when he brushed his lips across the hollow of her belly.

Her heart jolted when his mouth traced a shattering path to the inside of one slender thigh.

Her every thought gave way when the journey continued. His hands slid beneath her to cradle her buttocks. With the pads of his thumbs, he parted her soft down, exposing hot, furrowed flesh. Her eyes widened, for she had gleaned his intent. Her heart was near to bursting.

With the wanton blade of his tongue he touched the center of her core, circling that aching bud of desire and tugging it into his mouth, much the same way as he had sucked her nipples. And in so doing . . . he proved that he was far more learned than one might ever have imagined.

And immensely more talented as well.

Time stood still as he tasted her again and

again, his mouth divinely tormenting. Tasted her until she was slick from his tongue, slick with desire.

Primed and wet and wanting, he heaved himself up over her again. Their bellies rubbed; his expression was scalding. Lean fingers slid through her hair, turning her face up to his. His mouth opened over hers.

Her gasp echoed in the back of his mouth. His penetration was almost agonizingly slow this time. Little by little, inch by inch, he advanced, the head of his rod encased in velvety folds. She felt rather than saw a lightning thrust of his hips; her breath suspended high in her throat, she waited for that instant of pain.

But he'd readied her well—so sleek and slick and wet that when he split the barrier of her maidenhead and pushed home, she felt but the slightest sting.

By the time she released the air in her lungs, it was gone.

But Aidan was not. He was inside her—such a strange realization. The pressure was immense. Intense. She didn't know that Aidan had plunged as far as he dared, as much as she could take.

He released her lips and turned his head ever so slightly, nuzzling the hollow beside her ear. "All right now?" he murmured.

Fionna nodded. It spun through her mind that he'd certainly ravaged her powers of speech tonight. It also spun through her mind that she couldn't take a breath without feeling him—all of him.

"Are you sure?"

His mouth grazed hers. The huskiness of his tone nearly made her come undone. "I am," she whispered, and then again, "I am!"

Her arms twined around his neck. Her cry seemed to release a frenzy inside him. He expelled a ragged breath. Hearing it, seeing the way his flesh stretched taut across his cheekbones, it came to her how great was the control he'd exerted over himself.

"Fionna."

The hot, melting way he said her name made her want to cry.

"Watch," he whispered hoarsely. "Watch me make love to you."

No power in the heavens could have made her look away as he withdrew—all the way so that she saw the passionate sheen of her body's juices glazing his rod.

Her eyes widened. Coarse dark hair mingled with soft, chestnut curls, a sight that was incredibly erotic. Even more erotic was when he plunged again, gliding deeper this time, harder. She couldn't tear her gaze away. She was both amazed and stunned at the way male joined female, feeling the walls of her passage yield—soft tender flesh clinging tight and wanton to hard male steel. Everything inside her went wild. Every part of her was melting, every fiber of her being.

With a helpless little moan she caught the sides of his head. She wanted to tell him how wonderful he made her feel. But the power of words had once again deserted her. The pleasure was climbing, spiraling high and fast, taking her by storm. Unable to hold back, her hands slipped to his shoulders. She clutched at him; sensation gathered there, in the very center of her body, the place he possessed so fully. Had she surrendered? Or had he? she wondered vaguely.

Eyes closed, she flung her head back. Release was close. She could feel it coming, shivering throughout her body. His head dropped low. He kissed the arch of her throat. "Fionna," he said, his tone almost raw. "Fionna!"

Her nails bit into his shoulders. The walls of her channel contracted around him, again and again and again, sending spasms of release hurtling through them both.

Chapter Fourteen

The demon was trapped. Or perhaps we were. I laid my finger on the knob of the door. An unearthly chill seized me, the whole of my body. And somehow I knew what we were meant to find...

Demon of Dartmoor, F.J. Sparrow

Aidan wasn't particularly proud of himself. The reasoning part of him called him the biggest fool in all London. He'd taken a lady—one who was a virgin no less—on the sofa in his drawing room.

Christ, he might just as well have hiked her skirts to her waist and taken her up against the wall!

Another voice reminded him that at least the cushions had been soft as down.

At least it hadn't been the floor.

That had come later.

And at least it was carpeted, a most exquisite carpet—with a far more exquisite partner beneath him.

Ah, yes, but he'd proved himself quite the romantic lover, he reflected wryly. He'd demonstrated the utmost charm and finesse in giving the lady her first taste of a man.

Well, at least his intentions had been, well . . . of a most romantic flavor. The stage had been set—wine, roses, the fire burning low.

Did you bring me here to seduce me?

He had—yet he had not.

Liar, mocked a voice in his head.

Yes, there was the fact that he'd wanted it almost since the first time they'd met. But tonight—well, it wasn't the cool, calculated decision it seemed. He had *hoped* she'd let him make love to her.

The last thing in the world he expected was that she'd let him.

After all, this was Fionna. Tart-tongued, sharp as a tack, never one to do anything she did not want, ever one to go her own way . . .

He'd just never expected she would melt against him as if he were all she ever wanted.

And that was the catalyst. It wasn't just the overwhelming need to make her his. It was her willingness, the trust she placed in him.

And once he had her in his arms—*naked* in his arms—well, he'd lost control. There was no other way to put it. He knew he'd never make it to his room. Hell, he wouldn't have made it up the stairs.

She did that to him. No matter that he'd wished otherwise . . . a woman's first time with a man should be slow, sweet, and tender, shouldn't it?

And yet he'd known it would be like this between them—hungry and stirring and passionate, hot and sizzling. The minute he felt her beneath him, it was like flint to tinder.

He hadn't meant to be so impatient, so desperate, so wild and rushed. He meant to be slow and careful and easy, but for one blinding moment—that unforgettable instant when his shaft prepared to plunge home—a haze of blood-red desire flooded over him, sweeping him along with it.

His jaw tensed. Thank heaven she'd had the presence of mind to curtail him. Why, he would have surely cut out his heart if he had hurt her, ruined this first time with her.

No, it probably wasn't particularly gentlemanly to lie sprawled out with a lady in his drawing room on the rug before the fire. Thank heaven he'd given Alfred orders that the servants not be allowed to start their work until well after dawn. At the very least, he supposed, perhaps he should take her to his room after all.

He chuckled softly to himself. That hadn't

worked the first time. He'd tried it, and look where they had landed!

And after the second time, they were both too spent to move.

Fionna lay curled against his side, her head pillowed on his shoulder. He'd tugged a light coverlet over her. He was feeling just a tad proud of himself, for he knew he'd pleased and pleasured her well. But he had best stop his boastfulness, lest it turn around and bite him right back.

Did he regret it? The answer thundered in his breast, pounding through his veins.

Lord, no.

The better question was whether or not *she* did.

Aidan eased back so he could see her face. He'd thought she was dozing; she was not. Her eyes were half-closed, the shadow of her lashes crescents on her cheeks.

Yet he sensed something that sent a flicker of disquiet through him. "Are you all right?" he asked softly.

"I'm fine," she murmured.

"Are you sorry?" Aidan had to know. And he would be aware if she lied. He captured her chin, bringing her gaze to his. His hold tightened so she couldn't turn away.

Her cheeks turned pink, but she made no effort to avoid his regard. "No," she said, her lips tremulous. "I'm not sorry it happened."

"Tell me again," he said softly.

"I'm not sorry it happened, Aidan, I swear!"

Her face was scarlet. "I . . . it's what I wanted."

Still he scoured her face, not releasing her until he was satisfied.

Her head returned to its berth against his shoulder. But the contentment that had marked the quiet aftermath was suddenly marred by something he could neither see nor feel—yet hovered between them like an intangible wall of stone.

His arms tightened possessively. Protectively. "I can hear you breathe," he said huskily. "I have felt the beat of your heart matched against my own. We have become one in the closest, most intimate way a man and woman can be together. There are times I know you as well as my own heart. Yet there are times it's as if I know you not at all. And so I find myself forever pondering your thoughts. You reveal so little, Fionna. And so I wonder if there are mysteries, secrets that I cannot see—things that you refuse to let me see."

She eased away so that she lay on her belly, her chin propped atop the backs of her hands. So very close, yet separate. He should have expected it, he realized. But he curbed his impatience.

Silence prevailed. There was a curious air about her. She wanted to retreat back into herself; yet with every instinct he possessed, it was almost as if he could see her fighting within herself.

Just when he thought she would refuse to answer, she did.

"I rather suspect everyone has mysteries," she

said after a long silence. There was nothing in her tone that gave any hint to the scope of either her thoughts or feelings. "Some little secret we wish to keep to ourselves, that we prefer no one else know. Is that so wrong? It's human nature, I think. No one should be able to see everything in someone else. No one should allow everything to be seen. It would leave one too vulnerable, I think."

She was evading him. Throwing up her defenses, sealing herself in.

Shutting him out.

"I think I would very much dislike regarding everyone as an enemy," he offered casually.

"I'm surprised you don't, considering you were a soldier."

"Perhaps that's why I don't, love."

Her head turned almost sharply. "Is that what you think I do, Aidan?"

Easing to his side, he propped his head on his hand so he could gaze at her. "Sometimes I think you do, sweet. And no, it's not wrong to keep some things wholly to oneself, though I rather think it would be nice to share one's thoughts with another—the right person, of course. One's hopes and fears and just silly little things. I would regard it as a gift, I think. A privilege. To know—at some moment or other—exactly what that other person is thinking . . . I think it should engender feelings of care and closeness and devotion. My sister shares that with her husband. My parents had it. I doubt it's ever easy for anyone. But I should like someday to have that closeness with someone." *With you*, he almost said. "Wouldn't you?"

Her gaze skidded away for the merest heartbeat. He saw the way she swallowed, the glaze of tears that rose to her beautiful amber eyes, swiftly blinked away before she thought he could see them.

But he did. He did, and though it was like a blade in his heart, his own frustration nearly consumed his patience. He sensed the contradiction inside her as if it were his own. Something was tearing her apart. What, for God's sake. *What?* He couldn't force her to tell him. God, certainly not now, not in this moment of softness. She'd come to him tonight and, by God, he wouldn't lose her.

His fingers combed through her hair. "Fionna?" he said huskily.

She lowered her lashes so that he could no longer make out her expression. She gave a tiny shake of her head. Her whisper emerged haltingly. "It's not a question of what I want. It's not a question of what I don't want."

Long, languid fingers smoothed the valley of her spine, clear to the rise of her hips, then back again. "And if I said you can have what you want?"

"I can't," she said painfully. "And do not ask me why, Aidan. Please do not."

He wouldn't let her go so easily. Snaring her naked waist, he turned her back against him once more. She simply buried her head against his chest.

"We all have demons, you know. And no," he said dryly, "I do not mean the *Demon of Dartmoor.*"

At least that succeeded in luring a smile from her. Their eyes connected.

Her smile faded, all too swiftly. "Even you?" she said tentatively. "Do you have demons?"

"Yes," he said, and his attempt at a laugh was an abysmal failure. "Lord, yes."

All at once the tables had been turned. He was aware of Fionna scanning his features, probing in a way he wasn't used to. Instinctively he sought to shield himself.

But Fionna was no fool. "Something happened," she said slowly. "When you were in India? In the Regiment?"

Time ticked away. Aidan had never doubted her powers of perception. He hadn't realized they were quite so keen, however. Alec knew the truth of all that happened there—no one else. Yet beneath Fionna's direct query, he knew he wouldn't lie to her. The possibility never even entered the realm of his mind.

"Yes," he admitted finally. "Something happened."

She ran her fingers lightly up and down his arm, a caress? he wondered? Or a gesture of comfort.

"Will you tell me, Aidan?" She turned her liquid gaze up to his.

Christ, who could resist her when she gazed at him so? Aidan released a pent-up breath. "I was twenty when I joined the Highland Regiment," he said softly.

Her eyes widened. "So young."

"Not so young," he corrected. "I warrant most of the Commonwealth's soldiers are just boys. And a career in the Regiment was what I'd always wanted. I would have joined when I was younger but for my father's advice. He thought I should complete my education." He offered a half smile. "Wisdom comes to those who wait, you know."

"He sounds like he was a very wise man."

Aidan nodded. "He was. So out of respect for him, I waited. And he was right, for as it turned out, I was the Empire's prodigy. Its greatest tactician, some said, during the last decade. I was ambitious and made the most of it. My strengths were recognized, and so I rose through the ranks quickly."

A faint, teasing light appeared in her eyes. "Was your reputation well deserved?"

"It was. That's the hell of it. I was good, and I knew it." His eyes darkened. "But that proved my downfall as well."

"Go on," she murmured.

"There remains much unrest in India, among so many factions. I expect it will soon explode again, for the natives hate the British occupation. I can't say I blame them, but it's not my place to judge. I was sent there to perform my duties—to the Punjab—and so I did.

"There were small skirmishes almost daily. Then they began to increase, more often and more deadly. The number of British casualties rose dramatically. There was a man named Rajul, you see, a shrewd, rebel leader. He was like a snake, striking suddenly, when and where it would do the most damage, slipping away like— like a ghost before we could catch either him or any of his followers."

He knew Fionna's gaze hadn't left his face. Deliberately he chose not to look at her.

"It became a game of cat and mouse, the two of us pitted against each other, each determined to outwit the other. I was determined to catch him, to cut off the head of the snake. It was more than foe against foe. It was"—he floundered for the right word—"like an obsession."

Aidan's voice took on a note of hardness. "My men and I had a small base in the mountains, roughly a hundred men. We were awaiting the arrival of more soldiers. But one of our scouts was told by a native that Rajul was two villages to the north, that he would be spending the next few nights in the tent of the tribal leader."

He released a breath. "I was—ecstatic. I wanted Rajul badly. So very badly. I ignored the voice in my gut that warned it sounded too easy. The voice

that warned we should wait for the arrival of the
rest of the company—they were less than half a
day's march away—and then determine that the
information wasn't just a ruse. But I was afraid Rajul would escape again, as he had so many times
before. And knowing he was so close . . . I decided
to move ahead immediately, that very night. I left
half the men behind to defend our camp. The rest
I took with me to the village where Rajul was re-
ported to be hiding. My intent was to leave most
of the men on the perimeter of the village while
a small group could sneak in during the dead of
night and seize Rajul while he was asleep, when
everyone was asleep, and capture him when he
least expected it. Before he could slip away again
the way he had so many times before. But he was
one step ahead of me, Fionna."

She frowned. "Rajul wasn't there?"

Bitterness swelled in his chest. "Oh, he was
there. Waiting for us, his men flat on their bellies behind every rock, scattered atop the ridge,
all around us. The village was deserted. We were
surrounded. Outnumbered by at least three to
one. It was a bloodbath."

She made a faint sound. "How many—"

"Forty-seven. Forty-seven of the Regiment's
best men were slaughtered because of me."

"Oh, no," she whispered in horror.

"Oh, *yes*." His self-disgust rang out. "I scarcely
even considered the possibility it was a trap—an
ambush—before I discarded it. I told myself that

good as he was, I was better. That's what comes of believing oneself invincible."

"No!" she cried softly. "It wasn't your fault. You couldn't have known—"

"I *should* have known. It was my life's work. Planning. Strategizing. *Anticipating.*"

"Oh, God." Her voice caught as she looked up at him. "Is that when this happened?" She ran the pad of her thumb beneath his left eye.

He nodded. His gaze avoided hers; he feared the condemnation he might find there.

"You still feel guilty, don't you, Aidan?" Her voice came very softly.

His mouth twisted. "How else should I feel?"

"You did your duty, Aidan. Defended—"

"I did not defend those men. I failed them. All but three." It was a brittle denunciation. He sat up, a sinewed arm stretched out, staring broodingly into the fire. One fist clenched unknowingly.

He felt the muscles in his throat go tight. "My men depended on me to lead them," he said, his voice gritty with emotion. "They looked to me to protect them. Of course I'd sent soldiers into battle before, and yes, some died. But this was different. I wasn't concise and deliberate, as I should have been, as I had *always* been. I was reckless and arrogant and I was *greedy*. It wasn't *duty* that compelled my decision. A part of me wanted what no one else had been able to achieve. So yes, I failed them."

"What about Rajul? Was he killed?" Fionna sat

up as well, tugging the coverlet around her nakedness.

Aidan's lip curled in a sneer. "Escaped. Yet
again. And I knew he was somewhere out there
laughing at me because he'd made a fool of me.
But do you know the Crown's reaction to my attempt to capture Rajul? Another medal. Another
promotion for Colonel Aidan McBride. They
hailed it a glorious victory since more than half
the rebel forces were killed. But it wasn't pride
I felt. I was ashamed. Ashamed for having been
careless when I should have been cautious. It
was a mistake, Fionna. Going after Rajul was a
huge mistake. I rarely made mistakes, and this
was one I simply couldn't live with. And so I resigned my commission. Gave up my career. But I
didn't leave India. At least . . . not right away."

Fionna sucked in a breath. "You went after him,
didn't you? You went after Rajul."

Aidan nodded, the lines of his face stone-hard.

"For six months I tracked him. Dogged him as
he had dogged me. And when I found him, I put
a bullet in his head. He was laughing. *Laughing.*
Because he knew he'd gotten the best of me." At
last he looked at her. "Does that disgust you?
Make you sick inside? Knowing you've just lain
with a murderer?"

Her lips parted. He shook his head, stopping
the protest he knew was coming.

"Yes, Fionna, it was murder. It wasn't justice
I wanted. It was revenge. And—I thought it

would be enough, knowing Rajul was dead. That I killed him. But it wasn't. I still had the blood of all those men on my hands. I still *do.* I tried running from it. Hiding. It took another six months before I could face my family. To this day, Alec—and now you—are the only ones who know my shame. My guilt."

He sucked in a breath and glanced away. "I'll never forget that night in the Punjab. I'll live with it forever. But I learned something. I thought I was infallible. But I learned that no one ever is. I learned that life's lessons are never-ending. I was angry, so very angry! But I was afraid, too. Afraid of dying like so many of my men. And that makes me a coward as well, doesn't it?"

"No. No! You're no coward, Aidan McBride. What happened was—" Her shoulders lifted helplessly. "I don't know what to call it. Simply part of war, I think."

Very slowly she knelt before him. The coverlet pooled around her knees. Gazing directly into his eyes, she framed his face with her hands.

"No," she whispered again. "No coward here. All I see is a man brave enough to look inside and see himself so clearly." There was the merest pause. "A man who has punished himself far too long already, a man who is *still* punishing himself." She shook her head. Very gently she smoothed the lines scored beside his mouth. "It's time to stop, Aidan. It's time to let yourself heal."

He moved suddenly, snaring her close and tight. "Then help me, sweet." The words were a hot, muttered plea against her lips. "Help me heal. Help me *now*."

Falling back, he pulled her beside him, anchoring her between his thighs. His kiss was fiercely devouring, but her lips opened beneath his, as ardent as his.

Her hair streamed over her back and shoulders. Aidan dragged it aside and pressed his mouth on her nape. A purely masculine pride shot through him as she shivered with delight.

She was beautiful. So beautiful he was consumed by desire as fiercely as before, overcome with the urge to plunge inside her again and again. The second time they'd made love, he was afraid she would be tender and sore—thrice was a dire certainty. But he couldn't stop himself, the passion throbbing in every part of him. His feelings for her were too intense, too wild. His hand on her nape, he captured her mouth once more. An arm about her back, he guided his rod between soft, silken thighs, rubbing her cleft, letting her feel the rigidness of his erection. Her eyes widened; it was as if he could see her heart stop.

Her legs went wide. Aidan groaned and clamped her against him. He was shaking with need. God help him, he couldn't stop. He couldn't stave off his desire. Not now. Not yet. And when he plunged deep, her silken heat and warmth surrounded him, sending him to a place where nothing existed but the two of them.

A short time later they finally rose, searching about for their clothing. Aidan laughed a little when they found it halfway across the room. Fionna picked up her slippers, dangling them from her fingertips while Aidan sought to find her drawers for her.

The night was bitterly cold. They hurriedly walked the short distance from his home to hers. A freezing wind eddied around them. Snow was falling. With the wind blasting, it was like needles of ice against their faces.

"Good heavens," Aidan muttered. "This must surely be the coldest night of the year."

Fionna didn't answer. She couldn't; her teeth were chattering too much.

At the rear of the shop, she turned to him.

"Let me see you inside, love."

"No," she said, chuckling a little. "You know what will happen if you do."

"Yes, that's precisely what I was hoping." He allowed a slow, wicked grin to crease his lips.

Fionna gave him a little push. "I'll be fine. Hurry home before someone sees you."

"No one will see me. It'll be dark for more than an hour yet."

Fionna wrinkled her nose. "Off with you, you scoundrel!"

Aidan dragged her into his arms for a long,

rapturous kiss, then drew back. "I'll see you to-morrow," he started to say, then stopped. "No, wait. Today. I'll see you later today. Dinner?"

She nodded over her shoulder, key in hand, anxious to be inside.

Aidan waited until the door was closed, then walked away. Crossing the street, he paused.

One last look, he thought, glancing up.

Upstairs in her apartments, the glow of a lamp flared brighter. Through the frosted pane, he glimpsed the shadowy outline of her form as she started past.

He frowned.

All at once she halted, then spun slowly toward the window . . .

In that indefinable instant when Fionna turned the key in the lock upstairs, something inside her clanged a warning. An eerie prickling skittered over every inch of her body. Before she had shivered from delight.

Now it was in dread.

The door was unlocked.

She sifted back through the last hours. Had she locked it when she and Aidan had left last night? She couldn't remember. But she was a creature of habit, a woman of routine.

This was ridiculous. She quelled the rise of panic. So what if she'd forgotten to lock it? Aidan had been with her. His presence was distraction in the extreme!

Trying to act as normal as possible, she stepped inside her parlor. She glanced around. Nothing was amiss. Faith, what an idiot she was!

But she'd left the lovely, lace curtains ajar. How stupid of her, and on such a frigid night! She started to close them.

It was then she saw the words.

Never forget you belong to me, my love.

It drummed slowly through her mind, echoing inside.

In some faraway corner of her brain, she recalled the window had been wet and steamy when she left; she'd noticed it just before Aidan arrived.

Never forget you belong to me, my love.

Now the words were frozen, icy crystals scrawled across the pane.

In blood.

Never forget you belong to me, my love.

She touched it. Cold penetrated clear to her soul. As if there were ice in her blood.

A sickening fear twisted through her. A quickening fear.

A vague sense of unreality descended. Hardly aware of what she did, she rushed for a cloth from the kitchen, darting back into the parlor. She scrubbed and scrubbed, rasping, ragged sounds tearing from her throat. It was no use. Finally, she flung the cloth aside. The thunder of her heart jolted her entire body.

In a frenzy she scratched and clawed, digging

into the words, the ice. Her nails ripped. Her fingertips hurt. And dry sobs ripped from her lungs as she grabbed the cloth and wiped and rubbed until there was no trace of the words.

Her strength sapped. She sank helplessly to the floor. Curling into a little ball, she wept.

She was wholly unaware of the door crashing from its hinges downstairs. She didn't hear Aidan's feet pounding up the stairs.

"Fionna! What the devil? What's wrong?" Sinking down, he hauled her into his arms. "Was someone here?"

She cringed, pointing toward the curtains. "The window," she managed. "Look at it."

"Sweetheart, I am looking at it. I don't see anything. What am I supposed to be looking at?"

"It was there, I tell you!" she screamed. "It was there! Someone was here! Someone wrote on the window!"

"Fionna, I don't understand."

Fionna stared over at the window. There was no blood. There was nothing.

A horrified inevitability clutched at her insides. She clutched at Aidan's jacket.

Oh, God, what had she done?

What a fool she'd been. She had erased it all.

She began to scream uncontrollably.

Her thoughts were a wild jumble in her brain. Disjointed. Frantic. No one had seen. No one but her. Only she had seen the dead flowers. Seen the writing. No one had *ever* seen anything, heard footsteps in the dark behind her, no one but her.

She thought of her mother. Had her mother's infirmity of the mind passed on to her? Had she imagined everything? The feeling of being followed. The footsteps. The book of spells being misplaced in the bookshop, the dead flowers, the writing on the window. She wrote of demons and murder. Perhaps she had culled it—all of it—from the darkest corners of her mind.

Somewhere in the distance, someone still screamed. Shrill and stark.

"Fionna, stop! Have you gone mad?"

No wonder Aidan called her mad. Perhaps she was.

"Don't!" she cried. "Don't call me that!" She slapped him, hard. "Don't you ever call me that!"

Hard hands closed over her shoulders. He shook her. "Fionna!" he shouted.

Her head slid back. Her scream caught halfway up her throat. She stared at him numbly. The bruised hurt in her eyes made a band tighten around his chest. Her state alarmed him.

Stung to the core, Aidan closed his arms around her and rocked her against him. She was shaking so violently she felt she would surely break apart.

"Calm yourself," he murmured, over and over. "It's all right."

At length he drew back, sponging the tears from her cheeks with the pads of his thumbs. "Perhaps a physician should be summoned," he said quietly.

She clutched at his shirt. "No. Aidan, *no.* I don't need one. I swear I don't need one."

His eyes searched hers. "Then tell me what this is," he said very quietly. He pulled her up onto the sofa.

Fionna stared at her hand, engulfed within his, so warm and strong, perched on his thigh.

"The door was open. I thought I'd locked it, Aidan. Perhaps I did. Perhaps I didn't."

She could feel his gaze, settled on her face. She wasn't aware he was thinking how easy it would have been for someone to gain entry. The right tool and the tumbler and spring would twist as easily as oil. This he kept to himself, though.

"I went to pull the curtains shut. I thought I'd closed those as well—no, I *know* I closed them. But there was writing on the window. Blood on the window. It was written in blood. Frozen."

"Good heavens," he said curtly, "it sounds like something out of one of your novels."

Hearing him say it made her cringe.

"What did it say, Fionna?"

"'Never forget you belong to me, my love.'" Her tone was very low. She could barely stand to repeat it.

Aidan said nothing.

There was a protracted silence. His gaze had

narrowed on her. His expression gave away nothing.

Fionna's lips quivered. Her throat grew hot. She battled the threat of tears. Inwardly, she berated herself. Why was she so weak? Raven was never weak. F.J. Sparrow's characters were exposed to all manner of events that were frightening and intense and evil. And yes, they were afraid, but in the end they always triumphed, they always won.

Only this was real, and this was *her* . . . and wasn't about imaginary characters and imaginary demons. It was not a game. Yes, she wrote of all things sinister, of danger lurking about every corner. She reveled in creating it.

But she did not want to *live* it.

"It was there, Aidan. I swear it was—"

Two fingers against her lips stemmed the protest. "You don't have to convince me, Fionna."

She blinked. "You believe me?"

He slanted her a faint smile. "Is there any reason I shouldn't?"

A rush of guilt swept over her as she thought of Mama.

"The night we met you thought someone was following you, Fionna. Another time as well. What else has happened? Anything else out of the ordinary?"

A shiver shot through her. "I think so," she admitted. "But I couldn't be sure until tonight." She told him of other times she'd felt the eerie sensation of being followed. Watched. "Remember the day at the shop? The book of spells was not where it should have been."

"That could be a bit questionable, love."

Her eyes flashed. "Do not call my memory into question, Aidan!"

He debated no more. "Anything else?"

Fionna bit her lip.

"What, sweet?"

"One night when I returned home from my walk, there were dead flowers on the doorstep."

The way Aidan's expression tightened made her uneasy. All at once she felt ill.

She couldn't help the thought that crept into her mind.

Only one other person besides her mother knew that she was F.J. Sparrow.

Aidan.

But had he known far longer than she realized? Was this just a sick game?

Her mind balked. But that couldn't be. He'd been with her the entire evening. She discounted it immediately, despising herself for daring to even think such a thing.

"What?" His laugh was black. "You're considering the possibility it was me?"

Fionna bit her lip. "Only for a moment," she said, her voice very small.

"Well, I suppose I deserve that." He got to his feet and paced the room. Stopping before the fireplace, he rubbed the back of his neck, then gazed at her. His features remained tight.

Fionna wet her lips. "What is it?"

"It's nothing," he said curtly.

"It is. Tell me, Aidan."

"Very well, then. I wish to hell you had told me this when it happened."

His censure hurt. Until now she'd kept at bay her own fears, wrestling with them. But tonight had proved that these were certainly not supernatural forces at work but altogether natural. It wasn't some *thing*, but some*one* who was responsible.

"I didn't know for certain. There was every chance—but for the flowers—that it was my imagination . . . But the writing tonight . . . there was someone here, Aidan." She shuddered. "And whoever it is . . . it was not an endearment. He wants me to know he was here. It was a message," she said slowly. "Or a warning, do you think?"

"What I think"—his tone was decidedly grim—"is that you have an admirer."

Fionna shuddered.

Aidan's arms immediately closed around her. "Here, stop that," he said gruffly.

Fionna's arms slid around his waist. She rubbed her cheek against his chest, loving his strength, the utter safety of his arms locked tight about her back.

His breath stirred the soft cloud of her hair. "Perhaps the police should be called in."

She stiffened. "No."

He sighed. "Fionna, be reasonable."

She started to pull away. He didn't allow it. Craning her neck, she stared up at him mutinously, her hands now fisted on his chest.

"I won't even consider it. Not yet, Aidan. There would be too many questions, questions I refuse to answer. What if I were forced to disclose that I am F.J. Sparrow? I can't do it. I won't. It would be devastating to my career."

Aidan's mouth tightened.

She gave a little thump on his chest. "No!" she reiterated. "I can't risk it!"

"All right. But if anything else happens, I shall have no choice—"

"It's not your choice at all, Aidan. It's my life. My decision. Mine."

His expression was one of ill-concealed annoyance. He wanted to argue. Fionna was prepared to as well, for she would not be dictated to by anyone.

"As you wish then," he said finally. "Now come." He led her to the sofa and pulled her down.

Nestled tight against his heart, Fionna shivered once more.

Such brave words. Such bravado.

Until tonight, she hadn't thought herself in jeopardy. But now everything had changed. She hated feeling as if she were some kind of prey!

As if a ghost had followed her, a ghost that was now literally a shadow on the fringe of her life.

Raven and Rowan fought creatures of the dark every day. But they always emerged victorious, she thought, the frail over the overbearing, the victory of good over evil.

The thought of that horrid message made her blood curdle. And all at once nothing could warm her, not even Aidan.

For now she feared her life would never be the same.

That the darkness was no longer her haven . . . but her hell.

Chapter Fifteen

There were tracks, traces of frozen blood that
turned my stomach. I felt my veins turn to ice,
for it is here he dwells, this faceless demon. Deep
in the bowels of the earth.

Where he thinks we cannot find him.

Demon of Dartmoor, F.J. Sparrow

There was no question of leaving Fionna alone
that day. Aidan stayed until Glynis clambered up
the stairs later that morning.

Glynis rapped on the door. "Miss Hawkes!"
she called anxiously. "Miss Hawkes! Oh, praise
all the saints, there ye are, safe and sound. Why,
I was so frightened when I saw the door downstairs, dangling from the frame, it is—"

Fionna had already sprung up from the cozy
little nest she'd made against Aidan's chest on the

sofa. Aidan untangled his ankles and stretched upright in a more leisurely fashion.

Glynis's mouth fell open. Her eyes flew wide. Fionna's face flamed crimson. Aidan would have wagered a fortune that the whole of her body was the exact same color. He'd have very much liked to inspect—and confirm—for himself the possibility.

Glynis hadn't moved since she'd laid eyes on Aidan. Aidan gathered up his coat and pressed an airy kiss on Fionna's mouth. "I'll be back shortly," he told her. "We're going away for the day, you and I. Dress warmly."

Impossible as it seemed, Glynis's eyes grew rounder still. Aidan did not pass her; instead, he bowed low, caught the maid's hand, and brought it briefly to his lips. "You must be Miss Barnes," he said with his most disarming smile. "How very delightful to make your acquaintance, Miss Barnes." He gave her a wink. "Don't tell anyone, but I'm going to kidnap your mistress for the day."

Fionna confided later that the little maid remained just as dazzled until the very instant she left.

Back at his town house, Aidan summoned Alfred as he changed his clothing. He had informed Fionna he would make the arrangements for a discreet, reputable locksmith to come and replace the door to her apartments and change the locks to both her residence and the shop. Surprisingly, she'd made no argument. Even if she had, this time he'd have insisted. He would not have her burdened any further. He also imparted instructions to Alfred on another matter.

Fionna had already divulged that she planned to close the shop today. Aidan was glad there was no need to make that particular argument.

When he returned, his carriage was directly outside the bookshop. Though the sign indicated that the shop was closed, he saw Fionna through the window and summoned her.

She was dressed in a warm brown traveling gown trimmed with fur, and the color brought out the gold flecks in her eyes. Aidan admired her figure, then tipped her face to his as she descended the last step. She met his regard with unswerving directness. She was tired; the shadows beneath her eyes gave it away. But while he knew she was hardly well rested, he was glad to see she had recovered her self-control. Her strength was one of the things he admired most about her.

Slender brows rose when she saw the carriage. But she didn't miss a step as he handed her inside. He swung his body up and settled beside her. He tossed his top hat on the opposite seat and turned to her.

"Well," he said lightly, "where shall we go?"

"I thought I was being kidnapped, sir."

"Well, you are. But you are being allowed the privilege of being asked if there's anywhere in particular you would like to go?"

Fionna's heart caught. *All the way to Gleneden,* she longed to cry. She remembered the night he'd first suggested he might kidnap her.

If I should kidnap you, he had said, *why, we would not be seen for many days and many nights . . . I admit, though, I find the prospect quite fascinating. I'd take you to Gleneden, I think, where we would be far, far away from everyone . . . quite alone, you and I.*

How long ago that seemed. Yet in truth, it had been only a few weeks.

In that uncanny way he had, he always knew her every thought. She knew it for certain when she spied the smile lurking at the corners of his mouth.

"North?" he murmured. "To Scotland?"

Fionna tried to stifle a smile and didn't succeed. Which in turn, only encouraged him.

He slid an arm around her shoulder, drawing her close. With the other he tossed her stylish little hat so that it landed precisely beside his on the other seat. That, of course, enabled him to lower his mouth to her ear, nuzzling the tiny little hollow there.

"I could take you all the way to heaven if you like," he murmured suggestively.

Fionna couldn't resist. "You already have, remember?" A finger on his cheek, she led his mouth to hers, boldly taking the lead. When he sucked in a breath, she knew she'd startled him.

It was a very long time before he raised his head. "Now that we're done circling the square," he said with a dry chuckle, "tell me true. It's a lovely, sunny day, too lovely to stay in the city. Is there somewhere you would like to visit?"

"Home." It slipped out before she even realized it; there was certainly no need even to think about it. "Odd that I should say that, isn't it?" she mused aloud. "I am home, aren't I?"

"Not so odd at all. When I think of home, I think of Gleneden. I think it's always thus. One thinks of home as the place where one grows up. Where we lived as children." A pause. "Is that where you'd like to go, Fionna? To Southbourne? To the village where you grew up?"

"I'd like that," she said softly. "I'd like that very much."

Soon they were rolling out of London, past soot-laden snow into the countryside. Aidan tucked a fluffy lap blanket over them. Puffy white snowdrifts piled high beside the road. The sky was pure azure. Fatigued as she was, Fionna didn't want to sleep. She needed the fresh air. She needed this day.

She needed *him*.

At the thought, her heart stumbled. An arrow seemed to shoot straight through her breast. This couldn't last forever. She couldn't *have* him forever, and greedy though it was, she wanted him with her at every opportunity.

They ate a hearty luncheon at an inn. A short while later, the farmsteads sprinkled outside the village came into view. Fionna pointed out the river where she used to fish with her father.

Her cheek pressed up against the glass of the carriage, she showed Aidan the small manor house where they had lived. The gates were closed by the present owners, but Fionna pointed out the window to her room, the room where she'd stayed up half the night and written *Satan's Path*.

Circling back toward London, the horses approached the churchyard. The bell tolled the hour from the tower and Fionna glanced up.

There, slogging through the snow, was Vicar Tomlinson. Fionna gave a soft cry.

"Would you like to stop?" asked Aidan.

Fionna hesitated. If she didn't, and Vicar Tomlinson chanced to see her through the glass, he would think it strange. "Certainly," she murmured.

The driver skillfully brought the vehicle to a halt. Aidan helped Fionna down the steps. Vicar Tomlinson had twisted around to stare curiously. He gave a hearty greeting when he recognized her.

"Fionna! Fionna, it's been so long, child!"

Fionna embraced him wholeheartedly. Gentle and scholarly, she had always considered him a friend—why, almost family—as had both her parents.

Fionna introduced Aidan. The men shook

hands, chatting briefly. Then, Vicar Tomlinson paused and glanced at Fionna.

Aidan cleared his throat. "Perhaps the two of you would like to walk alone for a few moments. I should like to admire the stonework of the church. I believe it's quite remarkable."

Vicar Tomlinson nodded toward him. "Your lord seems a fine young man."

"He is a very good man." She flushed a little, then waited. Fionna sensed he wanted to ask after her mother.

But he surprised her by saying, "Fionna, perhaps it is none of my affair, but I visited your mother recently."

Fionna blinked. She recalled her mother telling her Vicar Tomlinson had visited. She'd thought it was merely Mama's mind wandering again.

"It's very kind of you to visit her," she murmured.

"I've always been extremely fond of your mother," he said with a faint smile. "The best soprano in the choir, I daresay." His smile faded. "Fionna, I must be direct. Your mother's condition is no better than before. Am I wrong?"

"I fear she only grows worse," Fionna admitted miserably. "I expected so much more by now. At least some improvement. Some days are better than others. But of late, it seems there is none. Indeed, it seems she only worsens. When Dr. Colson agreed to treat her, I was ecstatic."

"I, too, was convinced that he could help her," he admitted.

He seemed to hesitate.

Fionna frowned. "What is it? I have the feeling something is wrong," she said slowly. "Did something happen during your visit? Is there something I should know?"

"It's nothing like that. I-I am just very concerned at her lack of progress, Fionna. One cannot help but wonder if the treatment she receives is truly helping."

He referred to the daily tonic her mother was given at the institution.

Fionna's throat clogged tight. "I-I begin to fear that I must accept that her condition will never change. That *she* will never be the same."

"All the more reason to find out if another institution—another physician—might have more success. Again, it is your decision, but I cannot help but wonder if potions and tonics are the answer. Perhaps you might consider another facility."

From the corner of her eye she saw Aidan approaching.

The vicar touched her hand. "Whatever choice you make will be the right one. I will pray for her, child. And for you as well."

She hugged him again, then he and Aidan shook hands.

Climbing back into the carriage, Fionna sat

staring through the window for long minutes after they left the village.

Aidan touched her hand. "You're troubled," he observed quietly.

"No, I'm just being silly. Vicar Tomlinson and I were talking about . . . happier times. My father. And . . . my mother."

Aidan could have kicked himself. "Fionna, I'm so sorry. I didn't even stop to think that you might want to visit their graves. They're here in Southbourne, I presume? We can return if you like."

A spurt of guilt shot through her. These were dangerous waters she was treading.

"It's not necessary," she said quickly. "I-I think I should like to be alone when I do." Hot shame filled her. Never had she despised herself as much as she did in that instant.

They rumbled home toward London. The movement lulled her, emptying her mind until she leaned her head against Aidan's shoulder. She fell into a restless sleep.

Darkness had settled over the chimneys and towers of the city by the time they arrived in London. It wasn't until the horses slowed to a walk that Fionna roused. She stirred.

"Fionna."

Sleepily she pushed a stray hair from her cheek. "Hmmm."

"Will you come home with me tonight?"

She gaped.

"No, not for *that*. I simply dislike the idea of you being alone."

Fionna was silent.

"A hotel then, Fionna."

She took a breath. "I won't allow this—this interloper to control my life, Aidan. To control *me*."

"Somehow I thought you'd say that." His disapproval was clear.

Fionna pulled herself from the sheltering enclosure of Aidan's loose embrace and sat upright.

Her eyes narrowed. "There's a man in front of my shop," she announced sharply. "Look there. He walked away—Now he's coming back!"

Fionna's little nose was squashed against the window. As the carriage passed, the man glanced up, saw Aidan, and gave a little salute.

Fionna's head turned slowly. Realization crept in. "You know that man?"

"His name is Gates. He was under my command in India. Capital fellow, Gates. A veritable bulldog, I daresay."

Fionna's mind was still reeling when the carriage stopped. Aidan escorted her to the rear entrance. Fionna glanced both left and right.

Another man in each direction.

Lightly he touched her elbow. "Wait for me at the door," he instructed.

He walked swiftly to one of the men. There was a very brief exchange, and he returned.

In his hand were several keys. He opened the

door with one, handed it to her and pocketed the other.

"A precaution, no more," he said smoothly. "No need to panic." Aidan opened the door.

"Do I look as if I am panicked?" Indeed, she was rather incensed. "And by the by, I'll have you know I was quite capable of making such arrangements myself."

"So you were," came his smooth reply, "but now there's no need."

The tension swelled as they entered her home.

Fionna headed toward the kitchen. "I'll put on the kettle," she said curtly.

She didn't want tea; she suspected Aidan didn't either, but she needed to busy her herself. She could hear Aidan moving restlessly around in the parlor.

She returned with a tray filled with a pot of tea, cups and saucers, and a plate of sandwiches. Aidan sat on what had now apparently become his favorite chair, Fionna thought with a flare of annoyance.

Fionna poured and handed him a plate. China clinked. Minutes passed, and neither one of them spoke a word.

Tension boiled as surely as the kettle had boiled earlier. Silence cut the air as surely as a knife.

At last he pushed away his plate and saucer. Fionna could feel Aidan gazing at her. She looked away.

Lowering her cup to her lap, she stared into the

brew. All at once she was shaking. Shaking uncontrollably, and she couldn't seem to stop. The cup rattled against the saucer; hot liquid nearly sloshed over the edge of the cup.

She tried to stop it. She truly did, but suddenly every one of her emotions was spinning wildly away, and she hadn't a prayer of harnessing even one! She locked her jaw to keep it from trembling as well.

Aidan snared both cup and saucer from her hands. "For pity's sake, you'll burn yourself!"

His tone was the last straw.

Fionna surged to her feet, snatched up the tray, and headed toward the kitchen.

"Fionna. Fionna, please come back here."

She ignored him.

His oath burned her ears.

Her head swiveled back. He was on his feet, striding after her, his features as determined as hers.

"Leave me alone, Aidan! In fact, please leave!"

"I will not. Not until I know what the devil is going on with you."

She slid the tray onto the table near the stove. All at once tears streamed hotly down her cheeks. She couldn't contain them, and she despised her weakness. She turned away, praying he wouldn't see. Damn! He stood directly behind her now. When his hands came down on her shoulders, they hunched up defensively.

Bodily he turned her.

He stared at her, stunned.

"Why are you still here? I believe I asked you to leave, Aidan!"

"Fionna. Fionna!" Aidan was shocked. Bewildered. He understood last night—Christ, even he had been unnerved. Tempestuous she was, oh, yes! But she'd been so strong today. She was always so strong, so in control of her life, her world, most of all her emotions. To see her dissolve into tears like this was like being punched in the gut.

"Goddamn it, I did this, didn't I? I'm sorry! What did I say, love? What did I do?"

She dashed away a tear. Half a dozen more replaced it.

"Dammit, Fionna! Lend me a hand, won't you, sweet? I-I've blundered and I don't know how to fix it!"

Hard arms encircled her, holding her until gradually her trembling began to stop.

"You haven't done anything," she confided raggedly. "It's not your fault. It's not anyone's fault." Her voice wobbled traitorously. "There . . . there are times I don't know who I am. Times I don't want to *be* who I am."

He stroked her hair. "Fionna," he said quietly. "I don't know what you mean."

Of course he didn't.

And she couldn't tell him any more. What was the use?

How desperately she wished that time could

turn back. For her mother. For her father. When there had been life and joy for both of them.

And for herself and for Aidan. She ached with the need to go back to last night, to the thrill of being possessed by him. To those hours afterward when he'd held her tight, when she'd felt so safe and cherished, and nothing mattered but the magic of being with him.

What a fool she was. She couldn't be with Aidan. For now, yes. But not forever.

It was as if she'd been crippled. She couldn't change the past. She couldn't change the present, and she certainly couldn't change the future.

All she knew was that she couldn't risk Aidan discovering the truth about her mother. *Especially* him. The burden was hers. Hers alone. It wasn't fair to him, not when there could never be more between them. It wasn't fair to her, to *expect* more than there could ever be.

"Look at me, Fionna."

She didn't want to, yet somehow she couldn't stop herself either. His gaze probed deep into hers.

"I sense you struggling. Why are you so tormented? Do you think I do not see? Do you think I don't *know*?"

She shook her head. "Don't ask me those things, Aidan. Please don't. I have no wish to argue, Aidan."

"And why should we argue? Dammit, Fionna, just talk to me. Let me help you."

She made a low, choked sound. "No one can help me."

The anguish in her face cut him to the bone.

"Fionna! Stop hiding!" he swore.

"I am not hiding!"

"The hell you're not! There's something you're not telling me."

She tried to pull away. He loosened his grip, but wouldn't release her. He captured her chin so that she had nowhere to look but at him.

"I can't, Aidan. *I can't*. All I can say is that . . . I have obligations."

"Yes, yes," he said impatiently. "We all have obligations. We all have responsibilities."

"Not like this! There are things you don't know—"

She broke off . . . and broke away.

How impossible she was!

He swung her around, his blue eyes sizzling. He held her close. He held her hard. "You're hiding something," he said flatly. "I don't know what the blazes is going on, but something is. What are you hiding? *What?* I hate these secrets between us. There should *be* no secrets. Have you broken the law? Done something illegal? Are you hiding from the police? From someone else?"

She stared at him, stupefied. Aghast.

"What then? Are you in trouble? Are you being blackmailed? God, just tell me, Fionna! Tell me and perhaps I can help you. Perhaps my family can."

Her eyes filled with tears, nearly killing him inside.

She shook her head. Her face was deathly pale, but she pressed her lips together—holding her secret in, keeping him out.

Fighting him off.

He wanted to shake the truth from her. "What then?" he demanded. "For God's sake, just tell me!"

Fionna grappled for composure. Salvaged it. Conviction gathered full and ripe. He prodded, he probed like the tip of a rapier.

"You presume too much," she told him stiffly.

"And you tell me too little." His features were etched in bitter reproof.

"I think not."

"You said you trusted me." It was an accusation.

There was a stifling silence—a particularly bitter one on his part.

His jaw clenched hard. "I've bared my soul to you, Fionna, my *soul*. And by God, you are going to tell me what's wrong," he told her fiercely. "For now, I'll let it be on your terms. But you *will* tell me."

Inside, Fionna flinched from his unbending gaze. But outside—she would never show it. It was just as she'd said. No one could help her. No one could help her mother. Perhaps not even Dr. Colson.

"I won't be controlled, Aidan. And I won't be

told what to do, *Colonel*, as if I were one of the men under your command!"

"It's not command or control but concern that motivates me." His tone—his regard—was as icy as hers. "There's a distinction, Fionna."

"My life is my own," she said coldly. "I thought we'd established that. Now please release me."

Aidan neither agreed nor disagreed. He let her go. "Are you certain you won't let me make arrangements for a hotel?"

Fionna took a step back. She twitched her skirts into place, her chin as stubborn as her pride, he decided blackly.

"No. I won't allow this invader to control me, to try to frighten me from my own home. I've work to do, a novel to finish. Heaven knows I've lost enough time as it is. Besides, there's no need to fuss. I can take care of myself."

He stalked toward the door, then turned. "I've business in Southampton and Dublin for the next week," he growled. "I won't be back until next Monday, and dammit, I cannot get out of it. Just remember, you're not alone. My men—"

"I have no quibble if those men are outside at night. But I won't be hounded during the day, Aidan. I won't feel as if I'm being dogged."

Their eyes collided, but she frowned when he went to his greatcoat and reached into an inner pocket.

When he turned, there was a small pistol in his hand.

Fionna gasped, her eyes suddenly huge.

He pressed it into her palm, folding her fingers around the cold steel.

Fionna stared at it, still stunned. Swallowing, she looked up at him, her eyes huge. "Aidan—"

His gaze bored into hers. "Do not refuse me in this, Fionna. It will ease my mind if you have it. Now tell me, have you ever used a gun?"

"A few times when I was young," she said faintly. "I went hunting with my father on occasion."

"Excellent. I'll have Gates take you out and acquaint you with this one," he said curtly. "It's accurate at fairly close range. But one shot is all you'll have. Remember that."

Fionna was still reeling.

"Promise me you will carry it, Fionna. *Always.* Promise me." His tone warned he would tolerate no argument. Slowly she nodded.

"Trust no one, Fionna. *No one.* No one except Alec."

"Alec!" Panic sparked fearfully. "Aidan! You promised you wouldn't tell!"

"And I did not. But should you need anything, anything at all, do not hesitate to contact him. I trust Alec with my life, and so should you. Do you understand?"

Another nod. Her lips were tremulous. She felt suddenly abandoned. This was so unexpected. She hadn't realized he would be gone on business.

He was already at the door. "Lock the door behind me." He didn't glance back as he exited.

He was leaving, she thought numbly. Leaving!

And he hadn't kissed her—but oh, how keenly
she missed it. How desperately she wished he
had! It would drive away the pain, the ache in
her breast.

Make them forget their quarrel.

Stupidly—foolishly!—she slid to her knees,
buried her hands in her face, and dissolved into
tears.

Chapter Sixteen

He closes in. Ever closer, ever behind me. Behind us. I fear he is playing with me. Taunting me. Closing in, retreating. Icy shivers run over my skin. Needles of ice.

All that saves me is the feel of Rowan's fingers warm beneath my breast as he draws me near. Tight about my body, pressing me so his warmth surrounds me, every part of my body.

All that saves me is Rowan himself.

Demon of Dartmoor, F.J. Sparrow

Aidan went from Fionna's apartment to Alec's home. Alec had just returned from an evening at his club. He had just settled himself behind the desk in his study when Aidan strode in like a whirlwind. He headed straight to the whisky decanter.

Alec touched his fingertips together. "Well," he remarked, "I gather something is on your mind."

Aidan's anger was still too fresh to withhold. He downed the first drink and poured another. Only then did he seat himself across from Alec.

"May I hazard a guess? I believe this has to do with Miss Hawkes. You are perhaps experiencing—frustrations, shall we say—where the lady is concerned. You are perhaps experiencing . . . frustrations that involve—"

Aidan had yet to participate in the conversation. He glowered at his brother. "I will not reveal details of that particular part of my life—with that particular lady—to you, Your Grace. Nor to anyone for that matter."

"Nor would I ask you to," Alec answered mildly. "And you did not allow me to finish. I was about to say you are perhaps experiencing frustrations that involve matters of the heart."

Aidan expelled a long, pent-up breath. "Forgive me for playing the brute, Alec."

"Done. I've done the very same often enough over the years. A role we exchanged countless times, I daresay." Alec gave a half smile.

"That was when we were children."

"True enough, I suppose."

"And it wasn't about a woman. Well, there's Annie, of course. But not about—"

"The lovely Miss Hawkes."

Aidan nodded. He set aside the glass and rubbed his temples. His head ached abominably.

"I lost my head, Alec. I lost my temper. And I think I'm losing my heart."

Alec leaned back in his chair. "Is that so very bad?"

"It is when I've no idea if she feels the same," Aidan admitted. "Fionna, well, she doesn't wear her heart on her sleeve. She wants me. Then she does not want me."

"Hmmm. Only a woman can see the logic in that, I suppose."

Aidan took a breath. "She may be in danger, Alec."

Alec's smile faded. "What's going on?"

Aidan made a split-second decision. He'd promised Fionna he wouldn't tell a soul she was F.J. Sparrow. And he didn't. But he relayed Fionna's notion that she'd been followed, the bizarre message scrawled across her windowpane.

"That's not the least of it," Aidan finished. "There's something she refuses to tell me. Something she hides."

Alec studied him. "Well, you are the strategist. There has to be a way to find out what she's hiding."

Aidan said nothing.

Alec sighed. "For pity's sake, think, man. Regardless of how much you want to forget that part of your life, you were brilliant in the Punjab, and for pity's sake, don't tell me otherwise! Obviously you found many ways to penetrate, to overcome the enemy's forces—"

"Not always, Alec. You know that. Besides, I should hardly call Fionna an enemy." His smile held little mirth. "Quite the contrary."

"You know very well what I mean. How would you gather your information? I suppose," Alec said dryly, "that torture is out of the question here."

"Whatever makes you think I resorted to such tactics?"

Alec eyed him. He wasn't quite sure what to make of that.

"Well, what tactics would you resort to? What tactics *did* you resort to?"

Aidan made no answer. His features were very taut. Alec was quite sure he didn't want to know after all.

"The problem," Aidan said finally, "is that very few options are open to me. And the necessary tactics, well, they're hardly likely to win me the lady's heart."

Alec's curiosity overrode all. "All that aside, if you were back in the Punjab, what would you do?"

Aidan gave a brittle laugh. No, he certainly hadn't forgotten that part of his life.

"Let me ask you the same question, Alec. What would *you* do in such a case?"

The duke of Gleneden needed no time to ponder or consider. "I'd send in a spy," he said bluntly.

Smiling grimly, Aidan placed his hands flat on the desk top and rose to his full, imposing height. "Exactly."

The week seemed to drag on forever. On Sunday morning, Fionna shook off the snow from her parasol and entered the hospital. Her steps a rhythmic echo, she directed them down the corridor, trying to close her ears to the sound of someone screaming.

The screams were coming from her mother's room.

Fionna threw open the door.

Her mother's hair was wild and uncombed, her eyes red-rimmed and sunken. She still wore her night rail. Arms outstretched, her movements jerky, she turned this way and that, as if warding off some unseen predator.

She looked like a wraith.

"No! Stay back! Don't come near me. William . . . William! Make them stay away!"

"I'm sorry," said one of the nurses. "She won't let us touch her today, nary a one of us. We had to pull her from under the bed. She believes the beasties have come for her."

Fionna set aside her reticule, set aside her shock, though the price she paid was with every ounce of her being.

"Come, Mama," she began calmly. "Let us help you dress."

"You!" her mother cried. She pointed a bony, wavering finger at Fionna. "You are the one!" she accused. "You created them. You command them. You command them all! The devil, the demons. I know who you are! You're a monster, just like the rest of them! Don't touch me. Don't let her near me!" She began to scream again, shrill, ear-piercing screams that shattered the walls of Fionna's mind.

And every corner of her heart.

Bile stung her throat. Her insides twisted into an ugly knot. Self-loathing poured through her.

Had she done this? Was she responsible for her mother's condition? Had her novels of devils and demons sent her to a place where she felt she could not escape them?

Blindly she ran. Blindly into the light, no longer benign but obscene after what she had just witnessed. Her stomach churned sickeningly.

She ran into the bushes and retched.

Her head was still buzzing when she finally dragged herself upright. Tears sparkled on her lids. Her vision was a watery blur. She gazed neither right nor left, and so nearly collided with a tall figure.

"Miss Hawkes?"

She looked up. It was Dr. Colson.

"I just saw my mother."

He sighed. There was no need to say more.

"She wasn't in such dreadful condition when I last saw her." Fionna could barely speak for the tightness in her chest. Her tone was halting. "She did not recognize me then, or even the time before. But today she . . . I do not understand how she could change so quickly . . ." Her throat closed off.

"Unfortunate that you had to see her today. But I would remind you that her deterioration is not so sudden as you say. I fully agree, however. Her condition is alarming." He paused. "Miss Hawkes, I hesitate to tell you this, for I know it will distress you. Yesterday your mother attacked another patient."

Fionna recoiled as if she'd been struck. "No," she said shakily. "That cannot be." Her mother violent? It was as if . . . as if it were from one of her novels. After hearing Mama's tirade, she felt sick, sick to her very soul. She *had* done this. Through her writing. Her work.

"I saw it myself, Miss Hawkes." As ever, he was the voice of reason.

Fionna gazed at him painfully. "Dr. Colson, I think it is time that we consider another—"

He held up a hand. "Wait. I believe I know what you are going to say. But I ask that you hear me out, that you bear with me a bit longer. I've been experimenting with a new draught prepared especially for your mother's particular needs. I've been hesitant to tell you about it until I deemed the prospects encouraging. But I am pleased to tell you, Miss Hawkes, that I believe your mother could benefit greatly from this new treatment."

"Dr. Colson, it's been months, and there have been no results."

"This one is different. Results should be seen by the end of a week. Two at most. With your approval, I'll start it within the hour."

He paused expectantly.

More tonic. More draught. Fionna was growing tired of such promises.

She'd had such high hopes when they came to London. Yet now, it was as if there was no hope left.

Only disappointment. Only despair, and the taste was bittersweet.

Her heart felt dull and lifeless. Did two more weeks truly matter?

She nodded her agreement.

"Excellent," beamed the doctor.

An icy drizzle had begun to fall by the time Fionna reached home. She knew she should write, but she was exhausted. Tired of working. Writing. So tired of everything. But she had a chapter to submit soon else this month's publication of *Demon of Dartmoor* would be delayed. She couldn't chance that. She might need the funds even more if Mama stayed in Dr. Colson's institution. Even if she didn't, the hunt for a new facility must begin. Money was necessary.

It gave her a start when a tall figure rose from the chair. "Hello, Fionna."

She blinked. It was a moment before she recalled Aidan had retained a set of her keys.

A part of her longed to hurtle herself against him, to close out the world and everything in it, to lose herself in passion and surrender.

She set her reticule on the table beside the door and tugged off her cloak, a little puzzled. "I thought you wouldn't be back until tomorrow."

"I finished my business a day early."

He stepped close, lifting her face to his. "You've been crying," he said very quietly. "Why?"

She avoided his regard. "I've had several very late and unproductive nights. It's silly I know, but I've been fretting a bit."

"Is that all?"

Why was he being so insistent? "Yes," she lied.

"All has been well? No more messages? No threats?"

Her nod was jerky.

His fingers caught hers. He tugged her to the sofa.

"Why are you here, Aidan?"

His eyes flickered. "I promised I would not invade your sanctum without your permission. For this, I apologize. However, I thought the situation warranted it. It was either here . . . or there."

There was an odd note in his voice. Fionna looked at him sharply. "Here or there?" she repeated. "And I've no idea what situation you refer to."

Something surfaced in his eyes, something that made her heart begin to thud.

"The truth is, Fionna, I've had you watched while I was gone."

"Of course. Of course I knew your men were here at night—"

"Not just then," he interrupted, watching her closely. "Even during your . . . daytime jaunts."

"What? For heaven's sake, why? And by whom? Your cronies? I told you I did not mind if they were here at night, Aidan—"

He cut her off once more. "Gates followed you last Tuesday after you closed the shop. Again on Thursday, after the shop closed. Oh, and let us not forget today. Since I was home, well, I followed you today."

"Gates followed me," she repeated. "And you followed me . . . " All at once she felt crushed inside. "Why? Why would you do this? Treat me like a—a traitor!"

He ignored her outburst.

"You visited the same place each time. Tuesday, Thursday, and today. Three blocks north, two to the east, and north again. It's a red brick building at the end of the street, quite lovely, in fact. If one didn't know it was there, why, one might quite easily miss it."

He paused. "This is purely a guess, but given the regularity of the hour, I should imagine you've been going there for some time. Odd, that you never mentioned it to me. After all, as you once told me, you are a woman of regularity. I distinctly recall, the utmost regularity, you said."

A feeling of utter dread began to seep through her, mingled with a furious resentment. "How dare you. How dare you pry into my life like this! It's none of your affair where I go, when I go, and whom I choose to see."

"Yes, your life is your own, isn't it, as you persist in telling me."

His curtness stung.

"The situation is this, sweet. I knew you were hiding something from me. I simply did not know *what*. However, you should know I can easily find out what is in that building. And who. My cronies, as you call them, are quite skilled at discovering information—and extracting it as well. Gates in particular. After all, he was trained by me."

Fionna's heart seemed to stumble. She felt herself blanch. "Sweet heaven," she breathed. "What have you done . . ." She moaned. "Oh, Lord, what have you done? Are you telling me he *knows*—"

"He knows you visit *that* building. The one I

saw for myself today. That is all he knows. As for why, I wish to hear it from you. I wish to give you the opportunity to tell me yourself. That is why I am here."

Inside, she was crumbling. But by heaven, she wouldn't let him see it.

She disguised it, feeling betrayal burn inside her. Letting it burn like the red-hot poker of Satan himself.

She was on her feet before she knew it. "You bastard," she said feelingly. "You deceived me, Aidan. You had those men follow me, and you did not tell me! You told me you were in Southampton and Dublin, but perhaps it was just a lie—"

"Do not speak to me of lies! I did not lie to you, I simply did not tell you about my men! Indeed, I think you are the one who has been lying all along."

Her face was bloodless. She knew it. She'd been caught. Trapped. Devastation swept over her. She almost hated him for doing this to her, for making her feel so guilty when all she sought was to protect herself and her mother!

He arose, his expression taut. "It's time, Fionna, time for you to tell me the truth. What do you conceal? It's more than the fact that you are F.J. Sparrow. This is what you've been hiding from me all along, isn't it? Yet I cannot imagine anything that could be so horrible that you cannot tell me, that you refuse to trust me!"

"You've ruined me, Aidan. You've ruined *us!*"

He uttered an impatient oath. He caught her wrists when she would have raised them. "I have ruined no one!"

Panic swelled. She tried to tear herself away. He wouldn't allow it. He jerked her close, the strength of his grip like bands of iron.

"You have!" she cried. "You've ruined me. Me, and . . . and . . . "

"Who?" he demanded.

A thundering tension split the air.

"Dammit, Fionna! *Who?*"

"My mother," she said wildly.

He made a sound of scorn. "Your mother is dead."

And he was killing her with his questions.

"You told me the day we had Sunday dinner together. I'll never forget the way you looked. So sad. So anguished! And last week in the village you told me again when I asked if you wanted to visit your parents' graves. By God, we passed the graveyard where they're buried . . ."

Realization began to dawn. "My word, Fionna. Are you saying . . ."

"My mother is not dead," she said dully. "She's mad."

"Mad," he repeated, as if he still didn't comprehend.

"Yes. *Yes.*" Her voice was half-choked. "Must you make me say it? Pour it out as if it were nothing? As if it were of no consequence to anyone? My mother is mad."

His eyes widened. "No. Oh, no."

"Oh, yes!" She broke free of his hold, her hands balling into fists, her lungs burning fire. "Daft in the head, as people like to say. *Touched* in the head. And the place where she is . . . it's an asylum. An asylum for the insane."

Chapter Seventeen

If it is from here the demon came, then it is here he shall return.

I will make certain. We will make certain of it, Rowan and I.

Demon of Dartmoor, F.J. Sparrow

Of all the things she might have told him, that was the last thing in the world Aidan expected. And Fionna . . .

She had exploded. She was half-hysterical. She pounded on his chest. Dry sobs wracked the air.

"Now do you understand? Do you? What would the good people of England do if they knew the truth about F.J. Sparrow? They would be shocked to discover that *he* is really a woman. And then they would say that *she* writes of madness and murder and mayhem because her poor mother is insane. Was it *she* who made her mother go mad? Or was it her mother who made *her* go mad? That should go over well, shouldn't it? But I know the truth. It's my fault she's mad. I'm the one who made her that way. I am!"

He caught her hands, engulfing them in his own.

"Fionna. Fionna, stop. Stop, love. It's all right."

"It's not all right! It will never be all right." She was screaming. "I won't have my mother subjected to ridicule. I won't be gossiped about. I won't! It's up to me to protect her, Aidan. I'm the only one who can protect myself!"

Something had snapped inside her. Strong hands curled around her shoulders. He forced her head against his chest, subduing her, but not hurting her, closing his arm tight around her back until the wildness passed, and she stopped battling him.

And then he wasn't sure which was worse. Her strength bled dry, he pulled her down on the sofa. She lay against him, as if she'd been beaten and driven into the ground. Feeling her thus was like a clamp around his chest. His heart squeezed as she expelled a dry, jagged sob. She didn't cry. He wished she would; perhaps it would have been easier for her.

A long while later, she stirred. Aidan brushed his lips against the soft, stray hairs of her temple.

"Fionna," he said softly, "it's why you pushed me away, isn't it? So long and so hard."

He knew the precise instant tension invaded her body, but she didn't draw away. Perhaps it was because of the subtle tightening of his embrace—perhaps the not-so-subtle tightening of his arms.

It lasted but a heartbeat. She sighed, rubbing her cheek against his shoulder. There were no barriers between them now. Nothing but raw, naked truth.

"Why did you say it was your fault that your mother is mad?"

"Look at me, Aidan. I-I am a creature of the night. I thrive in the dark. In the night. Look at my novels. I write of darkness and devils and gloom."

Aidan wasn't sure he agreed, but he let it go. He paused, a little uncertain how to phrase this.

"Has it always been thus with her?"

She shook her head.

"When did it begin?"

"After my father died."

"A period of grief then?"

"Yes." The details emerged haltingly—how her mother withdrew into herself, her refusal to accept that her husband was dead. Fionna's search for a physician—a hospital—that could treat her. Her feeling of helplessness that she could do nothing to stop her mother's spiral down into a place where no one could reach her.

"There's been no improvement at all since you came to London?"

"None," she said bleakly. "She cries for William—that was my father's name—to save her. To rescue her. She called me Essie once, her sister. She didn't know me. Me, her only daughter. And today—" Her voice was so low he had to strain to catch the words. "Today she called me a monster. She-she screamed that I wasn't to touch her."

Slowly she sat up. Her beautiful amber eyes spilled over with tears. "That's how I know it's my fault. That I'm the one who made her ill. Her mind is all mixed up with monsters and fiends and demons—and me."

"That doesn't make you responsible," Aidan told her quietly.

"I think it does. Oh, I don't know how to say it other than . . . somehow, I think I've made her a prisoner of my own mind. That somehow it's all blurred in her own."

Aidan shook his head. "The mind . . . I saw things in India, sweet. Men who did not speak. Who cried as if they were infants. That doesn't mean she'll never improve, Fionna. Maybe not the same as before, but . . . better." How lame that sounded! But he didn't know how to comfort her.

"You didn't see her today, Aidan." Her voice grew lower still. "And it's not just that."

"What then?" He propped himself up on an arm.

"I tell myself I must be strong, lest her infirmity

take hold of me too. When I was being followed—Lord, I don't even know if I was!—I wondered if it was simply my imagination running wild. If it weren't for that writing on the window, I think I'd wonder if I"—her voice began to wobble—"if I am as mad as my mother."

"That is nonsense," he scolded.

A shiver shook her form. Aidan reached for her. "What is it?" he murmured against her cheek.

"It's not my imagination, Aidan. Someone *did* follow me."

"I believe you, sweet. I believe you." He drew back so he could see her. "Who knows about your mother's state? You, Dr. Colson, and now me. Anyone else?"

"Vicar Tomlinson."

"Yes," Aidan said slowly. "I thought so." He paused, his mind turning. "Who else knows that you are F.J. Sparrow?"

"Only my mother."

"Not the vicar?"

"No."

There was a strange look on his face.

Her gaze flew to his. "Aidan, what? What are you thinking?"

His face was shadowed. "I cannot say why, but I just have this feeling that someone else knows you are F.J. Sparrow, and that person may well be your secret admirer. Somehow I think it's all tied together."

Fionna sucked in a breath. "He visited my mother," she said slowly.

"The vicar?"

"Yes. My mother told me several weeks ago. I didn't believe her, but he mentioned it the other day. I've known him for years, Aidan. It's difficult to believe he would do anything to harm me, or anyone, for that matter. He's always been kind and generous. Why, he's the one who helped me with my mother when everyone else turned away."

"Maybe there's a reason for that."

"What?" She frowned.

"Fionna, you are not obtuse. Perhaps there's a reason he's been so kind. Perhaps that reason has to do with you."

His meaning sank in. Her jaw dropped. "But he's years older than I am," she objected. "Why, he's probably my mother's age!"

"He'd hardly be the first man to fall for a woman far younger, especially one as beautiful as you."

Fionna flushed with pleasure. Not at his reasoning that Vicar Tomlinson had fallen for her—that was ridiculous. But hearing Aidan say she was beautiful thrilled her to the tips of her toes.

"Do you think he knows you're F.J. Sparrow?"

"I don't see how."

"Nonetheless, I don't think anyone can be discounted." His tone was rather grim. "At this point, I still don't think anyone can be trusted," he emphasized rather forcefully. "And I don't want you going anywhere alone, Fionna. Not to the market. Not anywhere, unless I am with you."

Mutiny flared in her eyes. He pressed a finger against the softness of her lower lip. "I mean it, Fionna. I don't like this whole business. I don't like it at all."

Fionna was exhausted early the next morning. Aidan had stayed with her. Neither of them slept, nor did they make love; he just held her, and it was enough. No matter how hard she tried, she couldn't stop the thoughts from racing through her mind the night through.

And when he left, she finally cried herself to sleep.

When she woke and went to open the bookshop, she found herself glancing nervously out the window every few minutes, or whenever someone passed by. Twice when customers entered, she actually jumped as the bell sounded. She scolded herself soundly. This was ridiculous. It was the middle of the day. Nothing was going to happen.

At noonday, the door opened. The bell jangled. Fionna jumped.

The shade on the door slithered down.

The lock clicked.

In the very center of the shop, Fionna stood stock still. She didn't move. Good heavens, she couldn't. Her every sense pricked. Her eyes huge, she listened to the rhythmic click of boot heels on the wooden floor, footsteps that grew louder with every step.

Behind her now.

Oh, mercy, she couldn't move. Every muscle was frozen into place.

The book she held tumbled to the floor.

The next thing she knew, hard arms snaked around her waist. She opened her mouth to scream . . .

. . . a scream that was swallowed by a hotly familiar mouth. How the blazes he managed to turn her so quickly was surely the feat of a magician.

But that's how it always was with him.

Magic.

"What—" she managed between heated, hungry kisses "—are you doing here?"

"What I should have done last night."

Good heavens, they were on the floor. His hands were on the inside of her gown. Already it was half-undone.

"What I've regretted not doing all morning."

Her head fell back. With his teeth he dragged open the ribbon of her chemise, the movement almost feral.

With his hand he fumbled with the opening of his trousers.

He bent over her. His shirt hung open to the waist, torn open by restless, eager hands.

Her drawers were somewhere on the floor behind her head. And her nipple—she sighed in ecstasy—sucking strongly, warm and wet inside his mouth.

A strong hand snared one bare buttock. Fionna emitted a sound of pleasure. Her thighs were open. Damp and waiting. But at the last instant, with another swift move that astounded her, he twisted so that she lay atop him.

"Aidan." His name was half-stammer, half-plea. "I'm not sure how to . . . what to . . ."

Both hands now clamped around her buttocks, he showed her what she needed to know. "There, sweet," he breathed, "there's not much to it."

One single, gliding move found him planted to the hilt inside her. Her eyes flew wide. "I think there is," she said faintly.

And then there was no stopping it. Her fingers dug into his shoulders, she churned and thrust, while Aidan gasped and plunged. She buried her head against his throat. He arched his head and exploded inside her.

When it was over, Fionna realized she still lay sprawled above him. It had been a heated, hasty—and unquestionably lusty—union.

Still a little appalled at herself, she gazed down at him. He was smiling faintly, a crooked little smile that did funny things to her heart. A little mortified now that it was done, she slid off him. It was Aidan who helped her to her feet, helped her dress, and tucked the wisp of hair back into place behind one ear. He whispered that he would return later that afternoon.

Fionna was still in awe when she heard the lock open and the shade whisk up once more.

She, Fionna Josephine Hawkes, had just made love in the aisles of her bookshop. Between *A History of the Mongols* and *Victorian Flower Arrangements*.

Somehow she'd never be able to think of either the same way again.

The mood was far different later. They ate dinner out, then returned to Fionna's. Throughout the meal, she had the feeling there was something he wanted to say to her. Once they were in her parlor, she knew what it was.

"I've been thinking," he said abruptly. "I don't think it's wise for you to remain in London. I think I should send you to Gleneden."

Surely she hadn't heard him right. "I beg your pardon?" she said coolly.

"I'm sending you to Gleneden."

"You," she pointed out, her tone dangerously low, "are not sending me anywhere."

"Yes, Miss Hawkes, I am."

"I will not leave my mother," she said very quietly.

"So you refuse?"

"I do."

His jaw thrust out. "I rather thought you might. Look here, sweet. I told you last night, I don't like this. Any of this. I dislike leaving you during the day. At night, not knowing if you're in danger."

The tension had begun to spin out. Fionna didn't say a word as he got to his feet and began to pace, finally turning to face her, his feet splayed wide. Her eyes never left him.

"I am not," Fionna repeated even more quietly, "leaving my mother."

"If you won't go to Gleneden, then there is only one way I can protect you—"

Something was rising inside her, something she couldn't control. Something she couldn't contain. "You!" she burst out. "How can *you* protect me? How can a man who is half-blind possibly protect me?"

He froze. His eyes drilled into hers, like shards of ice.

Fionna drew a sharp, jagged breath. "Aidan. Aidan, I'm so sorry." Her voice was a mere breath. "I should never have said that."

She hadn't meant to hurt him. Truly she hadn't. But she knew she had by the terseness of his nod.

"As I was about to say, Fionna, I can protect you much better if you are my wif—"

"Don't," she cried. "Don't say it!"

Her fingers clamped together, straining. She gazed down at her lap. It was the only way she could say what she had to.

"Walk away, Aidan. Walk away now." She steadied her voice. She steadied her heart. Would he ever know how much this cost her? The conflict inside her was almost unbearable. It was as if she were being ripped apart inside. How unfair life was, she thought bitterly. She loved him. She loved him desperately.

But she could never have him. Never in this world.

Two steps brought him before her. He pulled her up. "Please do me the courtesy of looking at me when we speak."

She gazed at him through a blur of tears, but her chin climbed high.

"Walk away," she said again. "Don't look back. Don't ever look back."

His gaze was now burning. Burning into her. Clear to her soul. "Is that what *you* will do, Fionna? Forget we ever met? Forget we were lovers? Forget I was your *first* lover?"

And he would be her only lover, her heart cried out.

"I'm not doing this to spite you. I'm doing it to save you!"

"To save me! How?" he demanded. "Why?"

"Because my mother is mad, Aidan! Because you are *Lord* Aidan McBride. Because your brother is—"

"What the devil does that have to do with anything?"

"It has everything to do with it. Trust me in this, Aidan—"

"Trust! When have you trusted me, Fionna? You have never trusted me. You still do not trust me!"

"I've had to be strong, Aidan. I *must* remain strong. Lest . . . lest my mother's infirmity take hold of me, too."

"What the devil!"

"It's well known that weakness of the mind is passed on!"

"Rubbish," he said baldly. "Fionna, you are the most sane person I know."

There was a suffocating tightness at the back of her throat. "Am I? I told you last night. Consider the novels I write. Spectres and wraiths and creatures of evil."

He scoffed. "A vivid imagination. I believe I told you that the first night we met. Your novels are less about ghosts and goblins and ghouls than the triumph of good over evil. If you think your subject matter is lurid, then your fans are just as lurid. And you stray from the point, Fionna. Deliberately, I suspect."

His eyes had drifted to her mouth. If he kissed her, she would be forever lost . . .

His lips came down on hers. Hard. Hungry. So unbearably sweet.

She tore her mouth away.

"Don't. Don't make me want you!"

Aidan turned and slammed a fist on the table at his side.

It splintered in half—just as she was splintering in half.

"It's not an illicit affair I want, and neither do you!" he shouted. "And dammit, don't avert your eyes again!"

Fionna made a jagged sound. The path of her life led in circles, not to him. Never to him. Somehow she had to make him see . . .

"It's all we could ever have. And you're right—I don't want that! I-I cannot marry you," she choked out. "If my mother's madness should ever be revealed . . . it would be the ruin of all of us. You cannot take that chance. *We* cannot take that chance. If that happened, your family would be ostracized, Aidan. Society would be horrified if you—if you married into a family of madness. None of you would ever be accepted in your world. You know it as well as I.

"Would you do that to your family? *Could* you? Even if you could, I won't. They would be devastated. They would hate me. You would end up hating me. Not now, but in time, perhaps, you might wonder if I will become tainted . . . as my mother is tainted . . . if our children would be tainted."

He gripped her wrist. "Do you know what you're doing? You desolate my heart. You desolate my soul."

"Don't! Don't say that. Don't say anything! Just . . . just leave, Aidan."

His lip curled. "That's right, Fionna. Turn away. Run away."

"Do not taunt me!" she cried.

"You little fool! It's not just me you deny, it's yourself! Do you think to wile away your life alone? What kind of life is that?"

"Must I put it more plainly? I do not want you here, Aidan. I . . . do . . . not . . . want . . . you."

The look he turned on her was utterly fierce. She shrank back.

"Say what you will, Fionna. You need me. You want me. And I won't bow out of your life now, not while you're in danger."

"You have to. It's over, Aidan. *It's over.*"

"Is it? We shall see, sweet. We shall see. After the tune you've made me dance to, I'll be *damned* if I'll walk away now."

He stalked to the door. "I'll be here tomorrow to check on you. And for pity's sake, don't go anywhere alone!"

He was seething. Filled with a vile, near murderous rage.

As for his love . . .

Oh, but she could be so alluringly convincing. So sweet when she chose to be. He recalled the last time he'd seen her. She was so concerned, so much so that he alone saw the truth.

He alone saw what was inside her.

Did she mock him? he wondered. No. Even if it were true, once they were together, she would learn that his way was the only way.

Perhaps it was the influence of her lordly lover. His lip curled up in a snarl.

For they were lovers, of that he had no doubt. He came and went as he pleased. He was there into the wee hours of the night.

He would find a way to deal with him, even if it required dire measures.

In the end, it all came down to just one thing, the way it was in all of her novels.

A matter of life . . . or death.

He was the one she truly loved. Once they were together, she would know it.

He would forgive her this one indiscretion, he decided. To err . . . well, it was the nature of man. He was acquainted with the nature of man better than anyone.

Besides, forgiveness was the godly way—and he was well acquainted with God's will. Why, the illness of her mother was what brought them together. What made them close. Was that not a sign of God's will?

Yet Fionna must be made to see her folly. He would see to it. She must be punished. He thought of her mother . . .

She would say it was cruel, of course.

But it was necessary. She had crossed him, and

he would not be crossed. For now, well, the time drew nigh. He was growing bored with their little game. He was impatient for her. He'd waited long enough for his prize.

And he knew precisely how to bring her where he wanted her.

Into his waiting arms.

Chapter Eighteen

The wind howled, and the night raged. I saw him then, the demon of Dartmoor. Garbed in the robes of a vicar, he was.

But deep within the hood there was no face. Only darkness. Eyes that dripped blood, that glowed red as the devil's heart.

Lightning struck the demon. His form glowed like ashes. Deep within the hood, his head burst into flames.

I screamed to Rowan. The wind carried the sound away, but it didn't matter.

He was with me, my Rowan. As always, behind me, beside me, before me . . . wherever I needed him.

I need him now.

It was he who tossed me my book of spells. I lifted the crucifix from about my neck. High so that when lightning struck the demon again, a pearly white glow surrounded it.

"Cast out the wind, cast out the evil, cast out the devil!" I cried.

It was done. It was over.

The demon was gone forevermore.

Demon of Dartmoor, F.J. Sparrow

Fionna was still wiping away tears when she heard someone pounding at the back door. She jerked upright. *Aidan!*

She hurried down the steps.

It wasn't Aidan but a young boy.

"Miss Hawkes?"

"Yes. I am Miss Hawkes."

"I'm to give this to ye, mum."

Fionna gave the boy a coin, and he was on his way. Breaking open the letter, she read quickly.

Dear Miss Hawkes,

I write to you of a matter most urgent, one I believe you will understand cannot wait until tomorrow. I regret to tell you that your mother was not in her room when the evening meal was delivered.

A search of the premises has proved fruitless.

I should like to request your presence at the hospital at once.

It was signed by Dr. Colson.

Her heart nearly stopped. A cry broke from her lips. *Not again,* she thought helplessly. *Oh, not again.* Mama was missing. She had wandered before. But that had been in the village. Here in London, why . . . she might never be found! Even in the village, why, if it hadn't been for Vicar Tomlinson. . .

Vicar Tomlinson again. Was he the one who had followed her? Who had watched her? She knew he visited London at least once a week. He had for years now.

Aidan had told her he would stop by later. After their row, she couldn't be sure that he would stop by at all!

Snatching her cloak from the hook, she ran down the stairs and hailed a hack.

It was true.

Mama's room was empty.

"Miss Hawkes! There you are!"

It was Dr. Colson. "Good news! Your mother has been found! I have a carriage waiting near the rear entrance."

Fionna hurried after him, breathless by the time they rushed out into the frigid night air. The coach was there; a lantern burned on the hook near the cab. Where the devil was the driver? she thought furiously.

She reached for the handle.

"Miss Hawkes. Wait."

Fionna didn't want to wait. She was anxious to be off, to see that her mother was all right. But she curbed her impatience, for she knew he was as concerned as she by her mother's disappearance.

"Yes?"

He set aside her parasol, took her hands.

Fionna glanced up. An odd sensation settled in, for his dark eyes were gleaming.

She had expected his familiar reassurance.

What she got was something else entirely.

"You knew it would come to this, didn't you?"

"What? Please, Dr. Colson, my mother—"

"Your mother is well. As well as can be expected anyway." There was an almost sinister sound to his laugh. "She's simply been moved to another room."

"What?" she said faintly. His expression frightened her. It was as if *he* was mad.

"Oh, come. Do not look at me so! I've loved you for so long now. My love, I've waited for you so long."

My love.

Fionna's blood curdled. Icy prickles climbed the length of her spine. In that instant, she knew it was he who had followed her. Who watched her. Who had written in blood on her window . . .

"I see what's in your mind. It's always been so. Yes, my love, it was my blood. I pondered cutting off the tip of a finger to leave as my gift to you, the way the housekeeper did in *The Devil's Way*. I have the skill, you know. The means. I thought of sending a note which said . . . *I give myself to you. You would have liked that, I think.*"

Fionna's stomach churned.

"You're mad," she breathed, "as mad as your patients. Why, more so!"

"Nay, my love. I'm brilliant at my work, just as you are in yours. It's why we are meant to be together."

In shock she heard him go on.

"Did you enjoy our little games? You weren't quite certain who followed you, were you? What you heard . . . I knew you would love the mystery, though. That's what made it so delightful.

"I loved you from our very first meeting, why, here in this hospital, when you first brought your mother. But a confession, my love. I admired your novels long before you brought her here to me. And when your mother told me you were F.J. Sparrow . . . it was but another sign we were meant for each other."

He'd always been such a calm, convincing influence. What a fool she'd been! His admiration had turned into an obsession. He was as deranged as those he treated. And now she'd played directly into the hands of a madman!

She must think. Try to find some way out of this. She tried to wiggle free of his grip. His fingers tightened around hers like iron manacles. She nearly cried out in pain.

His eyes glinted. "I know about your lover McBride," he said suddenly. His laugh was gloating.

"Perhaps I'll cut off *his* finger and send it to his mother." He threw back his head and laughed. "Or perhaps I'll cut off something else instead! Then he won't be capable of sticking his cock into any other woman, let alone mine!"

Fionna flinched at his crudeness, but her blood ran cold. She was terrified of the malice she sensed in him. He meant to hurt Aidan as well.

"Do you think he'll come after you?" His laugh was chilling.

She couldn't let that happen. She couldn't let any of it happen.

"My mother. I-I should like to see her before we leave. To say good-bye. To tell her where we are going . . . where *are* we going?"

"Not yet, my love." His smile vanished. His eyes gleamed. "And there's no point in saying good-bye to your mother. She won't even know you're there. She's slipping away, you know. Why, who knows how much longer she'll be in this world?"

"No! You said there would be results. In a week. Perhaps two."

"I did. I simply did not say what the result would be. And then, dear Fionna, I shall be ever at your side. I'll help you bury your mother. I shall console you. No one could ever love you as I do."

"You said you would help her!"

"And I've tried! But she requires ever more laudanum to calm her. Laudanum is a powerful drug, you know. And your mother is in a very weakened state. It's best to simply have done with it."

Laudanum.

Fionna reeled. She felt as if she were being strangled. His tonics. Tonics and brews and potions . . . witch's poison. Her mother had been his hold over her. And his hold over her mother was laudanum.

And now he meant to kill her mother, too. Perhaps he already had. Fionna swore, struggling against his hold. "Let me go!" Her reticule swung against her side, reminding her of the pistol inside. Thank heaven she'd remembered it. If she could just reach it . . .

His strength was too great.

"And your lover, the lordly McBride. Who knows how long he'll be in this world?" Colson grinned. To Fionna, he was like the devil's own hand. "If he comes after you, he'll regret it." He boasted. Gloated. "Indeed, I think I shall hunt him down—"

"You sick, twisted bastard," came a voice from directly behind Colson. "You don't need to hunt me down, because *I'm already here.*"

Aidan was furious when he left Fionna's apartment that night. Her jab had hurt.

You . . . How can you protect me? How can a man who is half-blind possibly protect me?

Bitterly he lashed himself. Perhaps she was

right. He certainly hadn't been able to protect his men against Rajul. Maybe she was right. When this was over, maybe he should just walk away.

But the certainty thundered inside him . . . By Jove, he wasn't going to walk away now, not while she was in danger.

And by heaven, whether she wanted it or not, he would protect her with his very life!

And yet . . . The strangest sensation plagued Aidan when he strode home that night. All he could think was that he should never have left her.

At home, he paced back and forth in his study. The longer he stayed at home, the more compelling was this strange premonition.

Closing his eyes, he let his mind take hold of his senses.

His eyes snapped open. Panic seized hold, a panic that was unlike anything he'd ever felt before . . .

In the far reaches of his mind, it was as if he could hear her calling out . . . calling for *him*.

She needed him.

Aidan didn't know how he knew.

That he did was enough.

He knew it for certain when she didn't answer his knock. Cursing, he let himself inside.

He paled when he read the letter from Colson. With a curse, he flung it to the floor.

Running home, he bellowed for his horse.

* * *

It was odd, the way it happened. That same sense of certainty swept over him, guiding him to where they stood—Fionna and Colson.

He came up behind Colson.

"You sick, twisted bastard," he sneered. "You don't need to hunt me down, because *I'm already here.*"

His presence had the desired effect. Colson released Fionna. From the corner of his good eye, he was aware of Fionna grappling inside her reticule. His blood surged. She'd remembered the pistol!

But he couldn't see Colson, dammit. The slime was on his left, where Aidan's vision was fuzzy and blurred.

Fionna had dredged the weapon from her reticule. She clung to the grip, but the barrel was wavering.

He willed his thoughts into hers.

One shot. One shot is all you'll have.

But it was not to be. Colson spied Fionna holding the pistol. He wrenched it from her grasp and turned, searching for Aidan.

The pistol was in his hands, pointed at Aidan's chest. Colson threw back his head. "You can't have her, you stupid fool! She's mine!" Colson crowed.

Fionna, it appeared, had been totally dismissed.

A stupid mistake on Colson's part. Aidan was rather stunned . . . and wholly proud.

It all happened in an instant. Fionna seized her

parasol with all the frenzy of a woman protecting her own. She whacked Colson full on in the belly the way she'd once tried to do with Aidan.

This time she succeeded.

This time with a power borne of fury and fire.

Colson grunted with pain. His eyes went wide with shock. He clutched his belly and began to slump . . .

Just as Fionna's knee came up.

His jaw cracked like the sound of a pistol.

There was no sweeter sound on earth. No sweeter feeling than Fionna clinging to him with all her might.

"Aidan! Aidan, I knew you would come. I knew it!"

Aidan's laugh was breathless with love and laughter. "Remind me, sweet, never to cross you when you're holding a parasol."

Colson had been taken into custody. Aidan was quite certain that when his sentence was carried out, he'd not be seeing the outside of a prison cell for many a year. The police constable informed Aidan that the methods Colson employed to treat his patients would be thoroughly investigated. The night nurses had already revealed Colson's heavy reliance on laudanum—and how a number of other patients had died in his facility.

According to the constable, they would be checking the possibility that laudanum was involved in those deaths as well.

All the while, Fionna's mother had been locked in a room across the hall. She was now in a much different hospital. Fionna had been assured by a capable, efficient doctor that the effects of the laudanum were not permanent. The process would not occur overnight, but, he assured her, her mother would recover.

Both Fionna and Aidan were rather startled when Vicar Tomlinson burst into the room. Fionna glanced up from her mother's bedside.

"I was told she'd been brought here!" he cried. "Is she all right? Is she safe?"

Fionna smiled. "She will be now."

"Penelope!" he cried, rushing to the bedside.

Her mother's eyes opened. "William," she murmured. "You are here. Have you come for me?"

William. Fionna had to stop her mouth from opening in shock. Her father's name was William.

But she hadn't known that Vicar Tomlinson's was William as well.

Fionna suddenly understood that there had been more to the vicar's visits to the asylum than just the duties of his station. Once her mother was sleeping, the vicar explained how he'd fallen in love with her mother some months after Fionna's father had died. In light of her illness, he'd withheld his true feelings, for he wasn't sure how either Penelope or Fionna would react. That Vicar Tomlinson loved her mother was abundantly clear. And Mama's reaction when Vicar Tomlinson charged into the room was telling as well.

Fionna was glad—for both of them.

A short time later, Fionna kissed the vicar's cheek, kissed her mother's brow, and left with Aidan.

It was long after midnight when she and Aidan climbed the stairs to her apartment. He caught her fingers, squeezing them lightly.

Fionna squeezed his in return.

She would never let go, she thought achingly.

In her parlor, she turned and clung to him, her embrace tinged with a sort of desperation.

He gave an odd little laugh. "Fionna! What is this?" He smoothed the back of her head.

Fionna lifted her face. "I've been such a fool." Tears choked her voice. "Aidan, I'm so sorry! I never wanted to push you away, ever. I wanted you always, and I hope that you can find it in your heart to forgive me."

"Oh, but there is much more than forgiveness in my heart, love. Much more indeed." His expression tender, he guided her eyes to his. "It's time I asked that question you would not allow me to ask earlier."

Fionna's heart skipped a beat.

His smile faded. His gaze slid over her features, one by one. "I love you," he said softly. "Will you be my wife?"

She threw her arms around his neck. "Yes," she

said, half-laughing, half-crying. "Oh, yes. I love you, Aidan McBride. Do you know how very much I love you?"

"I think I would like you to show me." He captured her mouth in a hungry, arduous kiss. Reluctantly he dragged his mouth away.

"You love to shock your readers, don't you?"

Fionna blinked up at him. That wasn't quite what she'd expected him to say. But then she smiled, a rather secret little smile.

"Actually, yes. I do so enjoy shocking my readers."

His eyes were glittering blue fire. "Then shock me," he whispered.

Fionna was only too willing to oblige. Slipping from her garments, she assisted him in divesting his.

A finger in the middle of his chest, she marched him back toward his favorite chair.

Sitting on his lap, their limbs all a-tangle, she splayed her hands wide across the dark fur on his chest, coasting them down his belly to tangle in the thick nest between his thighs.

Her mouth followed, her lips hot on his naked skin.

She sank to her knees on the floor.

Aidan went very still. No. He could not believe that she would . . .

His hands twisted in her hair. It was the most incredibly erotic sensation in his life. Her tongue danced and circled, down to the very root of him and back up, tasting and exploring that most sensitive part of him.

He gritted his teeth until he could stand no more.

He caught his hand in her hair and pulled her up and onto his rod. They were both frantic, twisting wildly in perfect union, until at last he exploded inside her, spurting wildly again and again and again.

"Fionna," he gasped when he was finally able to draw breath again. "My word, you do have the devil in you."

"Well," she teased, "you did ask me to shock you."

"Speaking of the devil, where the hell did you learn *that*?"

"From you. And—"

He cocked a brow high. "And?"

She pursed her lips. He was still inside her, soft now. "Do you recall the time you came into the bookshop looking for . . . a particular book?"

"Yes, of course. *The Devil's Way.*"

"Not that book. Not that time." Her smile was purely wicked. "The next."

Aidan's brow furrowed, deep in thought. "The next," he murmured, "was when you gave me such an upbraiding for . . ." His eyes widened.

"No," he said.

"Yes."

"Yes?"

"Yes, indeed. Vatsyayana's *Kama Sutra.*"

"You wicked little witch!" She could feel him swelling inside her. "No wonder you proclaimed yourself so learned the first time we made love." He reflected rather thoughtfully. "Do you realize, we've made love on a sofa. In the aisle of your bookshop. This very chair. But never"—a glint appeared in his eyes—"in a bed."

"I do believe that should be remedied, sir."

And so it was.

Epilogue

Over a year later, much had changed.

While Aidan longed to insist they wed immediately—why, the very instant he discovered Fionna loved him—of course such a thing was not possible.

Even if it had been, Fionna had longingly expressed her wish that they wait until her mother had recovered sufficiently to attend their wedding.

Aidan gave thanks that her recovery was swift—within the month, in fact. So it was that on a glorious spring day in March, Aidan and Fionna were married in the tiny church in Southbourne by Vicar Tomlinson. The vicar beamed before the ceremony. During their loving exchange of vows . . . and most certainly thereafter as the vicar sat next to the blushing bride's mother—

Who was about to become a blushing bride herself, and very soon.

Knowing her mother was in safe hands and back in her beloved village of Southbourne, Aidan and Fionna set off on their honeymoon.

Oh, how Fionna squealed on their wedding night when Aidan finally revealed what he'd managed to hide from his bride . . . the details of their honeymoon. Fionna had assumed they would go to Gleneden for a week of seclusion.

Not so.

Instead Aidan left his business in the capable hands of his manager, overseen by Alec. Knowing that Fionna had always longed to travel the world, how could he possibly deny her?

And Fionna gave all that was in her heart to give, a heart near to bursting with love for her new husband.

Their honeymoon lasted for months. Their first stay was in Italy, at a villa where warm, azure waters lapped the shore below. In time they moved on to Egypt, where Fionna rode upon the back of a camel and laughed with all the zest of a child.

He took her all the way to India.

And it was there that Aidan finally left behind his demons. It was there that he closed that painful chapter of his life.

And truly began the next.

It was there, too, that each suspected their child had been conceived.

Back in London, given that they'd just learned they were expecting their first child, they decided to buy a bigger home in the country, and the city as well. Fionna had closed the bookshop while they were away, but she'd hired a new manager only today.

Fresh from her bath, Fionna seated herself at the desk in their bedroom, dressed in a sheer white gown and matching robe. The first snowfall of the season had arrived that evening; already the ground below was covered in crisp, glittering white.

A smile played about her lips as she gazed out the window. It reminded her of the night she'd first met Aidan.

Aidan sauntered in and closed the door, stripping off his robe on the way to the bed.

"I am going to write a letter to Mama and William," she said, "and then I am going to finish up the very last chapter on *The Scourge of Scotland*." She had worked part of the time while they were away, for it was in her blood. And it was a good thing she had, for apparently her readers were clamoring for more-more-more of Raven and Rowan.

Aidan got up to read over her shoulder.

She turned and gave him a little push. "Stop

that! That is an author's worst enemy! Perhaps I'll put a curse on you."

Aidan chuckled. "What! Remember what my mother said the night of Alec's dinner party when you first met everyone? It appears the family is already cursed anyway! Besides," he complained, "I know you've kept Raven and Rowan panting after each other throughout yet another novel. I only want to know if those two have finally become lovers."

"Only the author knows," he was informed with a severe frown. "You know that. Now back to bed with you."

A few minutes later she tipped her head to the side, tapping the feathery quill against her lips.

"I've a thought," she mused aloud. "I think I shall write a children's story next. What do you think? Of course I'd have to assume another pen name. But I think it would be quite fun, don't you?"

"Aye." Naked, Aidan watched from the bed with smoldering eyes. He grinned. "But come tame this monster first!"

Good Girls Do

Just because a woman is brought up a proper lady, doesn't mean she isn't harboring some very improper desires. And just because a lady may have led a more . . . *colorful* life, doesn't mean she hasn't got a heart of gold. In fact, we're willing to bet that within the hearts of the most well-intentioned beauties beat the kind of passion that conventional society cannot contain . . . and only a rare gentleman can capture.

In the coming months, Avon Books brings you four captivating romances featuring heroines who live by their own rules when it comes to matters of the heart. Turn the page for a sneak preview of these spectacular novels from best-selling authors Jacquie D'Alessandro, Christina Dodd, Victoria Alexander, and Samantha James!

Coming January 2008

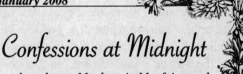

Confessions at Midnight

a brand-new *Mayhem in Mayfair* novel
by *USA Today* bestselling author

Jacquie D'Alessandro

Though Carolyn Turner can't believe the Ladies Literary Society of London would choose an erotic novel as their reading selection, she also can't help but read the tantalizing Memoirs of a Mistress *at least a half dozen times! Suddenly the lovely widow is tempted to surrender to her newly fueled fantasies when in the company of roguishly sexy Lord Surbrooke, a man no proper lady should be seen talking to, much less kissing. . . .*

Are you warm enough?" he asked.

Dear God, ensconced with Lord Surbrooke in the privacy provided by the potted palms, Carolyn felt as if she stood in the midst of a roaring fire. She nodded, then her gaze searched his. "Do . . . do you know who I am?"

His gaze slowly skimmed over her, lingering on the bare expanse of her shoulders and the curves she knew her ivory gown highlighted—skin and curves that her normal modest mode of dress never would have revealed. That openly admiring look, which still held no hint of recognition, reignited the heat the breeze had momentarily cooled. When their eyes once again met, he murmured, "You are Aphrodite, goddess of desire."

She relaxed a bit. He clearly didn't know who she was, for the way he'd said "desire," in that husky, gruff voice, was a tone Lord Surbrooke had never used with Lady Wingate. Yet her relaxation was short-lived as that desire-filled timbre pulsed a confusing tension through her, part of which warned her to leave the terrace at once. To return to the masquerade party and continue searching for her sister and friends. But another part—the part held enthralled by the darkly alluring highwayman and the protection of her anonymity—refused to move.

To add to her temptation was the fact that this anonymous interlude might afford her the opportunity to learn more about him. In spite of their numerous conversations during the course of Matthew's house party, all she actually knew of Lord Surbrooke was that he was intelligent and witty, impeccably polite, unfailingly charming, and always perfectly groomed. He'd never given her the slightest hint as to what caused the shadows that lurked in his eyes. Yet she knew they were there, and her curiosity was well and truly piqued. Now, if she could only recall how to breathe, she could perhaps discover his secrets.

After clearing her throat to locate her voice, she said, "Actually, I am Galatea."

He nodded slowly, his gaze trailing over her. "Galatea . . . the ivory statue of Aphrodite carved by Pygmalion because of his desire for her. But why are you not Aphrodite herself?"

"In truth, I thought costuming myself as such a bit too . . . immodest. I'd actually planned to be a shepherdess. My sister somehow managed to convince me to wear this instead." She gave a short laugh. "I believe she coshed me over the head while I slept."

"Whatever she did, she should be roundly applauded for her efforts. You are . . . exquisite. More so than Aphrodite herself."

His low voice spread over her like warm honey. Still, she couldn't help but tease, "Says a thief whose vision is impaired by darkness."

"I'm not really a thief. And my eyesight is perfect. As for Aphrodite, she is a woman to be envied. She had only one divine duty—to make love and inspire others to do so as well."

His words, spoken in that deep, hypnotic timbre, combined with his steady regard, spiraled heat through her and robbed her of speech. And reaffirmed her conclusion that he didn't know who she was. Never once during all the conversations she'd shared with Lord Surbrooke had he ever spoken to her—Carolyn—of anything so suggestive. Nor had he employed that husky, intimate tone. Nor could she imagine him doing so. She wasn't the dazzling sort of woman to incite a man's passions, at least not a man in his position, who could have any woman he wanted, and according to rumor, did.

Emboldened by his words and her secret identity, she said, "Aphrodite was desired by all and had her choice of lovers."

"Yes. One of her favorites was Ares." He lifted his hand, and she noticed he'd removed his black gloves. Reaching out, he touched a single fingertip to her bare shoulder. Her breath caught at the whisper of contact then ceased altogether when he slowly dragged his finger along her collarbone. "Makes me wish I'd dressed as the god of war rather than a highwayman."

He lowered his hand to his side, and she had to press her lips together to contain the unexpected groan of protest that rose in her throat at the sudden absence of his touch. She braced her knees, stunned at how they'd weakened at that brief, feathery caress.

She swallowed to find her voice. "Aphrodite caught Ares with another lover."

"He was a fool. Any man lucky enough to have you wouldn't want any other."

"You mean Aphrodite."

"You *are* Aphrodite."

"Actually, I'm Galatea," she reminded him.

"Ah, yes. The statue Pygmalion fell so in love with was so lifelike he often laid his hand upon it to assure himself whether his creation were alive or not." He reached out and curled his warm fingers around her bare upper arm, just above where her long satin ivory glove ended. "Unlike Galatea, you are very much real."

Coming February 2008

Priceless

the classic novel
by *New York Times* bestselling author

Christina Dodd

*One of the celebrated Sirens of Ireland, spirited Bron-
wyn Edana is known for stunning titled society with
her courageous exploits. But once betrothed to nobleman Adam Keane, she finds herself at the center of a
shocking conspiracy that could rock the British realm.
Now she faces her most daring adventure yet: risking
it all for the only man she would ever love. . . .*

Adam drew her outdoors, into the heated darkness. A
great bonfire leaped in the middle of the square, an-
swering the flames atop the hill, calling in the summer.
On a platform, a swarm of instruments—violin, flute, and
harmonica—squalled. The players cajoled off-key bits of
melody, then whole bars of music, and at last, inspired
by the occasion, a rollicking song. Although Bronwyn
had never heard it before, its concentrated rhythm set her
foot to tapping.

With a tug of his hand, Adam had her in the center

of a circle of clapping villagers. "I don't know how to dance to this," she warned.

"Nor do I," he answered, placing his hands on her waist. "Have a care for your toes."

She had no need to care for her toes, for Adam led with a strength that compensated for his limp. He kept his hands on her waist as he lifted her, turned her, swung her in circles. Under his guidance, she relaxed and began to enjoy the leaping, foot-stomping gambol. The community cheered, not at all distressed by the innovative steps, and the whole village joined them around the bonfire.

Girls with their sweethearts, men with their wives, old folks with their grandchildren, all whisked by as Adam twirled Bronwyn around and around. Bronwyn laughed until she was out of breath, and when she was gasping, the music changed. The rhythm slowed, the frenetic pace dwindled.

She saw Adam's amused expression change as he drew her toward him. His heavy lids veiled his gaze, and she knew he'd done so to hide his intention. She wondered why, then felt only shock as their bodies collided.

Shutting her eyes against the buffet of his heated frame against hers, she breathed a long, slow breath. The incense of his skin mated with the scent of the burning wood, and beneath the shield of her eyelids fireworks exploded. She groaned as her own body was licked by the flames.

Before she was scorched, he twirled her away, then back, in accordance to the rules of the dance.

There were people around, she knew, but she pretended they weren't watching their lord and lady. She pretended Adam and Bronwyn were alone.

Ignoring the proper steps, Adam wrapped himself around her, one arm against her shoulders, one arm at her waist.

Her hands held his shoulders. Her fingers flexed, feeling the muscles hidden beneath the fine linen. She could hear his heart thudding, hear the rasp of his breath and his moan as she touched his neck with her tongue. She only wanted a taste of him, but mistook it for interest, for he scooped her up.

Her eyes flew open. He'd ferried them to the edge of the dancing figures, planning their escape like a smuggler planning a landfall. A whirl and they were gone into the trees. Looking back, she could see the sparks of the bonfire, like a constellation of stars climbing to the sky.

This was what she wanted, what she dreaded, what she longed for. Since she'd met Adam, she didn't understand herself. His gaze scorched her, and she reveled in the discomfort. His hands massaged her as if he found pleasure in her shape; they wandered places no one had touched since she'd been an infant, and it excited her. Even now, as he pulled her into the darkest corner of the wood, she went on willing feet.

He pushed her against the trunk of a broad oak and murmured, "Bronwyn, give me your mouth."

She found his lips and marveled at their accuracy. His arm held her back, his hand clasped her waist; all along their length they grew together, like two fevered creatures of the night.

Coming March 2008

The Perfect Wife

the classic novel
by *New York Times* bestselling author

Victoria Alexander

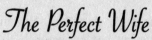

When the Earl of Wyldewood decides he is looking for a proper wife, Sabrina Winfield bargains for the position of his convenient bride. This fiery beauty will do anything to protect her family, even if it means playing into Nicholas Harrington's arrogant ideas about how a woman should behave. But the passion in the infuriating earl's touch shatters any illusions Sabrina has of keeping her heart safe. . . .

Sabrina stepped forward and gazed up at him. The glittering heavens reflected in her eyes, and Nicholas had to stop himself from reaching for her.

She drew a steady breath. "Since this is to be a marriage of convenience only and privately we shall continue to live our separate lives, and since you already have an heir, I will expect you to respect my privacy."

"Respect your privacy?" he blurted, stunned. "Do

you mean to say you will be my wife but you will not share my bed?"

"That's exactly what I mean," she said earnestly. "I shall be everything you want in a countess. I shall be the perfect wife. But I shall not share any man's bed with other women, and I shall not give my favors to a man I do not love."

She stepped back. "I suspect you would never wish the public spectacle of a divorce; therefore, if we do not suit, we can have the marriage annulled, or we can do what so many do and live completely apart from one another. If these terms are unacceptable to you . . ." Sabrina tilted her head in a questioning manner. "Well, Nicholas, what's it to be?"

He stared, the silence growing between them. He had thought she'd be the appropriate wife for his purposes the evening they first met. But now he wanted more. Much, much more. The light of the moon cast a shimmering halo about her hair, caressing her finely carved features, her classically sculpted form. She was a vision in the misty magic of the black and silver shades of the night. He could only remember one other time in his life when his desire for a woman had been this overpowering. Irrational, instinctual and, ultimately, undeniable. He would take her as his wife, terms, conditions and all.

"I have a condition of my own," he said softly. "If we decide we do not suit, it must be a joint decision. We must agree to separate."

"Is that all?"

The moonlight reflected the surprise on her face.

Nicholas smiled to himself. Obviously, she did not think he'd accept her outrageous proposition. He nodded.

"Then as acting captain of this vessel, Simon can marry us. Is tomorrow acceptable?"

"More than acceptable." He pulled her into his arms.

"Nicholas," she gasped, "I hardly think this is an auspicious start to a marriage of convenience."

"We are not yet wed," he murmured, "and at the moment I find this wonderfully convenient." He pressed his lips to hers.

The pressure of his touch stole her breath and sapped her will. She struggled to fight a sea of powerful sensations, flooding her veins, throbbing through her blood. How would she resist him? If he could do this to her with a mere kiss . . . she shuddered with anticipation and ignored the distant warning in the back of her mind; it was not to be.

He held her close, plundering her lips with his own. Instinctively, he sensed her surrender, knew the moment of her defeat. Satisfied, he released her. Lifting her chin with a gentle touch, he gazed into eyes aglow with the power of his passion.

"Until tomorrow."

It took but a moment. Nicholas noted Sabrina gathering her wits about her. Noted her transformation into the cool, collected Lady Stanford. She was good, his bride-to-be, very good.

"Tomorrow." She nodded politely, turned and walked into the darkness. He rested his back against the rail and watched her disappear into the night. Her scent lingered in the air, vaguely spicy, hinting of a long-forgotten memory. A smile grew on his lips and he considered the unexpected benefits of taking a wife.

Nicholas, Earl of Wyldewood, was a man of honor, and he would abide by their bargain, abide by their terms.

All, of course, except one.

Coming April 2008

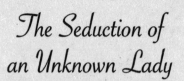

The Seduction of an Unknown Lady

an exciting new novel
by *New York Times* bestselling author

Samantha James

Fionna Hawkes values her independence as much as she does her privacy. Which is why she must resist Lord Aidan McBride, despite his persistent desire to know her better. Fionna not only has her secret identity as horror writer F.J. Sparrow to protect, but her family as well. But who will protect her from this bold nobleman's charms?

*Y*ou are the talk of all the neighbors, Lord Aidan—"

"Please," he interrupted. "It's Aidan. Just Aidan. The formality is not necessary. After all, we've been in each other's company in the dark before."

Fionna gasped.

"Miss Hawkes, you surprise me. I didn't think you were a woman easily shocked."

His eyes were twinkling. Fionna's narrowed. "I think you meant to shock me."

He chuckled. "I do believe I did."

For a fraction of an instant, his gaze met hers with that boldness she found so disconcerting. Then, to her further shock, his eyes trickled down her features, settling on her mouth. Something sparked in those incredible blue eyes; it vanished by the time she recognized it. Yet that spark set her further off guard . . . and further on edge.

Fionna wet her lips. If he could be bold, then so could she. Her chin tipped. "I should like to know what you're thinking, my lord."

His smile was slow-growing. "I'm not so sure you do, Miss Hawkes."

"I believe I know my own mind." Fionna was adamant.

"Very well then. I was thinking that I am a most fortunate man."

"Why?" she asked bluntly.

Again that slow smile—a breathtaking one, she discovered. All at once she felt oddly short of breath. And there it was again, that spark in his eyes, only now it appeared in the glint of his smile.

"Perhaps fortunate is not the best way to describe it." He pretended to ponder. "No, that is not it at all. Indeed, I must say, I relish my luck."

"Your luck, my lord? And why is that?"

"It's quite simple, really. I relish my luck . . . in that I have found you before my brother."

Fionna's cheeks heated. Oh, heavens, the man was outrageous! He was surely an accomplished flirt—but surely he wasn't flirting with her.

"And another thing, Miss Hawkes." He traced a fingertip around the shape of her mouth, sending her heart into such a cascade of rhythm that she could barely breathe.

Nor could she have moved if the earth had tumbled away beneath them both.

He dared still more, for the very tip of that daring finger breached her lips, running lightly along the line of her teeth. "I am immensely delighted," he said mildly, "to discover that you are most definitely *not* a vampire."

No, she was not. Still, Fionna didn't know whether to laugh or cry. Ah, she thought, if he only knew . . .

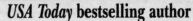